GW00599285

Praise for Vanessa Hannam's othe

THE HOSTAGE PRINCE

On a minor episode of the English Civil V
two of King Charles I's younger children
Wight in 1650, Vanessa Hannam has bu..
combines history with imaginative fiction. An enthralling tale of divided
loyalties, personal integrity, greed, lust and chivalry, *The Hostage Prince* is
teeming with fully realised, memorable characters who linger in the mind
long after reading, in particular the protagonist, Lady Elisabeth Anne, whose
beauty and spiritual strength bring about the happy denouement. A remarkable
achievement.   Shusha Guppy, author of *The Blindfold Horse*

There is a charm and integrity about this novel of the English Civil War that
keeps you reading. The author has done her homework, and is thoroughly in
love with her subject. If you want an old-fashioned (in the best sense) historical
novel, then you need not look any further.
                Lizzie Buchan, author of *Revenge of the Middle Aged Woman*

I truly loved this book and can genuinely recommend it without a trace of
hesitation. It's provenance, too, is intriguing, particularly the heroine, Lizzie
Jones, the children's faithful servant – beautiful, intelligent, independent
minded and strong headed – with whom the reader and the hero fall in love at
first sight. Vanessa Hannam uses the story to good effect to write about social,
political and religious issues raised by the Civil War with rare insight and
balance.

Unlike most historical novelists – who tend to be carried away by the glamour
of the Royalist Cavalier cause – Vanessa Hannam manages to be very fair to
the Puritan Roundheads as well, who, as she sees it, give bread to the common
man, taking from the rich and giving to the poor, in the cause, in modern
jargon, of social justice.

There is also a rich measure of human interest and even, towards the end,
old-fashioned bodice ripping, deflowering and other sensualities. And, it has
to be said, these earthy parts of the book, at any rate to my innocent eye, seem
to be not one wit less well researched or less convincingly true to life and
authentic than all the rest.   Peregrine Worsthorne, *Country Life*

DIVISION BELLE

A passion for music, the strains of political life and a sense of women's ability to
cope with loss all provide a wealth of inspiration for Vanessa Hannam's novels.
                                        Country Life

CHANGE OF KEY

As an opera singer used to singing at the Opera House, I was astounded at the
insight of this book into a very difficult and rarely understood way of life. I
was, at once, gripped by the colourful characters and storyline, but it was the
little details that brought it all so vividly into focus – I did not want it to end.
Well done, Vanessa Hannam.   Valerie Masterton

Also by VANESSA HANNAM

The Hostage Prince
Division Belle
Change of Key

A Rose in Winter

VANESSA HANNAM

And clever brains
Will find the logic that constrains
Not only Words but Arts defined
By theories of a different kind.

WILLIAM RADICE, 1971

QUARTET BOOKS

First published in 2009 by
Quartet Books Limited
A member of the Namara Group
27 Goodge Street, London W1T 2LD

A catalogue record for this book
is available from the British Library

ISBN   978 0 7043 7163 7

Typeset by Antony Gray
Printed and bound in Great Britain by
T J International Ltd, Padstow, Cornwall

For John with love and thanks for
his encouragement and support

ACKNOWLEDGEMENTS

Grateful thanks must go to my dear friend Nicola Beauman for introducing me to Elspeth Sinclair, an editor and literary agent of absolute brilliance, without whose quiet determination and support I could never have embarked on the journey into history which is, and continues to be, so exciting and rewarding. Thanks must also go to Guy Penman and the London Library who have helped me to visit the daily lives of my characters. The greatest possible thanks to Naim Attallah and Quartet who are the publishers every writer prays for. And of course my family. Deike Begg's encouragement has never faltered. Of course I must not forget Samuel Pepys, whose diaries supplanted the newspapers each morning. I grew to like him enormously and to see that nothing in life alters – people are the same. It is just events that change them.

PROLOGUE

The merchant knew at once that the silks were the finest he had ever seen, even though he could not fully appreciate the subtle blend of colours in the oppressive gloom. The two men who had come to sell it to him watched as he caressed the gossamer silk through his rough ill kept hands with a satisfied smile. It fluttered, suspended for a moment in the fetid air, until it rippled to the floor like a descending bird of paradise. The merchant's wife rushed forward, putting down a clean white linen sheet on to which she carefully lifted the delicate fabric. Although the maid had replaced the rushes on the bare earth floor the previous day, the house dogs had messed in their customary place, and rats' droppings had accumulated under the large oak table, on which the remains of the previous night's meal lay uncovered in an unappetising mess.

One of the men, whose command of English was better than his companion's, briefly acknowledged the woman's gesture, annoyed with himself for not having noticed the filthy floors in the dim light filtering in a grey monochrome through the small dirty windows. The two men pulled more of the stuff from a sturdy, much travelled leather chest. Suddenly an unexpected beam of winter sunlight penetrated the gloom, illuminating the silk in a kaleidoscope of rich crimson shot with purple and dark mossy green. The merchant's wife caught her breath and gasped in admiration, but there was something about this which filled her with an almost biblical apprehension, as if these strange

7

men had brought with them something alien. She felt like Eve in the forbidden garden, but she knew better than to share her fears with her husband, knowing he would punish her for her interference.

The merchant thought carefully, the price asked seemed low for such quality.

'You say these are from Holland,' he said slowly, aware of the draconian plague quarantine on incoming ships.

'We have our ways; it is better you ask no questions, and all I will tell you is that so fine a stuff is rare,' one of the men replied, smiling slyly.

'It came from the Levant,' added the other man, as an afterthought.

The merchant did some rough calculations in his head; he could make a good profit on the fabrics, selling them to the Frenchman who made gowns for the ladies at court. He thought of Sir Miles Boynton, a wealthy city gentleman who was planning a lavish wedding for his beautiful daughter. The city had been agog with tales of its grandeur. It would not be too late to show them something so out of the ordinary. He had heard that the bride was to have an impressive dowry; this would be an irresistible addition.

'I will take them,' said the merchant quickly, eager to complete the transaction.

The men counted the merchant's gold carefully, biting each coin to be sure of its authenticity before securing the payment in two leather pouches strapped to their thighs. They knew that London was one of the most dangerous cities in the world despite the splendour of the court and the extravagance of the nobility.

As the men hurriedly left the house, travelling faster without the weight of the chest, a baby's mournful reedy cry caught their attention; a flurry of snow had begun to fall. Some ragged beggars, huddled in the doorways of the houses opposite, assumed a ghostly quality as the flakes began to fall thickly.

'Look at those poor bastards,' said one of the men gruffly,

gesturing towards the group. 'The King's brave sailors and their families just left in the bitter cold to starve like dogs.'

Dusk was falling and lamps were being lit outside every house. The men tried to quicken their steps, darting in and out of the shadows.

'These lights are the law in this stinking place,' said the first man, 'if they don't set them they get sent to prison.'

A boy approached them and offered to illuminate their way. The men dismissed him and hurried on. 'If you get caught without a light you'll be thrown into the Tower and serve you right,' the boy called after them.

An upper window opened and the contents of a chamber pot descended into the street, narrowly missing them; the body of a dead cat in the gully blocked the flow, sending it spilling over the street in a malodorous pool.

'These English live like pigs,' said the other man, putting his scarf to his nose, as they deftly picked their way through the stagnant pools of excrement and household waste; they were unused to the squalor of London, coming, as they did, from the well ordered city of Amsterdam.

'Watch your tongue, my friend,' answered first man. 'We must get back to the ship; we can slip through the guards now it's dark.'

They knew they ran the risk of being stopped by the constables who patrolled the streets at night. They had been warned that in the city there was a strict curfew after dark and none but midwives could be out on the streets unaccounted for.

As they walked on in silence, occasionally glancing over their shoulders, the first man thought about the large sum of money they had paid to smuggle themselves past the King's quarantine, and he consoled himself about the expense when he recalled the way in which he had found the cloth in the first place. A house of the dead in the best part of Amsterdam: the man had been a respected tradesman with a good business, but no family to leave it to now; besides, looting was usual in such circumstances. I may as well take everything, he had thought to himself.

If he didn't someone else would and it was a shame to let such fine cloth fall into the wrong hands, ruffians who could not even guess its true worth. The man in London would not regret buying from them.

* * *

The next day the merchant sent a message to the Frenchman and he promptly came to buy: he took most of the fabric and was unusually pleased with his purchase. For good measure he took it away in the old chest in which it had arrived. The next day, after some careful thought, he decided to return to the merchant to see if he had some more. The day was bitter as he set off for Drury Lane, but when he rang the big ship's bell outside the merchant's door, there was no reply.

The merchant heard the bell clanging, but try as he might he could not raise himself from his bed. The fever had come on the previous night and already he felt as if he was burning up in hell's furnaces, and then came the vomiting, dizziness and a pain in his head.

The merchant's wife had been away, attending their eldest daughter's confinement, and it was on her return, as she opened the door, that she noticed the sour smell of vomit. Her heart lurched as she remembered just such a smell from her early childhood. She knew, even before she saw her husband in the murky light of the curtained bed, it was the pestilence; someone had brought it and she thought of the two salesmen. She had warned her husband to be careful; a man could lose his head for assisting in breaking the King's laws. She had passed three such poor souls on their way to their end the previous week. The cries of the weeping families running beside the cart that conveyed the poor wretches to Tower Hill still rang in her ears.

'Wife, I am finished,' the merchant moaned piteously. 'Give me some water, and for God's sake go, take the children, before the magistrate has you locked in here, which will surely be your tomb.'

The woman loved her husband and, unlike him, as a child she had experienced the plague; two of her family had died but she had escaped it. The Lord would protect her a second time. She ran to the bed and pulled back the covers. He had torn away his nightshirt, and puss oozed from the bubo in his groin. His neck and breast were covered in small angry red spots.

'Husband, I know what to do,' she cried. 'I must cut the carbuncle and draw the poison out.' But even as she said the words she knew he would die an agonising death within hours. She thought quickly and called for the maid, no one must know that the plague had struck them; she would send the children out of the town while she nursed her husband.

'The girl has gone, she left the poor children . . . I was too weak . . . I . . . ' gasped the merchant, unable to finish his sentence.

Before his wife could answer him, she heard the bell clanging furiously below. She went cautiously to the door, unsure of what she would find. She opened it slowly and heard a cacophony of voices.

'It's the searchers, the plague has come,' shouted one of the neighbours.

She tried to slide back the thick iron bolt but the door was forced open. Two crones holding long white sticks followed by a constable pushed her unceremoniously aside, elbowing their way up the winding stairs to the bedroom. One of the city constables also waited in the doorway, covering his nose and mouth, while the two old women advanced towards the dying man, roughly lifting the covers with their sticks. The merchant screamed in agony as one of them stabbed the blackening bubo.

'There's no doubt it's the plague, the girl was right,' said one. 'The door must be nailed up at once.'

'The girl must be found and sent to the pest house, and nobody is to leave this house,' said the other. She turned to the merchant's wife. 'And if you've any sense you'll kill those dogs of yours,' she screamed, 'and the pigs in the yard, or the constable will do it for you. Salt them down, for if you live that's all you'll get once the door is secured, and may the Lord have mercy on your souls.'

The merchant called to his wife for water. As she held the cup to his lips a gush of blood flowed from his mouth into his tangled hair, and with a low strangled moan he died.

It was the old woman who found the children, and remarked with terror on the speed and ferocity with which this new strain of pestilence took whole families within a matter of hours.

*   *   *

The Frenchman had meant to return again to the merchant's house that afternoon, but he was overtaken by a sudden fever. All he could think of was getting back to his house in Bearbinder Lane.

On his return, his wife immediately sent their eldest child to fetch the apothecary. The children screamed in terror as he entered the room wearing a grotesque plague mask. Under the curved beak he swung an ornate incense-burning lamp.

'Mama, it's the devil,' cried the smaller of the children. The apothecary did not need to take a closer look. He backed hurriedly towards the door. He liked the family and his initial fear at what he had found gave way to a certain sympathy. He knew only too well that once the parish officers were informed they would all be sealed up with the dead and dying and nobody would survive.

He looked at the Frenchman's wife, she was a beautiful woman and two of her pretty children clung anxiously to her skirts. She soothed them quietly in French, and then collapsed to the floor by her husband's bed, weeping uncontrollably.

'You must take your children away from London at once, or you will all die,' the apothecary said urgently.

'I cannot leave my husband and he is too sick to travel,' cried the woman.

'Your husband will die within hours, I can find you a plague nurse, you must save yourself,' he replied perfunctorily. He knew the punishment for concealing the plague, but he also knew the Frenchman was rich by local standards, and his early concern for the family gave way to more practical matters.

'For a fee, my dear, I will give you time to go before I report what I have found.' He hesitated, momentarily discomfited by the expression in the woman's eyes. 'It is a big risk for me,' he mumbled, 'and I have my own family to consider.'

The Frenchman called to his wife in a faint voice. Seizing her hand as she leant over him, he struggled to speak. 'You must take all the gold in the chest and give the man twenty pieces; it is your only chance,' he rasped.

Soon afterwards, a slatternly nurse arrived, and, at her sick husband's insistence, the wife left to go to relatives in Norfolk. Her grief was beyond tears, beyond anything she could have dreamed of. As an afterthought she had hurriedly packed the chest with the rare silk her husband had purchased that week. She knew it was valuable. It might yet be their saviour.

The cloth was not all she took; she did not see the small brown rat that had nested in the bottom of the chest. He had thrived on the journey from Holland as he scratched at his fleas, and gorged on the cockroaches in the hold of the ship, and the rat had left something dark and dreadful behind him in the city of London. He took that darkness with him on the road to Norfolk. Even before the cart had got to the city gates, the fleas were making themselves at home on the fresh new blood of the Frenchman's wife and children, infecting them with the deadly disease.

PART ONE

CHAPTER ONE

London, March 1665

It was finished at last, the bridal gown she had dreamed of. Mary Boynton stood looking at herself in the long mirror in her mother's chamber. The two seamstresses stood back to admire their work, for it had taken the best part of six months to complete. Sir Miles, the girl's father, had demanded the best French satin for the over dress and Flemish lace for the under-skirts. The bodice, encrusted with seed pearls, was the most sumptuous they had ever made.

One of the girls couldn't help the tear in the corner of her eye as she looked at Mary, so radiantly beautiful and happy. 'A marriage made in heaven,' the bride's maid Jayne had told them. And just once, on one of the many occasions they had come to the house, they had seen the young man. How could anyone not be in love with him, they thought. To them this was high romance, true love blooming in the security of two happy homes, without a care in the world. Life as it was in fairy stories, and in this case it was a real-life fairy tale. The girls did not feel jealous or resentful, just in some curious way glad that somewhere, somehow, this was possible and that they had a part in it.

They had made the most beautiful dress ever created for the happiest day ever known. And, what is more, they were invited to attend both the ceremony and the feast. This was unusual in a family of such quality, but it was all down to the bride. She had insisted; they had stood embarrassed while she argued with her mother on the point. But Mary had won and the girls had

17

already ordered some new silks for their own gowns, a bargain, from the Frenchman in the city.

Some time later, when the family gathered in the parlour, the excitement of the day was cruelly shattered.

'May the lord save us, the red cross has come to London,' Lady Harriet Boynton announced as she swept into the room.

'How do you know, who told you?' cried Mary, seizing her mother by the shoulders. 'You know there have been rumours, you cannot be sure, people panic. It could be the smallpox.' Mary, with all her instincts sharpened, could not control the feeling of dread in the pit of her stomach; in spite of all the precautions the King had imposed, she knew full well the plague was an insidious enemy.

'Jayne was in Drury Lane this morning,' said Lady Harriet calmly. She always prided herself on her composure. 'And she saw the houses locked and sealed with everyone inside.' She went on, 'The sick and the healthy, there is nothing can save them now.'

Harriet was a large and buxom woman. Even so, she had not enjoyed the experience of childbirth and for many years now had denied her husband access to her bed and resigned herself to a life of self-centred middle age. But for all that, the remnants of her once famous good looks still gave a striking impression: she dressed with extreme care, following the fashion of the day with avid concentration. She still prided herself on her own magnificent red hair, and for that reason ignored the fashion for hair pieces and wigs which had recently arrived in London. Her maid had learned the art of French hairdressing – coiling and whirling the tresses about her mistress's head each day, and adorning the finished article with some new and eye catching concoction. Today, she had selected some jewelled osprey feathers, which jangled disconcertingly as Harriet spoke.

Her two elder daughters had married and moved away from home, and the proximity this had imposed between her and her youngest daughter, Mary, had not improved relations. It was at times like this that Harriet felt the premature death of her two long awaited infant sons very keenly.

She saw the fear in her daughter's face and knew exactly what she was thinking, and yet she did not feel the least inclined to stretch out a comforting hand to her daughter, but rather stared at her coldly, impatient with the girl's uncontrolled emotions.

Mary started to cry audibly as the significance of the information struck her. The wedding might have to be cancelled; London would empty of the rich and wealthy with access to other premises. Her shoulders started to heave as she sopped up the tears in her apron. Hearing the commotion, her father, Sir Miles, left his office on the ground floor and rushed up to the parlour where the three women stood in a cameo. His wife watched their weeping daughter with an air of stiff disapproval and the maid tentatively patted Mary's shoulder. He stopped for a moment to register the scene before enquiring what was causing such distress.

His daughter Mary looked up towards her father, and his heart gave the characteristic lurch it always did when he saw her youthful beauty. She had deep blue heavily lashed eyes, arched brows, and the same titian hair as her mother's, which always escaped her cap, as it did now. She was tall and perfectly formed, with an hourglass figure and dainty hands and feet. She had a way of talking in a rich mellifluous voice, suggestive of an older woman, with her chin slightly lowered and her eyes looking upwards, emphasising her heart-shaped face, which even in repose retained a slight smile. But her character was not yet formed and tears were never far away. Despite this fact, he did not reprimand her for these shows of weakness, knowing full well that life would soon bring its own learning curve, and that Mary had a strength and maturity she had not yet discovered. Sir Miles made little attempt to disguise the fact that he adored his youngest daughter. She ran to him and he automatically put his arms around her. He saw her mother turn her head slightly away in a gesture of annoyance.

'Haven't you heard the pestilence has come and it's rather too close for my liking; we shall have to make some decisions,' said Harriet firmly. 'I have been worried for days now but nobody would listen to me. We must call the servants and send word to prepare the house in Norfolk.'

Mary stood quietly in her father's arms, her mind racing; her wedding, the most wonderful day of her life – her marriage to her childhood sweetheart – was only days away. They had been planning it for years. The bridal gown was finished, it hung in her chamber under a linen cloth heavily scented with lavender brought from their country home in Norfolk. No expense was to be spared. The Church at St Olaf's was to be prepared with garlands of spring blossom from her aunt Judith Briott's gardens at Hampton Court.

All the guests had been invited, valuable gifts had started to pour in, even a silver porringer from Lord Sandwich, and Mr and Mrs Pepys had sent a pair of fine candlesticks. Her father was an important man. The family business provided the hemp for the manufacture of rope for the navy. Men's lives depended on sturdy rope and there were many scoundrels who cheated with inferior goods, but not her father, who, as her mother often said, 'Would one day let his principles be the death of us all.'

The wedding was to be a splendid occasion. The Duke of York, the King's brother, had been invited; Lady Sandwich had arranged for the wedding feast to be held in one of the halls owned by the admiralty; there was to be an entertainment with the latest craze of dancing on ropes; and some of the actors from the King's theatre were coming.

To Mary the idea of leaving London now was unthinkable. 'I won't go, this can't ruin my wedding, it's only a few more days,' she wept.

Despite his daughter's predilection to tears, which could be swept away in an instant, Sir Miles did not like to see women cry. His wife had learned not to weep because it merely resulted in 'one of Sir Miles's famous rages', but with Mary it was a different matter. To her he responded, at first with concern and then with panic. Ironically he had thought only recently that she was getting control of her emotions, she hadn't cried for a long time, not since her little singing bird was eaten by the neighbour's cat. This, he knew, was due to the sublime, almost dreamlike happiness she enjoyed awaiting her marriage to Anthony, the most excellent young man a father could hope for. And now the sight of her weeping upset him to the point of impotence; he did what he always did when he wanted some sound domestic advice, he sent for his servant Thomas.

Sir Miles was a great bear of a man, undeniably handsome despite his size and age; he had just turned forty three. He had thick sandy hair and a short clipped beard, his eyes were atavistically dark and flashing and so surprising in appearance that they commanded instant attention and authority. When Sir Miles spoke people listened, with the exception of course of his wife, who paid little attention to anything not directly in tandem with her own, what Sir Miles considered frivolous, requirements.

The servant Thomas had been close to the door, listening; he knew the summons would come. He was familiar with all local matters and had been on the point himself of coming to his master with the dire news about the plague. As he came into the room he bowed, as he always did, but on this occasion he raised his eyes to his master and mistress, a thing a respectful servant should not do.

'Is this true?' Sir Miles roared. 'You know everything. Are there houses boarded up in Drury Lane?'

'Yes, Sir,' Thomas replied.

'Well, man, how bad is it?' Sir Miles bellowed.

'There are houses boarded up and the red sign with those fearful words slashed in red all over the doors,' Thomas answered as steadily as he could.

'What words?' asked Harriet imperiously, doubtful of Thomas's account, since he had only limited knowledge of reading.

'You won't remember, My Lady, but back in the late King's time it was the same words they put, and My Lady is right, then folk stayed in the city and left it too late to get away.' Thomas paused for a moment wondering how best the words should be delivered. All eyes were upon him and, perversely, he was enjoying his moment of drama. 'May the Lord have mercy on their souls,' he finished in his most sepulchral tone.

Unnoticed by her family, Mary had slipped quietly from the room. Putting on her thick cloak against the biting wind and some of her wooden platformed overshoes to keep her feet out of the filth in the street, she began to make her way with grim determination to Anthony's house. There were some coins in the pocket of her cloak and to her relief she found a vacant coach. 'Take me to Bearbinder Lane,' she commanded.

'Are you sure, Miss?' the man enquired guardedly. 'That's not a place you should go to, the plague is there, half the houses boarded up already.'

Mary could feel her heart pounding in her chest. Despite the man's warning, she knew that she must find Anthony. He would know what to do, he always knew what to do.

'Just take me there if you please. I will pay you handsomely,' she replied, trying to keep the terror from her voice.

'Seeing as how you are a young lady on her own I'll take you, but I won't wait. Nobody with any sense would linger there, and I don't know what your business is, but if you were my girl I would stop you,' the man replied.

'Well, I'm not your girl and thank you for your warning but I have to go,' said Mary.

Her mind was racing. If the situation was as bad as it sounded they must marry at once, forget about the wedding, leave London. Anthony could come to Norfolk with the family. But one thing she could not do was to wait any longer, she loved him too much. They had saved themselves for the moment of joy when they would be husband and wife but now she wasn't prepared to wait any longer. After all, they might all be dead of the plague in a matter of weeks. She had made her mind up, they would find a priest and be joined at once with the blessing of the Holy Virgin and the Catholic faith for which so many had fought and suffered.

Mary had taken control of her initial unhappiness at the prospect of losing her splendiferous wedding. 'After all it is only one day,' she said to herself. They would have all their lives ahead of them. They would have a celebration when the panic was over.

The driver cracked his whip and the horses broke into a trot, normally impossible in the crowded narrow streets with their overhanging windows. Mary became aware that the place was deserted and a strange silence had descended, broken only by the sound of the horse's hooves. It was as they rounded the sharp corner into Bearbinder Lane that she saw that the imposing, intricately crafted iron gates which led into the courtyard of Anthony's family home were chained and bolted. She leapt from the coach into the thick mud and ran to the gates. Grasping them in both hands, she rattled them hysterically, screaming Anthony's name. There was silence, the thick oak double doors at the top of the wide stone steps were shut and across them were blazoned the devilish words Thomas had spoken in her parents' home. The thought flashed through her mind, how prophetically they brought meaning to the family crest above them, into which the words *Nil desperandum* were intertwined.

She felt a hand on her shoulder as she had sunk, weeping hopelessly, to the ground, her gown dragging in mud. Looking up she saw the coachman, and beside him stood a ragged fellow with a lantern.

'You can't stay here, Miss. It's getting dark and this is the constable who is guarding the house to make sure no one goes in or out.'

'The whole family's down with it,' said the man, looking Mary up and down lasciviously, 'with one taken to be buried at St Olaf's without ceremony. It's all that could be done,' he continued, as casually as if he were announcing the death of a few family hens.

The coachman caught the look in the man's eye with distaste.

He had a daughter of about the girl's age and he made up his mind that he would attempt to help her as he would his own child.

'I have to go,' he said kindly. 'I have a family of my own and I wouldn't leave a young lady of quality here on her own, best get back in the coach and I'll take you back to your home. There's nothing you can do here.'

He gently coaxed Mary to her feet; she fumbled for a handkerchief in the purse which hung from her waist.

'My future husband, my whole life, is in that house. If he dies, I want to die with him,' she cried. In her short life she had never known adversity of any kind, except of course when the cat ate her little canary, and now it was as if God had been saving his account; all the happiness she had accepted without question, as if it were her right, had been nothing but a cruel mockery, leading her, unprepared and unsuspecting, to this moment of supreme, unimaginable agony. She knew that he was dead; she didn't need anyone to tell her. It was only four days since he had held her in his arms, breathing into her hair of the gentle joy they would have together, and she had felt a surge of longing at the prospect of approaching consummation.

The driver lifted her into the coach. He had a rug under the seat for special occasions – it had once covered the elegant lap of Lady Castlemaine, the King's mistress. He pulled it out and wrapped it over Mary's knees; then he asked her exactly where she lived and she told him in no more than a whisper. In this awful moment she was born into her adult life.

CHAPTER TWO

Norfolk 1665

On March 4th, war was officially declared against the Dutch and for Sir Miles this was the final straw. 'We are ill prepared for such a challenge and it can only end badly,' he said sombrely to his family. 'We will pack up and get out of London for I fear we may well be invaded before the summer is out and what with that and the plague I will truck no argument. For once, wife, you are right.' And so the matter was settled.

It had taken no more than a few days to prepare the family for the great exodus to Norfolk. Some of the neighbours thought the plan was premature and that the outbreaks of plague were isolated and would die down, but Sir Miles had made his decision, in part to get Mary away from London and her grief. The journey took longer than the normal four days, since two of the horses cast a shoe and finding a blacksmith had proved difficult. Besides which, they found nowhere to stay at Colchester, as word of the plague in London had filtered to the countryside and the inn they usually stayed in refused to put them up, 'in case they brought the pestilence with them'. They had been forced to make a detour to find another place to sleep, where they had barely had a moment's rest because of the stench from the chamber pots overflowing on to the floors and the choking smoke from the landlord's primitive candles made from wicks floating in rancid animal fat. The soiled straw in the mattresses had impacted and, as Jayne informed them, they were not even fit for the vermin they heard scuttling in the dark corners of the rooms all night long.

Mary sat in the coach as if in a trance and nobody could get a word out of her. At one point Lady Harriet suspected her daughter might actually be sickening herself, but Jayne cared for Mary as if she were a small helpless child.

Jayne was well acquainted with grief, her own husband had died at sea serving the great Lord Sandwich. He had drowned in a few feet of water. In common with most sailors he had never learned to swim, taking the view that it would be quicker to drown than be eaten by sea monsters. She had been left penniless; her baby had starved with her, and died of the spotted fever. It was Sir Miles, with his kind heart, who saw her outside in the alley, begging for money to bury the child decently. He took her in and wrote to the admiralty, expressing his disgust at this state of affairs. He had persuaded the navy board to make some small provision for Jayne, which she sent to her old mother in the country while becoming part of the Boynton 'family' – a term which encompassed not only family members but servants alike.

Jayne had been taken into service with the Boyntons as a scullery maid, but Mary soon found out that she had some learning and could sing as sweetly as any lady. What with that and her gentle manners she had soon been elevated to Mary's personal maid in preparation for her new mistress's 'soon-to-be-married' status. She and Mary had become as close as sisters, a fact that had not escaped the attention of Lady Harriet, who did not approve of such familiarity with members of the lower orders. Harsh words had been exchanged between mother and daughter on the subject as on many others and Sir Miles had, as usual, taken his daughter's side. Lady Harriet had reluctantly capitulated. It was now, as she saw her daughter almost expiring of grief, that she had to admit the usefulness of the friendship between servant and mistress, and it was not without a certain envy that she observed the tender way Jayne held Mary in her arms like a broken bird.

'Don't worry, My Lady,' the girl had reassured her, as they

stopped to rest the horses and stretch their legs. 'She is young and even though she thinks her life is over, in time she will recover.' Jayne spoke with the resolution born of experience, and, looking at her, Lady Harriet had to admit in her resistant soul that she had come to admire the girl and even to depend on her constancy and good sense.

'I don't know what we would have done without that girl,' said Sir Miles as he walked a few yards with his wife, both of them stamping their feet to get their circulation going after so many hours in the cramped coach.

'Yes, but all the same,' said Lady Harriet stiffly, her breath creating a dragon-like vapour in the cold air. 'Mary's behaviour illustrates a lack of moral fibre.'

'And how, pray, are we to decide on the matter of moral fibre, Madam?' asked Sir Miles with a note of sarcasm.

'Well, husband, she informed me the other day that she might actually die from a broken heart. I have never heard of such a perfidious thing,' replied Lady Harriet testily.

'Well, wife, your dramatic and unpredictable daughter appears to be doing just that and perhaps just a little maternal love and understanding might prevent it,' said Sir Miles, arching his eyebrows in a gesture which implied that an answer to the suggestion might be welcome.

'Don't be ridiculous. Sympathy will only make matters worse,' hissed Lady Harriet, pulling her cloak about her in a gesture of irritation.

'I have not observed the situation being anything but improved a little as a result of all the care Jayne has been giving to the poor child. Just remember, wife, she loved this young man, and so did I. Mary knew we all pinned so much hope on the union,' said Sir Miles sadly.

'Really, Sir, you are becoming feeble minded, and despite all you say, enough is enough,' said Lady Harriet.

'Enough of what, wife?' asked Sir Miles, his voice beginning to rise. 'There is such a thing as genuine understanding. I suppose it is difficult for you to empathise with the shock of losing someone you love, upon whom your entire future depends,' he said pointedly.

'I don't care what you say; Mary is being disgracefully self-indulgent,' said Lady Harriet, determined to stand her ground.

Sir Miles stopped for a minute and looked at his wife. He began to see that perhaps she had a point. Many things crossed his mind at that moment as he saw out of the corner of his eye that Mary was sitting disconsolately on a bench outside the inn. He suddenly realised that his wife had lost the capacity to love; she had developed a hard and dispassionate view of life. Perhaps in these terrible times such an approach was necessary.

'I concede, Madam, that the whole world is in chaos. It isn't just Mary's own personal tragedy,' he said thoughtfully.

'Indeed it is not, Sir,' said Lady Harriet. 'The plague is killing hundreds every day. Do you not think that each of these deaths is someone's tragedy?' she asked reasonably.

'Yes of course it is,' agreed Sir Miles, 'and let us not forget that at the same time the fleet is out fighting the Dutch.'

'And those losses at sea are hardly mentioned any more,' added Lady Harriet.

The time had come to get back into the coach for the last part of the journey and Sir Miles continued his discussion with his wife as they all took their places in the coach. Mary decided to join in, anxious to hear if her father had gleaned any more news from the innkeeper.

'London had virtually come to a standstill,' he answered to her enquiry.

'It seems that most able-bodied men have been pressed into the navy,' offered Jayne, having heard the latest from one of the grooms. 'And now it is impossible to get anyone to do anything.'

'Yes, Jayne,' said Sir Miles, nodding in agreement. 'That's why most people with any sense have already fled the coop and gone to their estates in the country.'

'Those that are fortunate enough to have the chance,' chipped in Jayne, realising at once that she had over stepped the mark.

Harriet looked at her coldly. She didn't approve of conversing with servants and this, she thought, was an example of how they behaved, given half a chance; so she addressed her remarks to her husband.

'It is extraordinary that the court remains at Whitehall,' she said disapprovingly. 'I am sure it is because of the King. He has this unseemly desire to be among the people, but it won't do him much good if the entire Royal family perish from the plague, will it?'

'I commend the King,' said Sir Miles quietly. 'He is a brave man and I expect his little Queen is very nervous about it all, but one cannot but admire such devotion.'

Lady Harriet detected a deterioration in the dialogue and became silent, pretending to fall asleep, whilst in fact she was considering her position.

Lady Harriet detested the Norfolk house, but the onset of the plague terrified her and she had resigned herself to the fact that it would be many months before they could return to London, if God spared them. She sank back into the cushions, thinking gloomily of the next few months of what she regarded as interminable boredom.

Sir Miles soon fell asleep himself and awoke with a start as the coach arrived at the gates of King's Bircham village; they had travelled through the family estates, miles of bleak fens waiting for the hemp to be sown in May, now the sole domain of the few remaining winter geese and sea birds. They were passing the huge barns that housed the hemp after drying and threshing and then the low building more than a quarter of a mile long, the 'Rope Walk', where the crop was processed into 'the toughest rope in the navy'. It was midday and men were hard at work inside, singing in unison, songs that Sir Miles remembered from his childhood.

Within minutes they were at the gates of Sailing Hall; fresh snow had covered the roofs of the lodges at the entrance and smoke curled reassuringly from the chimneys. The house had been built in Elizabethan times, by the first Baronet. He had been knighted by Queen Elizabeth for his services to the navy and had founded the family fortunes by being one of the successful captains of a voyage to the spice islands of Banda, where his share of the pomegranate seeds, cinnamon and the nutmeg, so prized for its legendary prevention of the plague among many other medicinal qualities, had been sufficiently valuable to build the house and set up the family business. The first Baronet had been a brave sailor and then a naval administrator, and had observed the importance of good hemp, otherwise known by the botanical name of cannabis, for a seafaring nation dependent on the navy for its wealth. He had calculated the uneconomic arrangements made for importing it from abroad, and suspected it would grow well in the rich damp soil of the fens. It had been Sir Miles's father who had expanded the cultivation and created a formidable business and now that two of the present Sir Miles's daughters, Abigail and Margaret, were married to men whom he referred to as 'nincompoops', he had settled them with a large jointure and had planned to pass the knowledge of the business to Anthony Cowan, Mary's future husband, and hopefully to a grandson. With that he had made it clear that the Norfolk estate was to be left to his youngest daughter. He had loved his future son-in-law and he clearly felt Mary's loss more keenly than his wife did. In fact the more he allowed himself to think about it the more he realised his wife was, to all intents and purposes, a stranger to him.

They did not live as man and wife in the biblical sense, and above all they did not share a love of all the things Sir Miles thought mattered most, as was instanced by Harriet's reluctance to spend time at Sailing Hall. She preferred to spend her time in the brittle social life of London, where she falsely imagined herself to be a member of the inner sanctum of the 'hangers on', at the court. He had lost count of the months he had spent without her at Sailing Hall while she improved the house in London and spent her days socialising.

What Harriet did not know, of course, was that Sir Miles was not alone during those long summers and hard winters. It never occurred to her, and the more so because when he came to London he could play the gentleman as well as any, but his heart was in the fen country with the cry of the sea birds and the smell of salt and brine and the bitter wind coming in straight from the North Sea, and where he was nearer to Amsterdam than to London.

He looked at his daughter's drawn face opposite him in the coach; it had a blankness about it which he had never previously observed and it worried him profoundly. But as he was watching her he saw her expression change as they passed through the village; she lent forward, pulling back the blind in the carriage and peering out, and as she heard the men singing, the trace of a smile played on her lips. He bent towards her and took her hand, their eyes met.

'Welcome home, dear girl,' he whispered softly. 'This place will heal you; let it work its magic.'

Sailing Hall was one of many houses in the area built by a Dutch architect; the long straight drive bordered by a neat avenue of pleached limes drew the eye to a mellow red brick façade of rounded gables edged with ornate stone pie-crusted swirls. Either side of a circular flight of wide steps was a sheltered ornamental porch, above which stood the family coat of arms, a pomegranate and nutmeg held in the talons of a majestic eagle. At the rear of the house was a complicated network of shallow waterways through which the house was serviced, most of them connecting to Norwich and Colchester and, most importantly, to the busy port of Harwich. Even the coal for the essential fires that warmed the damp flagged floors and ancient stone walls was brought down from the Tyne on canals which then connected to the smaller tributaries that led to the Hall.

Ornate gardens with parterres and the new fashion of gravel

walks spread either side of the cobbled sweep below the steps. In summer they were ablaze with plants and flowers collected by Sir Miles's mother, whose love of intimate gardens of this type came from her Dutch ancestry. Her family had not been best pleased when she fell in love with the Catholic Sir Miles but she had come to love the place and was still missed by the older villagers.

Harriet of course had not liked Sir Miles's mother and this had certainly contributed to her inability to be happy at Sailing. Neither did she like the climate at Sailing, with its stark contrasts, bitter winters when nothing stood between the house and the always brown sea. She found the balmy summers, when the hemp blossomed in the surrounding fens and the garden fruited in abundance, of little interest either, preferring a landscape of grand city buildings and formal parks. Sir Miles pondered all these things as he brought his family to safety.

He was brought from his reverie by the gentle pressure of his daughter's hand in his, and he felt a small consolation, and thought, not for the first time, how life often provided an unexpected bonus when things were at their darkest. The family was together, he could spend time with his beloved daughter. He had adjusted to the fact that soon she would have been another man's joy, but now he would at least have her near him for a little while longer.

*　　*　　*

Two days passed and the weather deteriorated, an unusual cold spell brought more snow and March winds. The news from London was that the sickness had slowed down with the freezing temperatures, but many families had decided to flee and Sir Miles was glad he had made the decision to come to Norfolk. Despite his wife's dislike of the place she had begun to settle in, although her rows with the servants were a cacophony of shrieks, clashing pans and slamming doors.

Mary awoke early. It was still dark and at first, in the befuddled no man's land between sleeping and waking, she couldn't remember where she was or why she felt an icy grip of sorrow as her mind gradually completed the mosaic of the time and place and the reasons for her being there. She pressed her face into the sweet-scented linen pillow, and wondered how she could get up, dress and live out a day in the awful reality of just what she had lost. She still couldn't think about the possibility of a life that didn't encompass Anthony. She slowly got out of bed, her feet searching for her embroidered slippers, and then she saw Jayne asleep in the rocking chair by the fire. The coals burned merrily, a bunch of white hellebores graced the table on which her toiletries were neatly arranged and Mary knew that no one but Jayne could have paid such attention to detail and she must have stayed with her all night tending the fire while Mary slept. Fresh clothes hung from a screen by the door, a simple black mourning gown and starched white underskirts, another example of Jayne's careful housekeeping. She had perfected the art of bleaching in urine and lime and laying the garments to dry in the sun.

Mary watched Jayne's wide, serene face as she slept and thought about the selfless way the girl cared and tended her in her grief, when she had herself been deprived of husband and child, and she never complained, thinking only of the mistress she served.

Mary crept quietly across the room and placed the coverlet from her bed over the sleeping girl and set to dressing herself. She left the room and made her way into the cold passage that led to the gallery that looked down on the family hall; her father's dogs, Ned and Betty, two brown and white hunting spaniels, stretched luxuriously and thumped their tales on the rug in front of the hearth. The cavernous space was bitterly cold, unlike her cosy chamber, and she pulled her shawl around her as she ran the gauntlet of family portraits gazing enquiringly at her from the rich panelled walls above the barley sugar banisters.

Sir Miles had been up since five, working at his papers in his study. The dogs alerted him to the arrival of his daughter, and he went to greet her.

'I was just about to take the dogs out, there has been fresh snow. Would you like to take walk round the house with us, I have done a lot here and have some surprises for you,' he said brightly.

'Yes, Father, I would like that very much,' she replied at once, eager to get out of the house.

Sir Miles helped her into one of the many cloaks and shawls kept in a big oak chest inside the door. One of the house stewards, a young boy of no more than fourteen, came running to her with her outside boots brightly polished; he knelt down and helped her on with them using a gold and ivory shoehorn kept in the pocket of his green baize apron, and all without a word or ever catching her eye. Finally, he adroitly tied the laces.

Thomas, their London servant, joined them as if by osmosis. He shooed the boy aside and opened the huge doors for master and daughter. 'When you get back the fire will be lit and your breakfast will be ready,' he reassured them respectfully, as they went out into the crisp morning air, so cold that Mary caught her breath and pulled the fur of her hood tightly round her chin.

The light had come as quickly as it had receded the previous night and a clear low elliptical sunlight illuminated the beauty of the garden under its mantle of snow. The trees bowed gracefully, their branches decked in garlands of flashing white ice crystals that tinkled as they passed.

They walked in silence, the only sound the muffled crunching of their boots in the fresh snow. Sir Miles deftly pulled back a low-hanging branch blocking their path with the weight of snow and a flurry of flakes danced about them in a glittering vortex. Some alighted on Mary's hood. Her father carefully brushed them away and she leaned against him for a moment. The contact broke the silence between them and Mary was the first to speak.

'It seems so unfair, Father.'

'What does, my dear?' Sir Miles asked, expecting her to unburden herself about Anthony. To his surprise she did not.

'Well, there is Jayne who has lost her husband and baby and she never complains and, do you know, I have never asked her about it. All I know is what you have told me and it went in one ear and out the other, but her first thought is always for me. She cares for my every whim and when we go back to the house our day will be eased along by the servants: my clothes will be laid out, my water will be brought to my chamber, our food will be prepared and when I weep for my lost love and my lost life, Jayne will be there with a kerchief to wipe my tears and rose water for my red eyes and I won't suffer in the physical way she has done. When I worked my rosary last night I lay in my warm bed and I thought about my life,' she hesitated fleetingly, searching for the words, and then continued falteringly, 'I did nothing to deserve the happiness I had and now God has taken it from me.'

She had stopped walking and faced her father expectantly, waiting for him to deliver some definitive comforting words as he usually did. She took her hands from her muff and clutched her throat as if she might choke. Her thoughts and feelings were a jumble of incoherent fragments, and for the first time in her life she was being forced to find her own path through the uncharted waters of a vacant future, for which she now realised she was ill prepared.

'My dear daughter, you must not speak so,' Sir Miles started pragmatically, 'there is such a thing as just living the life God has given you; it would be a worse sin to make little of your good fortune. You have given me nothing but joy and I . . . ' Sir Miles hesitated, he wanted to say more, to speak of things he had never discussed with his daughter; he had often wondered if she knew how empty his marriage to her mother had become, how he had found consolation here at Sailing. He had seen the way Harriet had always tried, by some acid word or gesture, to darken

Mary's carefree life and had been constantly reassured by the way his mercurial, beautiful daughter had appeared not to notice her mother's constant barbs and endless complaining.

'I am glad at least that I have caused you no pain, dear Father, for I know Mother would not share your view,' she said pointedly, darting a look at her father.

'Your mother's bark is worse than her bite,' Sir Miles responded cautiously. 'I think it is the life she leads. It has worried me for a long time. The King is a good man and, God knows, I admire him, but the same cannot be said for his court, which has such an influence on people like your mother who want to be in the fashion, with no thought for the dire state of the country.'

'But it is ridiculous, Father, the nearest Mother ever gets is when she goes with Mrs Pepys to see the King and Queen dine in public and she thinks she knows him personally,' said Mary with more than a note of contempt in her voice. 'You see, Father,' she went on, 'we have had plenty of warnings and we have all invited Nemesis. Even the King . . . although you speak loyally. The plague is retribution.'

Sir Miles was amazed by the turn the conversation had taken. He had expected Mary to continue wallowing in her grief but instead she was casting her mind to wider issues. He saw her hands were blue with cold and, taking her arm, he guided her to his latest addition to the gardens.

'Put your hands back in your muff and pull your hood around you. We shall get out of the cold,' he said solicitously, as they approached the new fruit garden, a series of south-facing semi-circular walls set inside each other. It was warmer out of the wind and hungry birds were busily pecking at some haws on the juniper trees. Father and daughter were coming to a high wooden gate in the middle of the old yew walk that Mary could not remember.

'Now close your eyes, my dear, for I have something to show you,' said Sir Miles, taking her by the shoulders and leading her towards the gate.

They came upon Sir Miles's new glasshouse as travellers discovering a summer paradise in a winter landscape.

'When did you do this, Father? It is wonderful!' she exclaimed delightedly, her face lightening for the first time in days.

The glass building stood before them, glistening in the sun, arched and graceful like a Chinese pagoda. They opened the door and were at once assailed by a steamy fragrance of hot damp soil and lichen, mingling with sharp citron and exotic perfume.

'I did it last spring, it is heated by a furnace,' said Sir Miles proudly.

They sat on an ornamental seat in a bower of sweet-smelling jasmine. Mary lowered her hood, basking in the reassuring warmth, and she closed her eyes, revelling in the unexpected pleasure. When she opened them she became aware that they were not alone. In a far corner she saw a young woman; Ned and Betty yelped excitedly when they saw her and went bounding towards her as if she were an old friend. The woman had a basket on her arm, full of cuttings, and in her hand she held a mother-of-pearl knife.

When Sir Miles saw the woman he got up and went over to her. She curtsied and they had a brief conversation. She nodded in agreement, darting a look in Mary's direction, curtsied again and turned to leave them. As she did so Mary saw her father brush the woman's hand in a gesture of unmistakable intimacy, far removed from the formal exchange, and in a flash Mary saw that her father had another life, one about which she had never even thought or suspected.

They walked back to the house, talking haltingly of other things, but Sir Miles could tell that this was not the end of the matter, Mary would be asking him questions, maybe not now but soon. He would have to do her the courtesy of speaking to her as an adult and not the protected child she had been.

'Her name is Charlotte,' he said suddenly.

Mary took her father's arm. She had a curious sensation of

time rolling up into a vast ball, which exploded in front of her, revealing layers of things which she needed to comprehend, and it was the transient nature of their lives which had suddenly hit her. When her father touched the woman's hand with such tenderness, she had remembered a dream she had had the previous night. It came back to her in vivid detail; she was making love with Anthony, experiencing a euphoric joy, something for which she had longed but which Anthony had forestalled. As she recalled the dream she felt calm and restored and realised it had been with her in her subconscious from the moment of waking, as if she had seen a vision of a room previously locked but now open to her. There was so much she didn't know, so much she had never asked. It was as if she had a revelation, from now on she would seize each and every experience; she would not wait for life to shape her destiny; she would make it herself in every thought, word and deed. She took her father's arm. He looked down at her, his big shaggy head slightly bowed in concern.

'It is all right, Father,' she said gently. 'I understand, you have made something beautiful here. You needed someone to share it with.'

CHAPTER THREE

'What is that on your face?' Jayne asked Bess. The girl was one of the maids at Sailing, who had the misfortune to be instructed to take over the care of Lady Harriet. Her own maid had left her, refusing to embark on the journey to Norfolk, but in reality she had come to loathe her mistress, and had been meaning to hand in her notice for some time.

'Her Ladyship boxed my ears and slapped my face for no reason but that the soap was not as she was accustomed to,' wailed Bess, putting her hand to her reddened cheek.

'Like as not you'll have to get used to her Ladyship's ways,' said Thomas gloomily. He was not in the best of moods since the chamber pots from the 'garderobes' at Sailing were stained and unsightly and he had volunteered to scrub them with soda and lime. In London they did not have the space for the cubicles Sir Miles had installed at Sailing, but in Thomas's view they were more trouble than they were worth since the removal of the pots was a tricky business and spillages made extra work, and, besides, it made the business of collecting urine for the wash house even more difficult.

'What was wrong with the soap anyway?' asked the distraught girl.

'It's my fault, I should have told you. I will show you how to make it. I have the best castile oil for mixing with the potash got from burned seaweed to make the glycerine and we always put in some oil of almonds or civet musk. It's all in the household chests from London. Thomas will get it out and I will show you how to make it,' Jayne volunteered brightly. The last thing she wanted was for the girl to leave so that she would be saddled with the personal care of Lady Harriet.

The girl had the offending soap in the pocket of her apron. She got it out and looked at it in bewilderment. Jayne could smell the sheep's tallow fat from which it was made, crudely mixed with wood ash. She knew it could burn the skin in a matter of seconds, the mixture making so much alkali.

'I will go through her Ladyship's ways with you in detail and then you won't get into any more trouble,' said Jayne soothingly.

'Oh I hope you don't all stay for long,' grumbled Bess when Jayne had taken her through a list of household duties.

'You'd best get used to us, because in London they will be dropping dead again like flies when the weather changes; and they say that the stink of bodies is everywhere because whole families died and there was nobody to bury them properly, the poor souls,' said Thomas, hastily crossing himself.

'I don't understand it,' cried Bess. 'My mother always says "green winter, fat churchyard" but we had a right bitter winter last, the cattle froze in their stalls, so how could we have the plague?'

'Didn't you country people see the comet that lit the sky last December?' asked Thomas. 'It was the omen,' he went on. 'It warned us of dark things and like as not darker to come, I would say. The King went up to Tower Hill for many a night to watch it through his new glass. It's called a telescope.'

'What's a telescope?' asked Bess, wiping her runny nose on her sleeve.

'A long glass tube at least twelve foot long and all, and the King could see heaven itself as if it were a few feet away,' replied Thomas.

'Oh, tell us about the King and his Queen,' Bess cried excitedly, forgetting all about her red cheek.

'I will have no tittle tattle about the King,' said Thomas severely. Apart from the factor and two inside boys he was the only authoritative male servant and he was going to keep everyone in order.

'Well tell us about the navy then. My sister has a sweetheart who is a sailor. He was taken in the street when he went to London to sell his father's wool; they say he's off fighting the Dutch.'

'Aye and the pressing is a wicked thing. More than two thousand men and boys taken from their families, mostly bread winners who leave the wives and babes to starve, and the navy give them a so-called ticket to get the men's pay, which is not worth the paper it's written on,' Thomas explained, observing that he had a captive audience as most of the servants had gathered to listen to the tales from London which never ceased to amaze them.

'This war with the Dutch is a bad thing,' he went on doggedly. 'The common man sees no point in it and the navy is now commanded by the gentry instead of the Tarpaulins, that's men who up through the ranks who know the way of the sea ,' replied Thomas gravely.

'But why would the gentry want to go to sea and die of the bloody flux?' asked the wide eyed pantry boy.

'They do it for the prize money. Ther's no one to care for the poor men who die like dogs, and then there's the hundreds taken prisoner by the Dutch,' Thomas replied.

'And tell the boy what happens to them,' said Jayne.

'They rot in the Dutch jails, unless they turn coat and fight for the Hollanders and their brave captain De Ruyter who can rout all the English like the cunning fox he is.'

Thomas stopped, aware of the fact that his tales were probably nearer to Jayne's poor heart than his own. In all the months he had known her she had said very little about the loss of her husband. 'It's good, Mistress Jayne, you should ask about the navy,' he went on, gesturing in her direction. 'She has a hard tale to tell.'

'So tell us, please, Mistress Jayne,' Bess pleaded, knowing these London folk could tell her the truth of how things were. 'My sister cried bitter tears when her true love went to sea,' she carried on, 'but our mother says he will come back a rich man serving under the brave Lordship Albermarle who was the man called Monke who marched the Scottish army to bring back the King.'

'I do not know the truth of it,' replied Jayne warily, knowing that she would have little good to report, but not wanting to upset the girl unnecessarily. She had heard Sir Miles discussing the terrible state of the navy and the hopelessness of the gentlemen officers; and how Albermarle knew nothing of fighting at sea and was accused of cowardice by his men and how no money was sent to care for the English prisoners in Holland, unlike the Hollanders who sent a generous amount to see their own men would live to return to their families instead of perishing from starvation in a foreign jail. She shivered as she thought of the many sons and husbands suffering so.

'I am too busy,' she said perfunctorily. She had long ago decided that the best way of getting over the horror of her loss was to put it out of her mind, and she didn't see the point of talking about it.

'But you must,' Bess wheedled, 'for we all know you lost your man in service to the King.'

'Now there's an end to it, my girl,' said Thomas quickly, recalling that Jayne was reluctant to speak ill of the gentry, whom it was acknowledged had feathered their own nests while the poor struggled as much as ever.

There was a brief silence, broken by the hissing of a big copper kettle on the kitchen range and then Lady Harriet's voice. 'Are there no servants in the house?' came the clarion call, reducing the room to confusion.

Seeing the terror in Bess's eyes, Jayne put a kindly hand on her shoulder. The girl was trembling. Not for the first time Jayne had feelings of almost murderous intent towards Lady Harriet.

'Don't you go, Bess,' said Jayne. 'I will go to her and calm her down. You mustn't take on so,' she persevered encouragingly. 'She can't really hurt you and it's Sir Miles who rules the roost, whatever she likes to think. I will see to it that My Lady Mary knows of her striking you and she will tell her father and it won't happen again. He won't have his family beaten like some of his kind are apt to do. Why that Mr Pepys, the lady Harriet's so-called friend, regularly beats his people and his own wife.'

Jayne bustled into the great hall and, sweeping a low curtsy, addressed Lady Harriet in a falsely sweet voice. 'I am here, My Lady, for Bess your maid is indisposed, having mysteriously walked into a door and injured her head.' Jayne waited a moment while she observed Lady Harriett's expression change from confident superiority to nervous embarrassment. 'And now,' Jayne continued staunchly, loading the news with innuendo which did not escape Lady Harriet, 'for the moment the poor girl is rendered quite deaf and cannot hear at all, and I am to ask Sir Miles to send for the physician since such good servants are so hard to find, and your Ladyship has need of a fine girl like Bess.'

When Jayne returned to the kitchen she had a warm reception from the servants, all of whom had been listening to the exchange between herself and Lady Harriet, but discretion was just one of Jayne's good qualities and she brushed aside the approving comments about her dialogue with Lady Harriet. All the same, she knew a point had been made, although she wisely judged that the high ground might be lost by embarking on a below stairs assassination of Lady Harriet's character.

'Now, we must all get back to work, the master will be returning soon with Miss Mary and all must be ready,' she said briskly, as Thomas winked at her approvingly.

Jayne had unofficially taken over some of the household details, and went immediately to the parlour, to make sure everything was in order for Sir Miles and his daughter on their return from their morning walk. She looked about her with pleasure, thinking how much more this was to her taste than the fussy interior of the London house. The room was panelled in beautifully carved oak that the maids at Sailing took a special pride in waxing to a high sheen, which reflected the glow from the fire burning cheerfully in the enormous stone fireplace, either side of which, were a pair of high-backed needlepoint chairs, worked by Sir Miles's mother and walnut cabinets veneered in maple which contained Sir Miles's rare collection of pipes, each of which had a story to tell. He prided himself on having a pipe for every occasion, some of which had incurred the wrath of Lady Harriet, who considered them lewd, particularly the figures of Leda and the swan, so he kept them firmly locked and the key hung on his watch chain. The stone floors were strewn with thick tapestry rugs, a thing impossible in London since the filth from the streets would have soiled them in a day. In the country, walks were confined to the neat gravel paths, anything more adventurous was strictly supervised by attentive stewards with a selection of outdoor boots and shoes, which were always found waiting in the hall.

There were tall, arched leaded windows overlooking the garden, in front of which was a long, highly polished oak table where breakfast was carefully set for two. The room contained a heady mixture of pleasing scents, from the beeswax polish, jasmine from the glasshouse in a huge brass urn, and hyacinths planted in a large blue and white Delft bowl. There was more of this Dutch china about the room, particularly on a ledge where the panelling ended, which drew the eye to the intricately moulded ceiling covered with a dark patina from years of wood smoke. The room was not the domain of a lonely bachelor and spoke volumes about the people who enjoyed and tended it. There were many touches which spoke of a caring female hand, and not that of Lady Harriet.

Thomas came in, followed by William, one of the house boys, carrying a canvas holdall of logs which he carefully stacked beside the fire.

'The smell of this apple wood reminds me of my childhood,' said Thomas. 'I'm glad the master uses this in the best rooms instead of coal. I never could abide the filthy stuff, it's been the ruination of the city and what with the poor burning that greasy sea coal which belches such fumes as would choke a man, it's good to be here breathing clean country air.'

'That's all very well for you to say but with all the wood being taken for ships, without so much as a by your leave we would all freeze without it,' said Jayne.

'You're right as usual,' Thomas agreed. 'I saw the red arrow painted on some of Sir Miles's trees yesterday.'

'Yes, it was the King's men,' interjected the house boy, as he swept up stray bits of bark from the logs. 'They came last week and marked out the trees and they've done the same all over these parts. Even Squire Cater's. And there's no argument, and no compensation. What with that and the hearth tax, people are blocking up their fires and making do in one room; some spend time with the cattle at nights, when the weather's hard, just for the warmth of the creatures.'

Jayne pondered this as she fussed with the table settings, rearranging the pewter service and horn-handled cutlery. She made sure the special silver poker was ready in the fire to heat the master's ale on his return. Looking out of the window, she saw Mary and her father walking towards the house.

'The master is a good man,' said Thomas, joining her. 'It warms the heart to see him with Miss Mary, and the way he talks so gentle to her.'

Sir Miles had his arm about Mary's shoulder; he was at least a foot taller than his daughter and she nestled happily towards him. They slowed their pace as they came towards the house, obviously deep in conversation.

'Miss Mary is a comely wench, for sure,' said William, having joined them by the window, 'not like the mother. She's a right battle-axe. I reckon as not half the servants will leave if they have to cope with her for much longer especially after – ' he stopped for a moment as Jayne and Thomas stared at him disapprovingly, but secretly in agreement with his outspoken opinions, 'well you knows what I mean, after the other . . . ' he ploughed on bravely, 'we all like her, and no one in these parts can blame the poor man. After all, he's only human.'

Thomas was in two minds as to whether to cuff the boy's ears or to speak to him man to man. One thing was sure; he could not be party to a situation where the family business was discussed lasciviously with the lower servants. But these were hard times and such adversity broke down barriers with sensible country people and he knew that loyal 'family' must best think of their masters as flesh and blood in the service of God, even though he appeared to have forgotten them all. The plague did not discriminate between rich and poor, even the King had just lost his own brother and sister from the smallpox – and so soon after his joyful return from exile, it was a cruel thing.

'You should not speak of such things in front of Mistress Mary,' he said eventually.

'Oh, away with you, Thomas, we have all had our suspicions,' said Jayne in a practical tone, 'and such things are common amongst the gentry. What can you expect when Her Ladyship won't spend the time of day in the place which puts the fine clothes on her back?' she persisted. 'But none of that concerns me; my loyalty is to Sir Miles, who saved me from starvation, and mostly to Miss Mary, who has the makings of a great lady. I will serve her as long as God spares me, for I know she is cut from the same tree as her father and how she ever came from that woman I will never know.' She lifted her head towards the door as it opened suddenly, revealing an incandescent Lady Harriet.

CHAPTER FOUR

Norfolk, Spring 1666

More than a year had passed and life at Sailing had fallen into an uneasy pattern. News from London had been dire. The plague was virulent, ten thousand dead in a week. The carts collected the bodies in darkness and they were hastily buried in pits without ceremony or name. Lime was quickly spread over the tormented remains before they were covered in a thin layer of soil. The sickening stench of death pervaded the air.

By contrast it was a fresh and beautiful morning at Sailing, the gardens were in full bloom, the fruit trees abundant, and nature basked in an air of fecundity at odds with this human catastrophe.

Sir Miles had sent Jayne to fetch Mary to his study, for he had news which concerned him deeply.

'Good-morning, Father,' said Mary cheerfully. She had been in the gardens, gathering flowers for the house. Her happy appearance made it all the more difficult for her father tell her the decision he had come to. He knew how she had grappled with her grief over the loss of Anthony but life at Sailing had restored her. Even Harriet had stopped harping about the boredom of the country, as she blanched in terror at the stories from London. As for himself, his wife's presence had disrupted his routine considerably and this latest news was yet another blow.

'Sit down, my dear,' he said solemnly, regret almost overwhelming him when he saw the pretty picture his daughter made, sitting gracefully in her sprigged morning frock, the basket of flowers at her feet and her shining red hair tumbling on to her shoulders. Ned and Betty sat either side of her, their noses pressed in her lap as she fondled their ears. She looked at him with her honest gaze and knew at once what he was about to tell her. Something which would disrupt the pattern of normality she had created around herself. Like a life raft it had prevented her from drowning in the cavernous emptiness that the loss of Anthony had left in her heart.

'Tell me quickly, Father. What has happened?' she asked anxiously.

'The plague is upon us, my dear. I did not tell you before, hoping the stories were exaggerated. It has been in Colchester for some weeks and half the town is dead or dying and now it has broken out in Norwich, but, more worryingly, there are cases in the village.' He paused, waiting for Mary to assimilate the news. She put one hand to her brow, the other idly fondling the dog's ears. Sir Miles went on as he knew he must, sensing that she anticipated something of what he had decided.

'It is only a matter of time until one of our family is infected,' he continued levelly, 'and then, as you know, we shall be locked up.' He didn't stop because he had to tell it to her firmly and resolutely before she had time to weaken his resolve. 'I have arranged for you to go to your Aunt Briott at Hampton Court where you will be safer. The pestilence has died out there. The court returned from Oxford two months ago, so I am sure this is an accurate barometer.'

Mary thought quickly. The news had not come as a complete surprise. Jayne had told her as much on the previous day. Her Aunt Briott, her father's half-sister, had been a heroine in the family. Married to the son of the late King's silversmith, she had served his two younger children loyally during their imprisonment by Parliament and had been rewarded with a handsome fortune by Charles II. The woman lived in great splendour close to Hampton Court Palace and mixed frequently in court circles as she had another house over looking the Privy Gardens at the

Palace of Whitehall. She often spoke with the King, who stalwartly valued old friendships in a way not typical of his class.

Mary knew at once the efficacy of her father's decision, she recognised the frightful march of the sickness and realised that, given the circumstances, they had no choice. She was young and resilient and, besides, although life at Sailing had at first been her saving, being alone with her mother, as she was for much of the time, had begun to get on her nerves. Her mind raced at once to the prospect of what life with her aunt might have in store. Much as she would miss her father and Sailing and feeling part of the community which worked so closely with her father, on the land which had been in her family for centuries, she knew there was a life elsewhere. She had a curious feeling that something beckoned her, something far away on a bigger stage, away from her mother's stifling temperamental outbursts, narrow views and ridiculous chatter.

Being at such close quarters with the local people, as she had been recently with her father while he went about his work, had opened her to the way the majority of people felt. They talked of the King, whom they all loved; they said he was a people's King and spoke of the fact that he had provided a thousand pounds of his own money each week for the plague families locked in their houses; how he cared for the common man as no other monarch had done before him. But they bemoaned the fact that the King was surrounded by a dissolute court. They spoke of the war with the Dutch, of the great ships that went to the East to bring back spices and silks and of the King's Portuguese Queen whose dowry had brought the great ports of Tangier and Bombay. It was, ironically, these simple country people who had opened her eyes to the world outside, and she had become restless.

Sir Miles was more than a little surprised when Mary put up no objections to the plan, and everything was settled. It was decided that she should take Jayne with her and they would leave by water in a few days.

CHAPTER FIVE

Hampton Court, Late Summer 1666

Judith Briott had adapted well to her life after the Restoration; the King's gift had brought her unimaginable riches and as her own family were now grown up and her husband had died, she was only too pleased at the prospect of taking her charming niece to live with her. She liked the girl, and it had been a sadness to her that her half-brother's wife had been such a tiresome woman. Harriet moved in a circle of people who were not to Judith's taste, who, not to put too fine a point on it, deluded themselves into thinking they were members of the elite aristocracy. Judith knew better and floated modestly in and out of court circles with an enviable ease. It was this that paved the way for the suggestion she made to her niece on a bright summer morning a few weeks after her arrival.

'Mary, my dear,' she said happily, 'let us walk through the gardens down to the river. Jayne must come and we shall take the dogs.' She turned to Jayne, who was sewing in the corner of the beautiful drawing room, and Judith thought with pleasure how nice it was to have these two attractive women in her home.

In many ways Judith had taken over the friendship that Mary had so valued with her father. Judith followed the political situation with voracious perspicacity, and in the morning, walks would be an intriguing update of the latest situation both in London and at sea and with some racy gossip about the court. What Mary had not guessed was the reason her aunt educated her in these matters. She had plans for her niece and although Mary's beauty and grace were without question, she would need more than just her looks if she were to have the future her aunt envisaged. She had already judged the girl's intelligence and had found her an eager pupil.

Judith had engaged a tutor, who was teaching Mary Spanish, the language the Queen spoke to the King, and she was perfecting her French, since it was well known that the King would often break into this, his mother's native tongue, and those who could not comprehend it were at a great disadvantage. Judith had also engaged a dancing master to teach Mary the Bransles and the 'New Dance', the King's favourite, just arrived from France. The only dance Mary had previously been taught was the Corant, which Judith informed her was now decidedly out of fashion. Judith was delighted that after just a few lessons Mary was as skilled as any of the great court beauties.

They walked down a wide gravel path which led to the river where Judith had built a quiet arbour; they sat with the dogs, a troupe of Cavalier spaniels, some of whom had sired at least three of the King's famous dogs, from which he was inseparable. As the dogs ran amok, chasing outraged ducks and geese into the silky waters of the river, Judith began her eagerly awaited bulletin. A week ago they had recalled the great naval victory off Lowestoft the previous June, when the Dutch lost thirty ships to the English, but today the news was not so good.

'It is said that if the Duke of York, the King's brother, had pursued the Dutch while he had the advantage a year ago it would have been the end of this senseless war,' Judith informed them, 'but he let his chance go and now, after a year, the Dutch are as strong as ever they were under the great Admiral de Ruyter and we shall soon be chasing our tails again.'

'And so what is going to happen now?' Mary asked apprehensively.

'I heard yesterday that the Dutch are out again and, not withstanding great bravery shown by the Duke of Albermarle when he destroyed more than twenty of the enemy ships and killed the Dutch vice admiral Evertson, the Dutch miraculously recovered and chased the fleet back up the river and they had to surrender the pride of our navy, the *Royal Prince*.'

'What about the French, Aunt?' Mary asked. 'Surely they will have to declare themselves sooner or later?'

'You are right,' said Judith. 'It is my guess that soon the King will turn to the French and his uncle King Louis, for don't forget the King was virtually brought up as a Frenchman and he has his mother's blood. But they say Louis would drive a hard bargain, for all the brotherly love.'

'Oh, Aunt Judith, it is all so senseless!' Mary cried. 'When I think that my own grandmother was a Hollander and then we thought of them as brothers. What can it all be for when all we do is destroy each other, and why does the King support this madness?'

'It is all about money, my dear,' sighed Judith. 'The King has to dance to Parliament's tune and though he is by nature a peaceful and circumspect man, he sees this as the chance to become independent. The prizes can be very great and don't forget that is why he married his little Queen – the alliance opened great opportunities for trade.'

'I have heard it started when we took New Amsterdam in the Americas to get a share in the slave trade. The Dutch bring them from East Africa chained like animals in the great ships and the stench is carried for miles across the open sea,' said Mary.

'Yes, my dear, it is a sin that our people are being squandered for a trade in human beings, but it has gone on for centuries. Now Mary,' said Judith on a lighter note, 'I have something perfectly splendid to tell you, because one lesson we must all learn is that when life is at its lowest we must keep hold of what we can so that when happier days come we are prepared and all the minor details are in order.' She paused for a moment, cogitating, while she regarded her well-kept hands spread in the folded silk of her dress, recalling the time when she cared for the late King's children and her hands had been reddened by the hard work she had to do during their dreadful imprisonment.

'My dear, I have been watching you carefully in the last weeks and I have decided to seek a position at court for you,' Judith announced.

'Oh, Aunt, I can hardly believe it,' cried Mary, jumping up from the garden seat and clapping her hands excitedly.

'Well, believe it you must,' Judith insisted. 'Why do you think I have been grooming you in this way? You have been a good pupil. For a girl to hold a position at court, she must have an understanding of the country's affairs, a quality sadly lacking with your dear mother,' Judith paused, regretting falling into the trap of criticising her sister-in-law, especially in view of the other news, which she had decided to keep from her niece for the time being. Nothing must interfere with her immediate arrangements.

'The Queen has need of more ladies of the bedchamber and they must be Catholic,' she continued. 'The King has acknowledged the importance of the Queen's faith, even though, as you know, Catholics are to be removed from positions of authority, a thing which stands to denude the country and the navy of still more of its intelligent leaders.'

'Oh, Aunt this is so exciting!' cried Mary. 'I have only ever seen the King once, when he was walking in the park, and I will never forget it.'

'Well, I can understand that,' said Judith. 'He is the finest man I ever saw, and whatever they may say to the contrary, the Queen is a beautiful person, full of grace, and gentle and kind, and she is sorely tried by that – ' Judith hesitated, looking across the water, unsure as to how to proceed, 'that woman. You will have to be told about all this, dear child. I mean, of course, that creature Barbara Palmer, the brazen trollop that she is. She has the King in her power with her tricks and scheming. The Queen weeps bitter tears as the woman produces a clutch of the King's bastards and Catherine loses child after child, the last as recently as March when the court was at Oxford.'

'Do you mean Lady Castlemaine? Why do you call her Barbara Palmer?' asked Mary.

'Her husband, the cuckold he is, was given the title so that the King might elevate his mistress,' replied Judith acidly. 'But there are many at court who will not give her that respect; she comes from an evil family, the Villiers. The Duke of Buckingham is her cousin, as much a rogue as his father, the man will soon be sent to the tower for his arrogance. He gets so high that one day he will fall and it will be a long way down.' A glint of pleasure crossed Judith's face as she thought of the possible fate of the present Duke of Buckingham, and she recalled the well-deserved demise of his father, murdered like the criminal he was.

Mary listened to her aunt speaking so frankly, and with such visceral dislike, with mounting alarm. She wondered how she could conduct herself in the fast flowing and glamorous world at court where, she was beginning to see, you only had to scratch the surface to find a treacherous nest of vipers. Judith saw her niece's face cloud apprehensively.

'Now don't you worry,' she said reassuringly. 'I had to tell you these things because they are trenchant to the life you will have to lead, and mark my words you are more than capable of dealing with these people. The thing you must remember,' she added emphatically, 'is absolute and undying loyalty. You have to concentrate your mind on what you believe to be right. I would not even consider your entering the Queen's service if I did not respect her and admire her for her courage and decency. You will grow to love her as all her servants do, even the great Chancellor Clarendon serves her loyally, despite her Catholic faith, being a fervent protestant; and that is another thing you must guard carefully, my dear. But beware, and as in all things, keep your own council with modesty.'

'Who shall I meet first?' Mary asked, almost unable to comprehend what was happening.

'I have corresponded with Lord Clarendon,' said Judith. 'He arranges all matters for Her Majesty's court and he is satisfied with your credentials. We are to expect an interview in a few days, and this afternoon the dressmaker is coming to make you a suitable gown before you are to be presented to the Queen.'

Matters had moved on rapidly and it was only later, when Jayne burst into tears of joy, that Mary began to grasp just what was happening to her. Jayne was in a great state of excitement since Judith had informed her niece that even a humble maid of honour must have her own servant.

Later, the seamstress came to fit Mary for her new gown. 'There will be no more stiff and formal costumes such as we have been used to,' explained Judith. 'Ladies of the court have taken to the French style brought by the Queen Mother, Henrietta. You shall have a graceful, flowing dress and your hair must be worn in well-smoothed curls caught with a rose or some pearls. And, as you see, we have found the best silks and satins for you to choose from, and ribbons for the bodice.'

The gown was to be ready in two days, in time for Mary's first audience with Lord Clarendon and the Countess of Suffolk, Lady Castlemaine's aunt, who was the Queen's principle Lady of the Bedchamber.

It was only as Judith explained all this that Mary remembered the gossip Harriet had so enjoyed when the King had insisted that his innocent young bride have his mistress Lady Castlemaine as one of her ladies. She asked Judith about this later and the answer left her trembling with indignation on the Queen's behalf. She had begun to see a darker side of the handsome beguiling King. She asked herself how he could have inflicted such a humiliation on his young bride. She decided to leave the matter of Lady Castlemaine alone for the time being as Judith chattered on, explaining that the court was in mourning for the Queen's mother and the court would be in black, but until Mary entered her service it would be considered presumptuous to dress likewise.

Later that day, Mary walked to the river alone. The air was still, with the slight edge of a storm in a strangely purple hued sky. She had adopted a favourite place to sit and think, a fallen willow on the river's edge, where Judith had cleverly planted roses and honeysuckle. Wood pigeons cooed to their mates in the branches of the trees above and a pair of swans sailed gracefully past, followed by six half grown signets, at one with the tranquil water flowing timelessly to the sea.

The sight of the happy family so at odds with the human world of which they were disdainfully oblivious brought with it a wave of emotion for Mary. She thought of her love for Anthony, of all the evenings like this they had shared, of all the evenings they would never share, of all the babies they would never have, and of the map of her future which had been so cruelly erased by the death of the man she loved, and as she perceived it, the only man she would ever love. For one mad moment she felt a compelling urge to fling herself in the water and find peace in its dark green depths.

But then the small pearls of hope sown by her aunt that day pushed up through her consciousness like vigorous green shoots. Mary had an intense belief in her own destiny. It was part of the solid rock which her beginnings had given her, perhaps something to do with her father, with the courtesy with which he had nurtured the good in her. It was also to do with her Catholic faith and she wondered, as she had done so often recently, if there really was a God and for what purpose he had sent this incomprehensible suffering. It was this matter of faith that she now realised was the crux of the dichotomy facing the country. For it was the Protestant rich who had originally accumulated their wealth and power by seconding monasteries and suppressing the belief that had been her family's cornerstone.

She straightened her back and looked towards the setting sun as it shot its last elliptical rays across the water, the pungent fragrance of honeysuckle and roses, always so sharp at day's close, caressed her. She plucked some of the blooms and walked towards the water. The family of swans was quickly disappearing from sight as she gently cast the flowers into the fast flowing water. They were taken up in a little zephyr and went fluttering towards the bend in the river and out of sight.

'Goodbye, my darling,' she said softly before turning toward her aunt's house. Through the open windows she could hear Jayne singing her favourite Dowland song: 'Now, oh, now we needs must part'.

As she entered the room through the open garden door her aunt came to her and took her in her arms.

'Are you all right, my dear?' Judith asked, noticing Mary's anxious face.

'Yes, Aunt,' replied Mary. 'I have been thinking about my new life, and I have finally come to terms with Anthony's death. I must stop feeling sorry for myself. When I see how the world suffers I realise I have not accepted my own loss as God would have me do.'

'Remember, my dear,' said Judith gravely, 'it is not what you are or have been that God looks on with compassion, but what you want to be.'

'I will be what God wants me to be,' Mary replied guardedly.

CHAPTER SIX

Mary's departure had left Sir Miles with a void. His love for his daughter was an edifice built on many things, not least his disillusionment with his wife and two other daughters. The death of his two baby sons had taken from him the dream of handing the family heritage down to another generation of Boyntons. There would be no Boynton to live at Sailing after he was gone, no son to look after the village and continue the business which fed so many hungry mouths. He loved all the people who depended on him. He knew each family dynamic, their births, their deaths, joys and sorrows; and he knew they returned that love with a loyalty and respect which he saw as a God given honour.

Not once in all his years with Harriet had she acknowledged this or displayed any interest in it and when she had finally given up any pretence at producing a son his resentment had turned to indifference.

It was with this indifference that he had listened to her when she told him she felt ill. And then, after a few days, he had been called to her bed by Bess. 'You'd best come, Sir Miles, My Lady is very poorly and Thomas fears it is the plague.' The colour had drained from the girl's face and Sir Miles could only imagine her thoughts as she calculated the inevitability of contagion.

Harriet was propped completely upright on her Flemish lace pillows; the gentry never lay down flat, fearing the prone body was an invitation to death.

'My dear, you look very uncomfortable, surely you should take away some of the pillows,' said Sir Miles. He knew at once that it was not the plague which ailed her. He was familiar with the symptoms and Harriet's waxen face and sunken cheek bones heralded something quite different.

'We must send for the physician at once; I am quite sure it is not the plague,' he announced emphatically.

The girl gave an audible sigh of relief and within the hour the physician appeared. He gave Sir Miles a reassuring nod as he approached the bed for he concluded at once that it was not as the maid had feared. Sir Miles waited as the man talked gently to Harriet and then pulled back the covers to examine the patient. It had been many years since Sir Miles had seen his wife's naked body and he was shocked to see how she had lost weight. Her hip bones protruded sharply and the base of her rib cage gave way to a deep hollow where she had once been rounded and soft, but just below there was a strange and marked protuberance almost like a pregnancy. The thing which struck him most was a strange, almost feral, smell of decay. His mind flashed back to the time when he had loved and desired her, and, as if sensing his thoughts, she cried out as the physician pressed his hand into her belly and her eyes sought those of her husband, her face contorted with fear.

'Oh, husband, the pain it is so terrible, it is God's revenge for the way I have been,' she said weakly. He noticed her hands, the veins etching a map through parchment skin, and his heart contracted with a kind of dread. He knew that his wife was dying and their life together flashed past him in an unresolved story, now written with no chance of alteration or resolution. Was he as guilty as she had been, as he had always assumed her to be, he asked himself? Had he ceased to love her before he had met Charlotte or had she driven him from her bed? After that he couldn't remember, it all seemed so long ago, like another life. And yet here it was, his wife's journey at its end and he frantically asked himself if he could redeem them both in the few remaining hours or days she had left.

The physician took Sir Miles outside the room and they stood in a dark corner of the gallery outside his wife's chamber.

'It is a pernicious growth, Sir Miles; it will spread and ultimately consume her, poor wretch. She must have suffered it for some time,' he said in a hushed voice.

'I never suspected, why would I? My wife is a very private woman,' Sir Miles stammered.

'Did she not complain to you?' the doctor asked, with a faint note of accusation in his voice.

Sir Miles knew that Bess and Thomas were listening and he chose to ignore the question. It was pointless to try to explain a whole life-time of misunderstanding in a few words.

'How long has she got and what can we do for her?' he asked, regaining some of his composure.

'I cannot say,' said the physician cautiously. 'I recommend bleeding to relieve the congestion of the blood and some laudanum given in pounded snails and get her maid to shave My Lady's head, it will help with the fever.'

The physician said no more, he had other things on his mind. The pestilence had come and he was minded to leave the area, for there was nothing he could do for any of the poor souls and he had a daughter in another county where there was no sign of the pestilence. He would take his family and leave as soon as possible. Lady Boynton had been his last patient here.

Sir Miles thought about Charlotte, who had given him back his manhood. This was the woman he loved apart from his daughter Mary, who was the one beautiful thing he felt he had salvaged from his union with Harriet. But it was Charlotte who had lain with him in the summer meadows and she who smelt of new grass and spring blossoms, who walked with him through the hemp crops, and felt the Norfolk land in her bones. She cared as he did about the people who breathed the Norfolk air. But Harriet was still here and she had come to the end her days in the place for which she did not care. Considering all this, he walked downstairs and into the garden, making his way to the glasshouse, where he knew instinctively that Charlotte would be waiting for him.

She wore her old summer bonnet, and simple white country frock and the sight of her was, as usual for Miles, a healing balm. She looked up as he approached, her sweet happy face, unfashionably tanned, complimenting her dark blue eyes, and thick pale brown hair, a face of no outstanding beauty but one that attracted a second and a third glance just for the sheer pleasure of gazing at something so ordinarily at one with the world.

'I have heard,' she said, full of genuine concern. 'I am so sorry, I am praying for her.'

He went to her and she pressed her head to his chest. As her bonnet fell back he inhaled the smell of her hair and felt the warmth of her breast through his tunic. She knew, because they knew each other so well, that there was nothing he could say. She said it for him.

'I will be waiting,' she said simply. 'You must be with her, do what you can. It was a life, my dearest, she chose to live. We must respect her for that.'

'I loved her once,' he said gruffly. 'I will try to make her feel that I do so again, even if it is a lie, it may ease her suffering . . . but I never thought she would . . . ' he stopped.

'Don't say any more,' Charlotte murmured, slightly ashamed that even now, her mind had raced, and even though she felt sorry for Harriet ending her life with so little love around her, the woman's death would be her own salvation. Her own family had felt dishonoured by the fact that she was mistress to Sir Miles, instead of choosing one of the local men who would have given her security and children. She quickly curbed her thoughts, and resolved to be patient for just a little longer. She would not let Miles see how she felt, how eagerly she waited for an end to the insecurity she had brought upon herself by loving him.

'I feel curiously numb,' said Sir Miles. 'It is difficult to imagine Harriet dying; I hope I will be able to grieve, as a man should do for his wife.'

'They always say, when a husband or wife dies, it is the harder if they have been out of harmony,' said Charlotte by way of reassurance. 'You will do what is right,' she said confidently. As Sir Miles listened to her, he wondered, not for the first time, whether her confidence in him was as well placed as she thought . . . and he made up his mind that if he had a second chance for happiness he would not let it slip away. He would guard it like the Holy Grail. He left her and went back to his wife for as long as she had.

Harriet died a month later. In those four weeks their marriage experienced a kind of resurrection. As Harriet drifted in and out of consciousness, she imagined they were young again, and Miles nursed her with a devotion which amazed 'the family'. When the end came it was with a great peace. The Catholic priest came and said the mass and she slipped away as Miles held her thin hand. He felt comforted by the calm which had preceded his wife's physical death.

Mary returned briefly for a hastily convened funeral. Neither one of her sisters could attend, the elder being about to give birth and the other mysteriously indisposed. At first Mary had been shocked that neither could be there to say goodbye to their mother but her father convinced her that at a time when the country was in such crisis, it was the living who must take priority, and the matter was not mentioned again.

*   *   *

After what he considered to be a suitable interval, Thomas confided in Bess his hopes for his master. 'The world is in chaos, the master is alone,' he said thoughtfully. 'Now I hope Miss Charlotte comes to be mistress here before we are all dead. There is no point in waiting,' he added bluntly. 'He needs her. Folk round here have thought of her as the mistress for years, it was the other one . . . God rest her soul, who didn't belong.'

Thomas had long developed a way of communicating local opinions to his master by articulating them when he knew Sir Miles could hear and this was just such a case.

Sir Miles lost no time and the next day he took the coach to the farmhouse where Charlotte still lived with her widowed mother, and brought her to Sailing. During the night she stirred in his arms, and he woke, not at first comprehending the miraculous speed with which destiny had moved his life' and then he heard her quiet voice.

'Miles, my dearest, we will not be alone, I am with child.'

CHAPTER SEVEN

The Palace of Whitehall, September 1666

Following a successful meeting with Lord Clarendon and Lady Suffolk, Judith showed Mary the palace at Whitehall; it was the day before Mary was to make her first official appearance and she was decidedly nervous. As she walked demurely beside her aunt with her eyes modestly downcast, a throng of elegantly dressed people jostled around them. Most ignored them, but occasionally one of the ladies would give her aunt a cursory nod and then look at Mary in her plain frock with evident contempt, not withstanding her dress, some of the men looked at her with undisguised lasciviousness.

'Pay no attention,' said Judith dismissively, as one of the court gentlemen ogled Mary with insulting blatancy.

'Aunt, I can hardly believe it, the men wear paint on their faces,' remarked Mary, stifling a giggle, as one of them pouted a pair of red lips at her, with a lewd kissing noise.

'Yes, my dear, and they look like a lot of idiotic girls. It is the fashion,' Judith went on scornfully. 'But you can spot the ones who have any sense. They look like men, as God intended.'

'Surely the King does not paint his face,' ventured Mary, hoping that her first unfavourable impressions of the inhabitants of Whitehall, would not be universal.

'Of course not,' Judith assured her unhesitatingly. 'The King has no need of that kind of artifice, and you will see that none the gentlemen in Her Majesty's entourage do either. The late King would be horrified if he could see what this place has become. I sometimes think it must be a reaction to everything that happened during that dreadful time.'

Mary's spirits began to flag as they meandered through the vast rabbit warren of buildings and Judith explained exactly where everybody lived.

'Of course I cannot show inside the King's apartments, or the ones lived in by the King's brother, the Duke of York and his wife, and then there are the ones occupied by Prince Rupert, the King's cousin, and the Duke of Monmouth, his son by his first mistress, Lucy Walters. I sometimes wonder how it is all paid for,' said Judith, shaking her head despairingly.

'So does each member of the royal family have their own household?' asked Mary in amazement.

'They do,' said Judith. 'And of course there are the King's mistresses and their children, and all the hangers-on, the so called 'noble' ladies and gentlemen who seem to have found themselves a profligate lifestyle at the King's expense.'

'And does the King pay all the people who look after them?' asked Mary incredulously.

'You may well ask,' replied Judith through pursed lips. 'Each has their own separate establishment – kitchens, cellars, pantries, spiceries, cider houses, slaughter houses, bake houses, wood yards, and coal yards. I could go on forever, really the whole thing is quite ridiculous.'

'I fear I will never understand all this, let alone find my way about,' said Mary anxiously.

'Oh, yes, you will, just like all these other fine ladies and gentlemen,' said Judith purposefully. 'And now I am going to show you my favourite part of the palace,' she went on whilst stoically striding ahead.

She lead the way to a massive gallery running along the east of the palace between the river and what were known as the Privy Gardens, the private gardens of the royal family and their enormous entourage.

'This,' Judith said in a low voice, 'is where the King is prone to walk, with his troupe of dogs, making decision with his advisors.'

Judith went on to warn Mary of the hazards of the King's dogs who left a trail of messes, and sure enough in the distance Mary's heart raced as she saw the royal party, followed by two servants with mops and buckets.

'There is many a satin slipper ruined in this place,' Judith cautioned, 'But that is the least of the hazards you will encounter here, I am afraid,' she hissed darkly as she swept Mary into a side passage to avoid a premature meeting with the King. Judith knew full well that even in her plain gown Mary would not escape the royal eye.

'Why are they all in such a hurry?' Mary asked as she saw a great surge of people hastening after the King and his party.

'They are all off to the banqueting hall to be present when their Majesties dine in public,' said Judith.

'I am truly disappointed because I could hardly see anything through all those people, only the top of the King's head above the crowd. Is he really so much taller than everyone else?' asked Mary.

'My dear, he is head and shoulders above them all in every way,' said Judith wryly.

*   *   *

That evening Mary drew herself a little map, which she kept in her purse which hung from her waist. She tried to memorise it, and sleep evaded her as she considered not only the enormity of the place which was to be her home, but also the people within it.

Together with Judith she arrived with her boxes the following day to take up residence in the Queen's apartments, but the introduction was to be conducted with strict formality.

The timing was, as usual with anything in Judith's control, immaculate. The Queen's apartments were empty when Mary arrived. They were on the south side of the palace between the river and the long gallery, and the first impact took Mary's breath away.

'Oh, Aunt, look what a picture this makes,' she cried, as she gazed out on to the river through an ingenious concoction of parterres Charles had built on a lawn which projected into the river. Mary's eyes continued to widen in excitement as Judith pointed out the famous exotic sundial the King had erected, portraying the faces of the King and Queen, Prince Rupert and the Duke of York, with the river beyond, on which there was a constant hub of boats.

'Do you see the palace barges with the royal rowers dressed in bright red livery?' asked Judith, sharing some of her niece's excitement. It was a sight which still brought pleasure to her, reminding her of many happy times she had spent on the water as a young woman.

They walked slowly through the Queen's apartments, which led from one room to another, and although each was more sumptuous than the last, Mary soon calculated that privacy was impossible and comfort was not a priority in a place where appearance was all.

'The Queen sleeps on a fine feather bed similar to your own at my house at Hampton Court,' said Judith, 'but you will see the royal bedchamber later; now I will take you to your new quarters.'

They got to a mean little passage where several rooms abutted and one of these was to be Mary's. Her heart sank and Judith's words did little to lift her first impression.

'Here the royal servants are provided with hard pallets and few comforts, but there is reason behind this, the assumption being that you will at all times be at Her Majesty's service. You will soon get used to it,' said Judith brightly, as she patted the narrow bed, raising a cloud of dust. Mary smelt the rancid whiff of rat droppings.

Judith looked at her niece quickly, noticing Mary's expression and knowing full well that it would not take Mary long to find out that the life of a royal servant was full of stark contrasts, and her own family life as an ordinary middle class girl had much to recommend it.

'Aunt, this is not at all what I expected,' said Mary in dismay.

'I shall send a coach with some comforts for this room,' said Judith, casting her beady eye over the shabby coverlet and broken furniture. 'And, what is more, I will speak to the wretch who is to act as your servant and get her to clean this room thoroughly.'

'But where is Jayne to sleep?' asked Mary nervously. No mention had been made of accommodation for Jayne, who was to accompany her.

'I will arrange for another small bed to be put in the room,' said Judith. 'You cannot sleep alone in this place,' she finished with conviction, only serving to increase the sense of alarm which was beginning to overwhelm her niece.

As today was to be the first time Mary had officially attended court and she was to be formally presented to the King and the Queen amidst the full glare of the royal coterie, Judith hastily calculated they had some time before Mary would have to put on her new dress. She took a deep breath and embarked on a hasty explanation of the principal players on the stage Mary was about to enter.

'You must realise that all these people are greedy for power,' she began, 'and central to them all is the King. There is not one of them,' she stopped a minute, the pause emphasising what she was about to add, 'except for the good Chancellor,' she continued emotionally, 'who acts from the dictates of their heart.'

'So exactly who are these frightening people?' asked Mary, recalling the unfriendly atmosphere she had sensed from the moment of her first arrival. She had heard the gossip about the court as had most people, but putting a face to all these famous characters was a different matter and she listened intently to what her aunt had to tell her.

'Firstly,' said Judith, 'you must watch out for the Duke of Buckingham and you need to know a little about him. He lost his younger brother Francis, who died bravely fighting for the late King. But would it had been the elder who had been taken. Then we would have been spared this pernicious influence on our sovereign. The boys were brought up with the King and his brother James, Duke of York, after the murder of his profligate father, the first Duke, who wormed his way into their grandfather's affections with his beauty, wit and grace, and a prediliction for unnatural practices such as should not be mentioned in front of a young girl. Sadly he bewitched the late King likewise,' explained Judith obliquely.

Mary shuddered, she heard dark allusions to such matters in conversations among the servants, and did not want to appear naïve, whilst at the same time she did not want further elaboration. She was already sick with nerves, so she nodded her head knowingly and looked down at the floor.

Judith paused thoughtfully, an expression of distaste crossed her normally sanguine features as she thought about these things. Then she straightened her shoulders, as if to continue was an effort against her better nature, but she knew she must go on for her niece would be at grave risk if she did not understand these complex tangled webs. Judith knew that knowledge was the best protection for her niece and she knew so delicate a flower would be ripe for the plucking, if she were not on her metal.

'The gene continues with the son, the present Duke. He crawls nearer to the ground than a snake,' she went on. 'He, my dear, is hell bent on bringing down the Chancellor, Lord Clarendon. He conspires to do so with his cousin, the unmentionable Lady Castlemaine. They stop at nothing to discredit the Chancellor.'

'But why should they hate the Chancellor so much? He is such a gentleman,' asked Mary in bewilderment.

'There is a long history there,' Judith recounted. 'The Chancellor, Edward Hyde, as he was then, had already been Chancellor of the Exchequer for the late King. At the young age of thirty seven he was already experienced in affairs of state. He went into exile with the King and the Duke of York when they were mere boys of only sixteen and fourteen. He became like a father to them, and to the young Duke of Buckingham and his younger brother, but to the Chancellor's dismay, the boys fell into bad company at the licentious French court. The Chancellor provided the only guidance they ever had, and the young Duke of Buckingham hated him for that, and later the cowardly self-serving Duke, only two years younger than the King, deserted his childhood friends, and traded with Cromwell's Parliament to save his estates from being sequestered. But it rebounded on him,' Judith added with pleasure, 'and Cromwell sent him to the Tower.'

'At that time few people come out of the Tower intact. How did he keep his head?' asked Mary.

'With the devil's luck,' Judith replied. 'When Cromwell died, his son Richard did not have the stomach to execute the Duke.'

'But how is it that the Duke is so close to the King after all that happened?' Mary enquired with surprise.

'Oh, you can be sure he was there to welcome him at the Restoration, and His Majesty likes to be loved by all and forgave him and now he is as high as ever. But he has far to fall and it will not be long before he gets too big for his own good,' said Judith ominously.

'And tell me about the Chancellor,' asked Mary tentatively, knowing the enquiry she was about to make would not go down well with her aunt. All the same, she had decided that she must know the truth behind all the gossip she had gleaned. 'Is it true,' she persevered bravely, 'that the Chancellor conspired to marry his daughter to the Duke of York when they were all in exile and that now because our poor Queen is childless the Chancellor is grandfather to the future King of England. Worse, they say he deliberately brokered Charles's marriage with a woman who could not bear a child to this end. To insure his own blood line on the throne of England.'

'These are gross lies,' exploded Judith. 'The Chancellor is a man of honour and he did everything he could to prevent the marriage of his daughter to the King's brother, for he knew what would be said, but the girl got herself with child, and the luckless union became inevitable. But don't forget the girl bedded a man with no expectations, in hopeless exile, and fate made him the heir and his children the heirs to the throne. But the truth is that if it were not for the Chancellor and his wise council the King would never have regained his crown and negotiated with Parliament.'

'And does the King still listen to him?' asked Mary.

'I wish I could be sure. For now, as far as I can see, he alone is the voice of reason who urges the King for a peaceful settlement of this costly war with the Dutch. The King is at logger-heads with his son-in-law on the matter, since the Duke is a sailor at heart and will do anything to take to the seas. But that is enough,' said Judith suddenly. 'You will be able to judge these things for yourself soon and now we must get on to the more pressing matter of today.'

Judith took a moment to collect her thoughts. She looked at her niece, standing by the open window with a cool breeze wafting in the scents from the garden below, and felt an impulse to take her home at once, away from this place. For, recalling some of the dark and troubled history of her King, she wondered if she were doing the girl a kindness by introducing her into a world so far from the peaceful life she could have with her family in Norfolk. But in a flash, as if sensing her Aunt's doubts, Mary turned to her with a swirl of her satin skirt, her chin held high and her graceful neck balancing the thick coils of her hair. She raised a graceful wrist and waved it sweepingly as if to indicate a dismissal of anything unpleasant. With a satisfied smile, Judith observed something worldly and clever in her niece.

'I know you are worried,' said Mary breathlessly, eager to get on with the business of how she should conduct herself this morning, 'but I can assure you that you could not make me do anything I did not want to do.' She took Judith's hand affectionately. 'I want to see the world outside the confines of the life I have known. I would have been happy had I married Anthony but God had other plans for me. I will not let you down; I will serve the Queen as you served the King's brother and sister in their loneliness.'

'Very well,' said Judith finally. 'Let us get on with today. Just remember, Mary, look straight ahead of you, do not look at the courtiers as they stop talking and stare at you while you approach their Majesties. They do it to test your mettle.'

CHAPTER EIGHT

They proceeded to an ante-room outside the famous banqueting hall at the Palace of Whitehall, where the King and Queen had as usual been eating their midday meal in public. It was hot, the country enjoying an Indian summer, and Mary could feel the perspiration under her arms, and prayed it would not mark the exquisite dove grey taffeta dress her aunt had commissioned for her. The bodice was tight and pushed her breasts up past the lace frill at the top. At first she had been worried that the exposure was immodest, but on arrival at the court she realised her dress was demure in comparison to the other women. The dress had a loosely gathered train that dropped from her shoulders with flowery pink satin rosettes. She had rehearsed how she would retreat from the throne backwards without tripping over it, the whole operation requiring a deft flick of the wrist to catch the train whilst the head was still bowed, and the prospect made her nervous.

Her aunt had presented her with a pearl choker necklace secured with a little black velvet ribbon. She had decided to wear her hair swept back from her head and caught in a gold threaded net; the prolific tresses protruded either side of her face, framing her perfect complexion.

'You will be the most beautiful young lady at Whitehall,' Jayne had said when she had finished dressing, but now that she saw the magnificent women of the King's court, especially Lady Castlemaine whom she had encountered on her arrival dressed in an armoury of diamonds and magnificent black taffeta, as she was still in mourning for the Queen's mother, Mary felt anything but beautiful. She looked around with a sense of wonder at the magnificent ceiling painted by Rubens and shining inlaid floors polished from dawn to dusk by the feet of a regiment of servants wearing lambskin boots. Mary had seen them that morning gliding about as a group of silent skaters.

'If you think it's hot now, just imagine what it is like at night when all the chandeliers are lit,' said Judith, fanning herself vigorously.

They assembled in an informal group of chattering courtiers, all of whom ignored her completely, when suddenly Lady Suffolk, Lady Castlemaine's aunt, beckoned her to step forward, and she found herself approaching the King and Queen as if it was not her at all. Just as Judith had predicted, a stunning silence descended. All she could hear was the beating of her own heart, the swish of her train and the tap of her embroidered shoes on the polished floor.

She meant to look first at her new mistress, a small pretty figure with a strange bat-like hairstyle which dwarfed her childish face. But instead her eye was drawn by the handsome and saturnine face of the King. His dark eyes met hers, and to her astonishment she thought he gave her an almost imperceptible wink.

In years to come, when she grew to admire the man for his many brave and often underestimated qualities, she would remember that moment vividly. For now, she felt intoxicated by heady mixture of luxury and indolence; and towering above it all was the majestic presence of the King. His right arm was proprietarily draped round the back of the Queen's matching golden chair and his other caressed the impossibly long ears of one of the many little dogs sitting in various positions of abandon about his feet. He was wearing a long black periwig, a fashion she was later told he had adopted after his own hair had turned white overnight during the Queen's illness. She had nearly died of childbed fever after one of her miscarriages. With his large aristocratic nose and full lips it was the sheer animal attraction of the man that gave witness to his ability to be, as so many of his subjects described him, 'the People's King'.

The Chancellor, Lord Clarendon, lent forward from behind the chairs and muttered something to the Queen. She nodded and smiled towards Mary, who made a low curtsy before turning again briefly towards the King, as she had been told to do. She backed away as she had practised a hundred times. And then one of the little dogs decided to jump behind her. Missing her footing, she trod on the train. She faltered wildly and imagined herself sprawled at the King's feet and the ignominious end to her life at court. But a strong arm came from nowhere, recovering her as if she were light as gossamer.

'Do not worry, little grey pigeon,' a man whispered in her ear. She looked up at him gratefully and as she did so, she heard the mocking laughter of Lady Castlemaine. Looking towards her, she saw her whisper some comment behind her fan, resulting in a barely suppressed titter from her neighbours, which left Mary in no doubt that it was at her expense. As Mary continued to look at Lady Castlemiane, her chest tightened and for a fleeting moment, as the woman's eyes met hers, Mary saw a glimpse of something cruel. For Mary, at least, a lasting enmity was born.

Later, the court adjourned and various courtiers gathered in an ante-room where Mary felt even more isolated and nervous. There were people everywhere, chattering like canaries, and she was studiously ignored. As she became more and more hot and bothered she seriously doubted she would be able to hold her own in this strange environment. But, with perfect timing, the man who had so adroitly saved her when she tripped came purposefully striding through the throng.

'Now, allow me to present myself properly,' he said in a rich, deep, heavily accented voice. 'I am Fernando Duke d'Almanda. I am a senior advisor to Her Majesty, and I know exactly who you are. May I say you are a delightful addition to the court.'

Mary curtsied and extended her hand languidly, as Judith had instructed her to do when approached by a gentleman; he took it and raised it to his lips with a gesture resembling a kiss though his lips never touched her skin. As he gave her a formal bow, she had time to register him. He was of middling height, slim but sturdily built. He had not adopted the periwig but wore his hair tied back at the base of his neck with a thick black velvet ribbon. His coal dark eyes flashed piercingly as he spoke and as he fixed her with an intense gaze she felt herself begin to tremble. This was the second time in the space of an afternoon that she had felt the presence of a man in a way that made her blush: firstly the King, who had connected with her in a moment she still recalled with a sense of delightful unreality, and now this man who made no secret of his pleasure when he looked at her. He was doing so now, his eyes lazily travelling up and down from her satin shoes to her halo of hair and stopping at places in between. A few weeks ago she might have felt discomfited by his attentions but now she was grateful that this dashing stranger had rescued her from disaster. He had come again, just when she had felt at her most desperate.

'Thank you for what you did, I nearly made a fool of myself as I feared I might, and when they all laughed I wanted to fall through the floor,' she said ingenuously.

'Now that is what I like, someone who is natural,' he said light-heartedly. 'Of course it is a terrible experience when you first come to court, but think of how Her Majesty felt, when she came to England. She is still surrounded by idle, mischievous people and we, the few Portuguese who are left with her, are glad to see someone as refreshingly honest as you come to join us. You must be a true friend to her,' he said seriously. 'Believe me she needs them.'

Mary felt instinctively that she had found an ally in the Duke. She prided herself on being a good judge of character and she liked his confident honesty. Apart from that, he was a very attractive man and made her feel beautiful and had restored her self-esteem. With a mocking air he seemed to disregard the reactions of the other courtiers, a fact she found reassuring, since in a very short space of time, she had begun to see that all the surface glamour hid something tawdry and jaded. As if to confirm her opinion she saw one of the male courtiers blatantly urinating against some exquisite hangings as they were talking.

The Duke followed her wide-eyed gaze and gave a little chuckle.

'You should not be shocked, the personal habits of these people are quite disgusting. Look the other way,' he said. 'It's what you will have to do in this place, it is the dirtiest palace in Europe.'

It had taken Mary no more than a few minutes at court to realise that personal hygiene was not high on the agenda with the aristocracy, and bodily functions seemed to be no matter for modesty with the men or women alike; even now, the powerful smell of the filthy latrine known as the 'garderobe', a primitive wooden seat projecting outside the walls, wafted through the throng and she began to feel sick.

'Let us go to the window,' said the Duke solicitously, noticing her pale face. He took her arm but before they could move away from the throng Lady Castlmaine appeared, moving like a cat, her gown making a silken whisper as her hips swayed provocatively.

'A word of advice,' she said, smiling slyly. 'Such obeisance in front of the King is really not necessary. Why, upon my word, had the Duke not caught you, you would have been flat on your face.' As if to emphasise the point, she flicked her fan open with a clacking sound and then threw her head back in ribald laughter.

Mary felt the tears pricking behind her eyes. Her face changing from ashen pale to scarlet, she tried to find the appropriate response and caution gave way to anger.

'Your Grace – ' she began in a faltering voice.

The Duke hastily intervened, staying her words with a gentle pressure on her arm.

'Madam, surely better than on her back,' he retorted, on Mary's behalf lifting his heavy eyebrows mockingly. 'Now if you will excuse us the air hereabouts is very thick.'

'Sir, you will regret that remark,' gasped Lady Castlemaine, her entire body shaking with anger.

'I rather think not,' said the Duke crisply, taking Mary's arm as the crowd of courtiers made a path for him and his young companion with a palpable and hushed respect.

It was then that Mary realised an inescapable truth. If she were to survive in this new life of hers she would need a protector. The statement made by the Duke when he had defended her against Lady Castlemaine had in one sense saved her, but in another it had taken away her anonymity. For almost the first time in her life she recognised that events beyond her control had marked her out. She must acknowledge that simple fact or she would never survive. She knew for certain that she already had one formidable enemy in Lady Barbara Castlemaine. The Duke's timely intervention and way the King had looked at her had sealed her fate, she could not simply fade into the background, it was too late. Like a chicken in the coop, she had been marked out for the pecking order.

She looked at the Duke and wondered exactly why he had come forward to help her. His fine rugged face gave nothing away.

'Tell me, my dear,' he asked probingly, 'has it occurred to you that you have come to the court with very little protection. A young lady as beautiful as you are is very vulnerable here. The court could destroy you as ruthlessly as if you were just one of the King's little dogs.' He paused for a moment and then laughed, 'No let me say that again,' he carried on satirically. 'I am wrong. The King has a high regard for his dogs and of course the two legged bitches who share his bed, although for my part I have nothing but contempt for these women, especially when I see the grief it causes my Queen.'

'I would never marry a man who would treat me like that,' said Mary vehemently, 'but I suppose with royalty it is a duty to suffer as the Queen must do.' She looked away from the Duke, fearing she had already said too much.

The Duke waited, watching Mary carefully. It was a test. He knew he had spoken coarsely, and it was against his nature, but he had set himself a task. This girl had been appointed to serve his Queen. If she were to be of any use she would have to develop a tough carapace. He knew something of her background and realised that she did not come from the magic circle of aristocracy, and this accounted for her refreshing directness. She had not learned the dubious art of dissembling, and for a moment he thought sadly how she might quickly become like all the other women who surrounded the King.

'Who knows what goes on in the secret heart of a man,' said the Duke, reverting to her comments about the King.

'I am sorry, I spoke out of turn,' she stumbled.

'No, you did not,' he reassured her. 'But in spite of it all, I admire the King for the man he is, and for the courage he showed during his exile. How he settles his own conscience in his marriage is a mystery,' he finished with a sigh.

'And you, Sir, do you have a wife?' enquired Mary boldly, throwing him a sideways glance.

'I do,' replied the Duke, darting Mary a quick look. He noticed a faint blush spreading across her cheeks and continued swiftly, to cover her obvious embarrassment at so direct a question.

'The Duchess remains on our estates just outside Lisbon,' he said sadly. 'She suffers from ill health and cannot travel or she would have accompanied me to London.'

'I hope she will recover,' said Mary quickly.

'The country is good for her and she derives what little pleasure that is available to her from the beauty of the estate,' answered the Duke.

He thought of Magdalena, his wife, whose failing health had rendered her unable to have a child, and felt guilty as he compared her in his mind's eye with Mary, this young luscious girl, bursting with life, her future before her.

The Duke was a devout Catholic, like his mistress the Queen, and despite his own personal circumstances, he had not as yet been tempted to sample any of the many attractive dalliances so readily available at court. In an irrational moment he imagined making love to this new arrival. How tempting it would be. Then he exercised the self restraint with which he had been imbued since childhood.

'I came from a beautiful part of England,' said Mary, her voice severing his thoughts.

'Tell me about it,' said the Duke.

'Our family grows hemp,' said Mary. 'I already miss the feeling of being part of the land. It is so strange to be in a man made world, so removed from nature.'

'You mirror my sentiments exactly,' said the Duke. 'Our family is renowned for its wine, and the vineyards cover the hills for miles around. The Queen imports our wine and no doubt you will soon sample it. Even the King has become accustomed to its rich taste, and we also import tea from China, a beverage essential to the survival of any self respecting Portuguese lady or gentleman. So, you see, we are providers of essential luxuries,' he laughed.

As they chatted on in an easy way which surprised and delighted him, he couldn't help thinking how this little English rose had no idea of just what a poisoned chalice awaited her at court. She was uncorrupted and innocent, and, by all accounts, educated and intelligent. He was concerned at the thought of her purity and niceness being tarnished before it had even had a chance to shine. He would make Mary his own concern, and he would not allow this to happen.

His concerns had been shared by the Queen, and in her sweet way she had asked the Duke to look out for the girl. There were so few good Catholic families prepared to field a daughter to the dangerous inferno of intrigue and debauchery at Whitehall, she was worth guarding and, besides, the Queen had promised the girl's aunt, another Catholic who had been married to a Frenchman, that she would protect her in return for the service she had avowed the girl would give.

The dialogue between Mary and the Duke had not gone unobserved and without warning, a group of men swaggered towards them. One of them put an arm about Mary's waist and pulled her roughly towards him, taking her breath away.

'So, Duke, who is this little peach? Are you going to keep her all to yourself?' said the man, the stale smell of wine engulfing Mary's face. She tried to wrench herself away, but he held fast, to the gathering mirth of his drunken companions.

'Release the lady at once,' commanded the Duke, his voice shaking with anger.

'How dare you dishonour one of the Queen's ladies in such a way,' he went on, his hand instinctively going to the jewelled dagger in his belt.

'I surrender,' said the man in a sneering tone, holding up his hands. 'We wouldn't like to spoil his Grace's chances, would we, gentlemen?' he asked the other men, who, seeing the Duke's fury and indignation, began to pull the man away.

'Sir, I thank you, it is the third time you have come to my rescue in so short a time,' said Mary, with a sigh of relief. 'I thought I would be well able to . . . ' she hesitated, and he could see her lip trembling.

'My dear,' he interjected before she had a chance to go on. 'That was the Duke of Buckingham, about whom you will have heard many unpleasant things, all of them true, but he is just one who behaves in so shameful a way, you will have to learn to deal with it.'

'But surely . . . ' said Mary, shaking her head in disbelief. 'I mean, how can this be? He is the King's closest friend, or so I have heard.'

'Forgive me, I must come straight to the point with you,' said the Duke. 'The King's court is no place for a shrinking violet, and in your charming grey dress you did strike me as a beautiful grey turtle dove, did you not, my charming little grey pigeon? I could not stand by while you were insulted,' he went on. 'But the question is, can you remain as you are here in this place, and I must be frank,' he looked at her gravely, 'you need to ask yourself, do you want to?'

Mary looked about her, at the room full of painted women and foppish feckless men, and suddenly she caught sight of the little Queen, who had been talking to the King, gazing up at her handsome husband with undisguised adoration. He was listening attentively, when Barbara Castlemaine nudged his arm and whispered something in his ear. Mary saw clearly how the woman observed the success of her intervention with her sly vixen's eyes, and the Queen's crestfallen expression struck Mary's heart like a knife.

'You see what I mean,' said the Duke, who had also seen the exchange.

'Everyone saw it,' Mary hissed under her breath. 'For the Queen to be humiliated like that, it is unbelievable.'

'It is a fact of life that some men are incapable of fidelity,' said the Duke, shaking his head. 'But I have often noticed that it does not make them any less attractive, in fact sometimes it makes them more so.'

'I hope I never get used to this,' Mary blurted angrily.

'The King had a reputation for being unfailingly courteous to members of the female sex,' explained the Duke. 'Consequently his quiver of mistresses ran circles around him, but I do not think it will be long before even the King tires of Lady Castlemaine's audacity. She has become quite reckless.'

'It is shameful that the King is made a fool of by such a creature,' said Mary in disgust. 'My Aunt tells me he has just paid off her debts of thirty thousand pounds whilst his Queen is unable to order a new gown, is it true?' asked Mary.

'The court owes money to all the tradesmen who provide for them, and their families are facing ruin. Why even last week the King's harpist literally starved to death and he one of the greatest players in the world. His family couldn't even afford a decent burial. Such a thing could never happen in Portugal,' said the Duke.

Mary gave a slight shiver, despite the oppressive heat in the room. The thought of so much misery below the surface made her feel decidedly uncomfortable. As if he could read her thoughts, the Duke offered her his arm. She met his eyes and she did not attempt to draw away, a fact which did not escape the ever watchful eyes of the court.

'One thing is certain,' he said with a slight chuckle. 'His Majesty will be confident he will be plucking your little feathers, little dove, and that would be your undoing, so have a care, for there are few who can resist his charms.'

'He will not succeed with me, My Lord Duke,' Mary replied defiantly. 'I have made my decision and I kept my virtue with the man I loved more than life itself, though God in his wisdom took him before our wedding day.'

'I am sorry to hear this,' said the Duke thoughtfully. 'We all have our crosses to bear. One day we will talk further and you will tell me of the fine man you lost.'

'Thank you for your concern,' Mary acknowledged, unsure of his exact meaning.

'Life is hard, but now you must concern yourself with the present,' said the Duke briskly. 'There are many before you who have succumbed to the King's onslaught,' he said teasingly.

'Do not doubt me, sir,' Mary commanded. 'I do not think I will lose my honour for the brief notice of our promiscuous King. It will take a better and more respectable offer than that to tempt me from my maidenhood, and besides, there is such a thing as loyalty and Her Majesty is a noble woman. If I am to serve her, it will be with all my heart. I have not been brought up to the ways of this court. I have seen the sufferings of the common people and the joy with which they welcomed the King, and I hate that woman Lady Castlemaine and her kind, for they have made a mockery of the people's trust.'

The Duke began to see more than ever that Mary was a strong and determined young woman and that there was a great deal more to her than he had at first thought. Her comments about her virtue had been startlingly frank and not only been directed towards the King, but to any male who might approach. He had the feeling that she had detected the frisson of desire he had begun to feel for her. She was in fact the first woman who had inspired such feelings in him for a long time, so immured was he to feminine charms with the burgeoning pattern of duty which threaded his life on all levels.

It was not only his duty to his ailing, pious wife, to his family, to his estates, and above all to his Queen, but there was also the sensitive diplomatic mission which lay bound in the marriage between these two nations. It was of utmost importance. The war with Spain which had killed so many of his countrymen had been temporarily halted by the alliance and his country had prospered as a result. For all his apparent frivolity, the King was a dark horse, and although he appeared in many respects to have abandoned himself to the licentious life at Whitehall he had a beady eye on world affairs and used his apparent insouciance as a clever smoke screen.

Mary was also thinking hard about the King. She had already decided that his dark brooding looks when in repose gave a peephole into a deeper and cleverly concealed agenda. She remembered how he had bravely gone among the plague victims when all the rich had fled, and how he had been the only one who had done something to help them. And, besides, when he had fixed her in his powerful gaze, she knew he saw beyond the girl who had been plucked from her very different life to serve his little Queen. But she had also realised that his power over women and his ability to love even the commonest actress from the slums of the city gave testament to the years he had had to fight for his very existence when he was in exile, despised and pitied by the affluent courts of Europe upon whose charity he had depended for the very suit on his back.

'I expect you are attempting to work out all the characters you have met today, my little pigeon,' the Duke, as if reading her thoughts. 'Before we go any further, I would like you to call me Fernando when we are alone, for I expect we are to be firm friends. We both have the Queen's interests at heart and your robust views on the morals at court are in keeping with all of us who serve Her Majesty.' As he spoke he took her hand and raised it briefly to his lips.

'Very well, Fernando,' said Mary, smiling up at him, just as she saw her aunt's redoubtable figure advancing across the polished floor.

As they turned to greet her, Fernando's hand lightly touched her own and the contact lingered just long enough to give her a little flutter of something more than casual interest.

None of this was lost upon Judith.

'Ah, my dear niece, I see you have already made a friend,' Judith said knowingly.

Mary looked down demurely, afraid her aunt might disapprove.

'My Lord Duke, I see you have taken my niece under your wing,' Judith continued with considerable charm.

'Madam,' he replied formally, 'we can only thank you for suggesting your delightful relative to serve my Queen. I have told her that she can trust me and she will need supporters. It is in my Queen's interest to have good people around her.' Fernando spoke, with conviction, anxious to impress Mary's aunt. He knew about the role Mrs Briott had played in the King's life. She had been a trusted friend and had been handsomely rewarded. The King was well known for his loyalty to past allies, he would have given careful thought to the arrival of Judith's niece, and her appointment was not a random choice. Judith Briott's niece Mary would be a precious commodity in the maelstrom of the King's past, littered as it was with the frightful images of the despicable murder of his father and the destruction of his family. He was a man who wanted harmony at any cost, and for that he tried to be all things to all men, and women. It was the coldness of his mother Henrietta which had in some way contributed to his need for female company which might seem on the surface to indicate a fatal flaw in his character. But Fernando knew that nothing escaped the King's beady eye, it would be a fool who underestimated him. And exactly what the King would have in mind for his Queen's latest servant was still unclear, but Fernando had already taken the girl's interests to heart.

He looked at her, still courageously unperturbed by her first day in the limelight, and gave her an encouraging smile. She curtsied and followed her aunt to the Queen's apartments.

CHAPTER NINE

The Queen's gowns were heavily darned and mended and the hems were in tatters. As a result, Mary had soon learned that a major part of her job involved painstaking repairs. She had spent the first week cutting strips of silk and binding them to the bottom of the Queen's skirts. Mary had learned that despite the fact the Queen had brought the largest dowry ever to an English monarch – Tangier, Bombay and five hundred thousand pounds in gold – little of her promised allowance had been forthcoming and the Queen knew that she was impecunious, to say the least, and all this added to her sense of isolation.

The Queen, none the less, had made her apartments very charming with the things she had brought from Portugal, Mary's favourites being her green damask curtains and Portuguese rugs bound with silver and gold thread. There were olive wood tables and numerous stools for her ladies, covered with white damask. She had a series of exquisite tea services to accommodate the fashion of tea drinking she had brought from Portugal.

The late afternoon, just before her game of cards, was the Queen's favourite time of day and preparing the tea ritual at this time was one of Mary's duties. She had to light a little silver spirit lamp to boil the water, and the Queen would select the chosen tea from a large wooden case in which were numerous exquisite Chinese bottles containing a variety of teas; finally, it was drunk from tiny gossamer-thin china bowls, the mouth daintily dabbed with small linen napkins.

The silent pleasure the Queen derived from watching her new maid of honour as she went methodically about these duties was the connection which began to form a bond between the two women. At first the Queen said nothing, only smiling sweetly with a gracious nod of approval when all was ready. Of course Mary was not of the privileged few who sat with the Queen and made conversation over the steaming cups, but the day came when the Queen was not her usual self and asked for her tea to be prepared in her chamber where she would consume it alone.

Mary bade a servant move the paraphernalia to the Queen's bedchamber and discretely set about the preparations. The Queen sat by the table in a voluminous peignoir, her hair was unbraided and spread about her tiny shoulders in a dark curtain. Looking at her, Mary was struck by how small and childlike she looked. She also saw that her face was pale and there were dark shadows under her eyes. Mary realised that she was clearly unwell.

'Please, will you sit with me and we shall drink tea together,' the Queen said suddenly in a small voice.

'Of course, Your Majesty,' Mary heard herself say, trying not to sound surprised.

'You see,' said the Queen, leaning towards Mary and taking her cup, 'I am really very much alone here, and you are about the same age as me, and also,' she went on, the words coming quickly, as if she had been longing to say them for some time, 'I think you must feel as alone as I do in this place, because you are not like the others.' She stopped suddenly and stretched out her hand, placing it on Mary's own. 'I did not mean to be rude, what must you think?' the Queen said with a little laugh. 'It was merely that . . . '

'Indeed, Your Majesty,' said Mary quickly, 'I am not in the least offended; you are quite right, I am not quite like the others,' Mary spoke carefully, despite the open invitation to friendship, feeling a pang of concern that she might be accused of forgetting her station in conversing in such a way with the King's wife.

'I am so unhappy,' blurted the little Queen, fumbling for a handkerchief in her silken sleeve. Mary said nothing, but once again the Queen's perfect alabaster hand stretched in her direction, and this time, before Mary could stop herself, she took it.

'You see I so miss my family, my mother particularly. As you know, I am still in mourning for her,' said the Queen. 'Is your own mother living, Mary?' she asked.

'No, Your Majesty,' replied Mary. 'But regrettably, we were never close.'

'Well, I wish my mother were here now,' said the Queen, 'it is difficult to discuss the things which are so close to my heart, but maybe one day God will grant me my dearest wish . . . ' The Queen looked directly at her, suddenly withdrawing her hand, and Mary looked into her eyes and saw such anguish and pain that she almost cried herself. She knew without any explanation that the Queen was referring to her longing for a child, the thing which would rekindle the King's love.

'I must dress now,' said the Queen wearily. 'We will talk again, Mary.'

It was a dismissal, but as Mary withdrew she knew that the Queen recognised that she could trust her, and that this would be the first of many conversations.

A few days later she looked up from her sewing to hear the distinct sound of weeping in the adjoining chamber. She could hear the voice of the senior Portuguese lady, the Countess Penalva, one of the few of Catherine's original entourage who had been permitted to stay. Mary had a little knowledge of Spanish and although the Portuguese spoken by the Queen and her fellow countrymen bore little resemblance to it, she could distinguish a few words, enough to connect some derogatory adjectives connected with the name of Castlemaine.

Later that day, Mary could hardly control her excitement when Lady Suffolk summoned her to help dress the Queen, in order to accompany her to a formal reception for the first time, where they would be joined by the King.

Since their conversation, Mary had begun to see the Queen as a woman like herself, a woman with her own challenges and sorrows, desperate for friends in a dangerous court. Now, in private, she thought of her as a kindred spirit, not a lofty queen, and there she was, waiting in her dressing chamber, standing still as a statue in front of a large table covered in bottles and brushes. She wore a long white shift which came almost to the floor, under which her clothes would be arranged discretely, preserving her modesty; her magnificent hair was held back from her face by a thick white linen band. Several women busied themselves about the room; petticoats, gowns and items of clothing festooned the gilt chairs and two small screens either side of the fireplace, where a fire burned merrily, at odds with the sombre, almost ritualistic atmosphere in the room.

As Mary arrived, Lady Suffolk handed her an extraordinary garment with which she was told to help the Queen. It was a pair of long white trousers, trimmed with lace, to be worn under the petticoat. Mary had been told to remain silent unless spoken to and to avoid eye contact with the Queen and to keep her eyes down. But to Mary such an item of clothing was strange and almost shocking, since women wore no underwear, although Mary had heard tales of such items being worn by the actresses at the King's theatre.

'What is this?' she whispered at one of the other serving girls.

'The Queen's drawers. It's the fashion in Portugal,' the girl murmured. 'The poor lady has her courses again – and just when we all thought her prayers had been granted. It is a strange garment but it certainly has its uses,' the girl persevered knowingly. 'There are things you should know,' she went on, 'some say that the King has infected her with the French pox and that is the reason for her problem.' The girl stopped suddenly, noticing a daggers look from one of the Queen's Portuguese ladies.

'Come now,' she said hastily, 'you take one side and me the other and remember to look the other way while Her Majesty climbs into them.'

For Mary this was yet another thing to think about in her new life: women never wore anything but petticoats and stockings up to the thigh, except when they had their courses and then rags were suspended appropriately from a ribbon round the waist. Mary remembered that her mother had once told her that Mr Pepys had hit his wife when she had adopted the fashion of drawers from the French court, as it struck him as immoral. But even more shocking were the whispered comments of the servant. She knew very little about the pox, although she had been warned that the affliction was rife in certain circles, but the idea that the King could have given it to his innocent wife was something almost too upsetting to think about.

The silent ritual of dressing continued and Mary knew better than to indicate any memory of her conversation with Catherine. In public, a formal dialogue had to be maintained. Mary was well aware that if she were marked out as Catherine's confidante she would expose herself to unwelcome attention.

To her surprise, Catherine turned to her, and, singling her out, enquired after her health and wellbeing, using a more formal English than she had done in the intimacy of her chamber, with just a trace of the accent which it was said so amused and pleased her husband; apparently it still made him laugh to have her repeat the phrase 'confess and be hanged'.

Mary was not entirely sure that she should answer or just smile and curtsy, but the Countess Penalva nodded at her encouragingly, her stern face breaking into a smile, indicating that it was in order for her to reply.

'Your Majesty is most kind,' answered Mary, 'but I must confess I prefer to be in here with Your Majesty than in the public rooms, which I find quite daunting.'

Mary observed the Countess muttering in approval as she caught the Queen's eye. Catherine looked at Mary and gently patted her on the arm, 'I cannot blame you for that, my dear,' she said sweetly. 'I have a plan for you, something which is most important,' she went on. 'I know you are a member of the only true faith. How would you like to accompany me to mass this evening before the reception? You would enjoy the music; we are to sing a special mass for the soul of my dear mother who passed to the angels in March.'

'Oh, Your Majesty, I would be so honoured,' said Mary respectfully, sweeping the Queen a deep curtsy.

'Well, before we, go' said the Queen in a matter of fact tone, 'Lady Suffolk will provide you with a mourning gown. We will summon the seamstress at once. She is quicker than the English girls and can have a gown ready in a few hours. Will you permit me to choose the fabric?'

'Oh, please, Your Majesty,' said Mary unable to keep the excitement from her voice.

Mary knew that to be granted this unexpected honour was in effect to be made part of the Queen's innermost sanctum. Her mind raced. It was not a passing fancy – Catherine had clearly decided to make her a friend and the fact had been formally acknowledged. Mary felt a mixture of excitement and trepidation.

*   *   *

The following day Catherine was seated in her drawing room, surrounded by her ladies, enjoying her tea. Lady Suffolk, Castlemaine's aunt, was pouring the tea into the little tea bowls. The atmosphere was unusually happy and Mary felt that she was gradually settling in to her new life. Her new black silk gown was the most beautiful she had ever owned and Fernando had complimented her upon it and suggested a walk in the Privy Gardens after tea, if the Queen could spare her. Mary was looking forward to the event, although she felt a small frisson of concern, since the Duke was a married man and, despite the lax morals of the court, she had no intention of becoming just another of the famous Whitehall paramours, so lampooned among the people.

The chatter was all about the latest scandal involving the Duke of York. 'It is a disgrace. He visits his mistress, Lady

Denham, quite openly,' said Countess Penalva. 'These women are nothing but common sluts,' she said robustly, aware that her voice carried loudly, as she eyed Lady Suffolk. 'If it were my family I would be ashamed,' she ploughed on remorselessly. 'In our country we do not tolerate such things.' Lady Suffolk did not respond to this obvious dig at her niece, Lady Castlemaine, but continued impassively pouring the tea, although Mary noticed a violent flush begin to suffuse her neck, and the dish she was holding beginning to tremble slightly in its delicate saucer, making a faint tinkling sound in the quiet room.

Suddenly all eyes were upon the doorway and there was the figure of Lady Castlemaine herself, resplendent and smug as ever. A hostile silence descended on the gathering.

'Ah, Lady Castlemaine,' Catherine said graciously. She had learned to accept the presence of this hated woman in her marriage, and her love for her husband was such that she feared a repetition of the misery she had endured when she had fought the appointment of the woman as a lady of her bedchamber. The previous night she had prayed again for a child, and the constant presence of this fecund woman in her husband's bed cut her to the quick, but she was not a princess of Portugal for nothing, and she knew, with a deep conviction, that one day she would be rid of this evil serpent. But for the moment she would have harmony in her court.

'I am worried about His Majesty,' she said ingeniously. 'He stays so long with your ladyship at night and returns so late I fear he will catch cold.' Mary admired the Queen for her sanguinity but, just as she was enjoying the moment, Castlemaine threw in her customary missile.

'His majesty does not stay in my apartments so late, Your Majesty,' she answered brazenly. 'It must be with some other lady that he stays out so long.' There was an intake of breath from the scandalised onlookers.

'A word, madam, if you please.' It was the King's distinctive voice, shaking with anger and directed unmistakably towards

Lady Castlemaine. All eyes turned to the doorway where he stood imperiously, surrounded by the usual busy gaggle of spaniels. The room sank into a communal genuflection and all eyes watched as Lady Castlemaine glided slowly towards him, as if she had not a care in the world.

'You are a bold impertinent hussy, leave the court at once,' he boomed, his face twisted with anger and his body shaking. Mary had not imagined the King could ever reveal such a lack of composure, and his anger sent a shiver down her spine.

Lady Castlemaine tried in vain to retain some sort of dignity in the face of the King's wrath, but as she rose from her curtsy she shook so much that Mary hoped she might fall over. Her face was white and her upper lip tightened in an obvious attempt to conceal tears. She backed away without a word, as the room watched in unconcealed delight.

'And do not return until you are sent for,' bellowed the King, as Lady Castlemaine hastily retreated from the room.

CHAPTER TEN

Pudding Lane, September 2nd 1666

The baker was at his wits end. Commerce in London had been paralysed and the people were starving. The plague had more or less abated, but the war with the Dutch still raged and still the King and his court continued to play. There were no fit young men to help the baker, since the few who were left had been pressed into the navy. He had to rely on two spotty girls who were as good as useless. 'You should be grateful,' his wife remarked, fed up with the constant grumbling, 'people still have to eat and you will never be out of a job, and, besides, as you are the King's baker he, at least, pays you for bread. It is one thing they cannot do without, we should be thankful for small mercies.'

It had been ferociously hot and the work in the bakery tired the man more than it used to, but mercifully a refreshing easterly breeze had got up, and as it became darker, the heat of the day began to abate and the baker instructed the two girls to dampen the ovens, shut off the flues and get to bed. It would, as usual, be an early start, and the baker must go for more flour before sun up and the court had ordered double the usual quantity of loaves for the next day.

'Good-night, wife,' he murmured, as sleep began to engulf him. 'You are right to chastise me for my complaining; there are many worse off than us and our little ones and things can only get better. The Lord has had his revenge for our sins, and we must pray for an end to all this hardship.'

He closed his eyes and in seconds he was sound asleep,

dreaming of life when he was a lad in the green fields of Kent. He often regretted coming to London to seek his fortune, but he had built up a good business and he had just finished paying off the money he had borrowed all those years ago to buy the bakery. He gave a satisfied grunt and his wife snuffed out the candle.

The girls waited until the house was quiet, and then sneaked slowly down the narrow stairs. Two men waited outside in the dark street. The girls knew their master would whip them for having sweethearts but they were prepared to take the risk. The boys had promised to take them to the river, where they had a stock of stolen mead and the night was sweet. The gentle breeze had strengthened and who knew what romance lay around the corner after the long hot day at the baker's ovens.

'Did you remember to dampen the ovens?' asked one of the girls, as they stealthily shut the door behind them.

Of course the other girl had not remembered, even though it was her job this night.

'Hush up, will you,' was the reply. 'It can wait until we get back.'

As the girls made their way to the river without a care in the world, the easterly wind picked up with unseasonable force and, as the baker and his wife slept, it drew up the ovens. Soon the metal surrounds were shimmering white-hot and the lath and plaster walls in which the ovens were set had ignited. The other side of the wall was where the baker stored his faggots. He had often been warned about the possible dangers of fire and now, at the end of a long hot summer, the faggots were soon ablaze, sending showers of sparks dancing into the air, only to descend on neighbouring storehouses, which held tar, oakum and timber. Within moments the baker's house and the surrounding buildings were ablaze.

It was the shrieks of neighbours that woke the baker and his wife and family. They knew at once their only escape was the window. People had begun to scream and panic; the flames had become an inferno so great that the population felt powerless and became supine, staring at the flames without making any effort to put them out.

'Quick we must run for the river,' screamed the baker's wife, gathering her terrified children.

'No, I must save the girls, they must be trapped inside,' shouted the baker above the din.

Before she could stop him, her husband dashed back into the blazing house. She heard him calling the girls' names, and then, mercifully, he was at the top window, flames licking up at him from the floor below.

'Jump,' hollered a neighbour and, as if by magic, another man came, holding a big canvas cloth. They stretched it below the window and the man jumped. His wife ran to him. She cried out in horror as she saw him, his clothes completely burned off and his skin blackened and blistered. His eyes were bolting wildly with the pain. Crying bitterly, the wife did her best to calm him, as the two neighbours ran for water. They doused him and the man screamed in agony before falling into merciful unconsciousness.

The baker was a popular man, often was the time when he had given bread to a starving family with no mention or hope of payment, and this was the time when his kindness was to be repaid. His neighbours brought a cart and gently loaded him on to it. The next day the family were safely with relatives in Clapham. When the man recovered consciousness, he told his wife in a faint voice that his search for the girls had been a waste because they had gone. She wept when she realised her husband had risked his life for them; he had lost the fingers on his right hand and like as not would never work again. They were ruined. Slowly she had begun to piece together the reason for the disaster which had overtaken them, and for which they would get the blame. 'I saw the wenches leaving with two ruffians well before the fire started,' the good neighbour told her, and she knew at once that the girls had not dampened the fires. She vowed to track them down and have her revenge.

'Father, what has happened to your fingers?' cried the baker's little daughter. 'If I say a prayer will God put them back?' she asked.

'There is no God,' said the wife.

Within a few hours, whole areas of the city were destroyed: thirteen thousand homes, four hundred and thirty-six acres. It was impossible to say how many lost their lives, since the records were burned. Some said it was only a dozen but many disagreed, and the eventual deaths caused by ruin and starvation and suicide were impossible to calculate.

*   *   *

In the Palace of Whitehall, Jayne awakened Mary at three in the morning, 'Miss Mary you must get up. The city has been struck by fire and they say the flames are spreading faster than a man can run. We must waken the Queen,' she cried.

Mary ran to the window, and, sure enough, the sky above the city had an eerie glow. The court had begun to stir and there was a frenzy of activity. Confusion and fear abounded and some of the courtiers were hastening to leave as soon as possible.

The King made a brief appearance and announced that he and The Duke of York were going at once to find the controller of the city. Several of the ladies were becoming hysterical and this was an occasion when Mary saw Charles coming into this own. 'Nobody is in danger here,' he reassured them. 'Just stay where you are, my brother the Duke and I are going to take matters into our own hands. If there is any imminent danger, the appropriate action will be taken and the court will be evacuated.' He kissed his wife and left.

Mary felt sick to her stomach. Her family home was directly in the path of the fire. Since her mother's death, her father had hardly been to London, but he was planning to spend some time in the city the following month. For the time being, the house was being looked after by the loyal steward and his wife. Only the previous week Mary had been to check it all and been reminded of the many priceless family things in the house. She had an instant gut reaction that she must try to salvage her family home before it was obliterated for ever by the flames. Just as she was desperately forming a plan in her mind, she heard the strong voice of Fernando.

'My family home,' she blurted and he saw the flash of terror which crossed her face.

He did not hesitate. His reaction was swift and unflinching. 'We must hire some carts and save what we can. It is an adventure; we will do it together, my little pigeon.'

They dressed hurriedly, putting on their old working gowns, and went outside to the palace yard, where Fernando had miraculously assembled three large carts. Mary saw him press some gold into the hands of the drivers and, together with Jayne, they set off. At first the way was clear, but soon the streets were blocked with people fleeing from the fire. Mary's heart began to sink as she realised they stood little chance of making any headway, and then she remembered a route she and Anthony used to take on their exploits.

'I know another way,' she told Fernando. 'We must sit up at the front with the driver and I will show you.' Fernando's strong, rugged features were set against the background of a reddening sky and rosy dawn, signalling another perfect September day. He smiled at her encouragingly and not for the first time she recognised the confidence he exuded in all things. The air was thick with the smell of burning and the horses were displaying a reluctance to obey their masters, ears back and tails flying. Mary seriously doubted the poor creatures would ignore their animal instincts.

'Your Lordship, the creatures will not go much farther,' cried the driver, his voice only just audible against the hue and cry.

'It is just two streets away,' she replied, her heart pounding with relief as she saw the fire was still many streets way from their house in Bow Street. And as they drove through Covent Garden, away from the crowds heading down the Strand, she let out a scream of joy when she saw the house intact. She leapt from the cart and pealed the bell pull at the big iron gates. The faithful steward came running.

'Oh, Miss Mary, thank God. What are we to do?' he cried. 'Unless the wind stops we will lose the house. The people are powerless, there is nobody in control and they say looters are taking everything while they have the chance.'

The man's wife was soon behind him. 'We must go,' she screamed, sweat pouring down her face, 'we shall all be burned, we must get to the river!'

'You will do no such thing,' Fernando boomed, ripping off his velvet doublet and rolling up the sleeves of his silk shirt. 'We will form a chain and start loading the carts with Sir Miles's possessions and for each cart that is full I will give you ten sovereigns.'

As if by magic, at the mention of money other faces appeared and in a frenzy of activity the Boynton possessions began to appear from the house amidst much groaning and heaving, Fernando supervising the careful stacking with miraculous efficiency. 'You will see I have experience in this,' he called to Mary as she struggled with her mother's porcelain dinner service wrapped up in the linen from her parents' wedding chest. 'We had a forest fire near my vineyard in Portugal and we cleared our home. We lost nothing and neither will you.'

Miraculously, Fernando had produced more than a dozen carts and Mary laboured with the rest to save the contents of her home. As more and more desperate people emerged from the burning streets, making their way to the river with what few belongings they had managed to save from their homes, she wondered what apocalyptic force had been sent to bring yet another catastrophe to her beleaguered country. She recognised how circumstances yet again discriminated between the rich and the poor.

'Here, take this and wrap it round your mouth,' she heard Fernanado saying, as he handed her a kerchief from his pocket.

He tied it behind her head and she looked up at him gratefully, the air had become thick with the stench of fire, the dawn sky becoming darker as smoke covered the sky.

A desperate woman, pushing a handcart, came through the throng, crying out. 'Has anyone seen a small child?' The family pig and some pathetic sticks of furniture were perched perilously on the small cart, three other children in their night clothes clung to the woman's skirts, all were covered in smuts.

'I know this woman,' cried Jayne breathlessly, 'her husband was taken for the navy. She has been struggling to keep her family fed, God help the poor soul.'

Fernando went to the woman and asked her the child's name, then he lifted her up on to their cart where she could get a better view above the heads of the throng and, looking desperately about her, she spotted her child.

'There he is,' she shrieked, and at once Fernando bounded through the crowd and scooped the wretched child into his arms, reuniting him with his mother.

'Oh sir, how can I ever thank you? I might have lost him forever,' the woman wept gratefully, wiping her tear stained face on her filthy apron.

Mary had been trying to comfort the other children, all of whom were wailing uncontrollably .

'Where are you going?' she asked.

'To the river and then we are in God's hands,' the woman replied dully, with a look of abject despair.

'Where is your husband?' Mary asked.

'He was pressed, and I don't know where he is. We have lost our home, there is nothing left of it, I took in washing to feed the children since my man left. We have had nothing from him and now we have nothing again accept for Ned the pig, but there is many who would take him off me.'

Seeing the woman's plight, Mary delved spontaneously into the cart and pulled out her mother's collection of gold snuff boxes, in which, she knew, her mother had kept a stash of coins.

She rattled one of them and out fell several gold sovereigns. She pushed them at the woman.

'Here take these. There should be enough to get you lodgings for a few months and to feed the children, and take the box as well.'

Mary ran back into the now echoing house. Most of the rooms were empty of furnishings and Sarah was busy taking the last of the rich hangings from the salon walls.

'That is just about everything of value,' she assured Mary. 'The Duke says we cannot take the pots and kitchen crockery, there is not room, but don't worry, miss, for they are of no value and easily replaced.'

As she was speaking, Fernando had rushed into the room. He put a comforting arm about Mary's shoulders.

'Now ladies, we must leave,' he said categorically. 'You must not worry,' he said to Mary. 'I have heard that the King has taken control and there is a good chance that the fire will be halted before it gets here.'

'You have been so wonderful, how can I ever thank you enough?' said Mary. 'Nearly everything has been saved, and when I see it in all its finery, and I compare it with the loss that poor woman has suffered, I realise how fortunate we are in comparison.'

'We live in troubled times, but it was ever thus, and at least you had compassion for that poor woman, and whilst kindness is not in evidence at the King's court, it is my duty to look after the interests of those who serve Her Majesty,' he said gravely.

Later Mary could not believe what happened next, but for some reason she leant towards him and kissed him on the cheek. As her lips touched his skin, she smelt the heady maleness of him, a mixture of sweat and smoke with the faintest trace of perfume coming from his thick black hair. She felt her stomach contract, and a strange half forgotten feeling of desire, heightened by the drama of the moment and the way he had taken such a forceful role in her life. The emotion was not lost on him and he fleetingly caught her round the waist, catching her eye with a look which sealed the attraction between them.

Mary did not look back. She did not know if she would see her home again, but seeing the misery and suffering about her and the fear in people's eyes as they fled, leaving everything they had worked for to be consigned to the flames, she said a silent prayer for those who must have died and for the hundreds of people whose lives would never recover from this fateful night. They drove in silence towards the river with the cries of the anguished people ringing in their ears.

The carts were taken to Judith's house at Hampton Court to be stored in one of her barns, and Mary returned to Whitehall. The Queen was beside herself with worry, the fire still raged on unchecked and the King had not returned. Word came that he had ridden bravely to the flames with the Duke of York and together they had formed a plan in the absence of any of strategy at all from the controller of the city.

'The King is going to make a fire break,' said the Queen. 'But it means pulling down the houses owned by some of the richest people.'

She was in her private rooms, but most of her ladies had conveniently acquired the vapours, and Mary was one of the few who remained in attendance. It was the Chancellor Clarendon, who spent several hours each week closeted with the Queen, who brought her the latest news of the King. He stood beside her with an air of paternal friendship which belied his grim unforgiving demeanour. His thin scraggy legs in high heeled shoes and black stockings gave him the appearance of a strange old bird of prey, but Mary had developed a great respect for him. Having initially been hostile to the Queen he now treated her with the utmost respect and Mary and had also grown to admire the young Queen, who had an unerring grasp of politics, and a broad and wise understanding of the struggle for power which dominated the seas.

'Pray be seated, My Lord,' the Queen said politely. The

Chancellor gave her a courtly bow and then took a seat in one of the gold chairs next to her. His cadaverous features relaxed a little and he listened attentively while the Queen questioned him about the state of the fire. She spoke calmly, as she always did, and the room had an air of tranquillity despite the horror unfolding in the centre of her husband's kingdom.

'His Majesty always displays his finest qualities in an emergency,' the Chancellor said quietly.

'I am so proud of him, My Lord,' said the Queen with obvious emotion. 'But I hope he is not putting himself in too much danger.' She closed her eyes, as if shutting out a distressing vision.

The Chancellor patted her hand briefly, in a gesture of reassurance, much as a father would do to a beloved daughter. Mary and the other ladies withdrew to a corner and picked up their sewing. They began a quiet, murmuring conversation.

'The more I see of the man,' muttered Lady Suffolk, nodding in the direction of Lord Clarendon, 'the harder it is to believe that he conspired to marry his daughter Anne to the King's brother. He is far too clever not to have seen how his own position would be undermined by such a plan.'

'You are quite right, My Lady,' Mary intervened boldly. 'I find nothing in his conduct with which to reproach him.'

'That is as maybe,' ventured one of the new ladies. 'But the gossips say he knew the Queen would be barren and that is why he promoted the marriage, ensuring that his own grandchildren would inherit the throne.'

'Such gossip is disgraceful,' rounded Countess Panalva under her breath, darting an evil look in the girl's direction. 'You had best watch your tongue or it could get itself removed along with your silly little head.' The Countess's entire appearance seemed to assume the same ominously dark patina as her withered complexion; the austere black gown and her elaborate black hood relieved only by a few priceless pearls adding to the force of her onslaught.

Almost at once the girl dropped her sewing and fled the room in terror, leaving the group in an awkward silence, during which Mary made some useful conclusions. She had little doubt that the offending girl's bags would be packed before the day was out, and, determined to avoid a similar fate, she resolved to distance herself from any form of idle gossip in the future. The room returned to an uneasy calm and the other ladies withdrew, leaving Mary alone in the corner except for the indomitable Jayne who had been all the while serenely sorting the bright coloured silks for the sewing.

Without warning, the clarion tones of a female voice could be heard approaching in the corridor and then closer, in the ante-room outside the Queen's chamber. 'Lady Castlemaine,' was the response to the respectful enquiry from the footman outside. 'Open the door at once and announce me, you dunderhead,' the voice continued, at which point the door burst open, revealing the confused young footman and one of the Queen's own guards.

Without hesitation Mary made a fateful decision, which was to have resounding consequences for her future.

'No, My Lady,' she said firmly, trying to bar the door, for she knew the Queen would be upset by the arrival of Lady Castlemaine, but would be unfailingly polite in her usual gentle way.

'The Queen is conferring with the Chancellor and it is a private meeting,' Mary said defiantly.

'Out of my way,' was the lofty response.

'May I at least enquire of Her Majesty as to whether or not she wishes to receive you?' Mary persisted coldly.

'Who do you think you are talking to?' the woman stormed, her magnificent bosoms heaving.

'I dare not say,' said Mary boldly.

Lady Castlemaine ignored her. Making a note of the girl's insolence, she pushed past, a look of terrifying anger on her face. The Queen looked up; her face hardened even whilst she stayed her hand towards the footman and guard who bowed and stood discretely aside. Mary stood her ground, watching with delight as Her Ladyship's bosom heaved in a mixture of anger and discomfiture at such a public rebuff, the room now having mysteriously filled with Royal attendants.

Clearly emboldened by the King's recent dismissal of his paramour, and to Mary's delight, the Queen acknowledged the woman with unusual spirit.

'I had thought my husband the King,' she said imperiously, 'had sent you from the court. We have important business here and I would ask you to respect the King's wishes and withdraw immediately.'

The Chancellor rose to his feet, his face momentarily brightening at the humiliation of his hated enemy. He was about to speak when Lady Castlemaine prevented him.

'I come, Your Majesty, to enquire of the King, and to offer my services to Your Majesty at this difficult time.' Lady Castlemaine's voice was still shaking, whilst attempting to assume a sweet conciliatory tone.

Almost before she had uttered the words Lady Castlemaine realised her error. Lord Clarendon saw the Queen's face darken and he took his chance.

'Madam,' he said loudly in sepulchral tone for all to hear, 'your services to this court are to some of us abhorrent and inappropriate to the Queen's welfare, and at this time she must have her loyal servants about her while His Majesty, her husband, is fighting to preserve our city. We pray he is in God's care and in the eyes of that God you have no place here.'

There was a deathly silence in the room, broken only by the cheeping of birds in the gardens below.

Lady Castlemaine stood statue-still. Her face giving nothing away, she turned without so much as a curtsy. The Countess Panalva, who had also returned, hearing the commotion, muttered something in Portuguese at which the Queen caught her eye and smiled wryly. Mary curtsied as Lady Castlemaine swept from the room. The disgraced lady said nothing, but as she passed Mary, she stopped for a moment and looked her full in the face. It was a look such as Mary had never seen before, dark, menacing and ominous. For a minute Mary felt a shiver run down her spine. And then Countess Panalva came to her.

'You are a brave young woman. There is not much about the English court to admire, but you, my dear, are of a different breed. Your loyalty has been noted.'

Mary curtsied and kissed the woman's proffered hand.

*   *   *

The fire raged on for four days. The King and the Duke of York fought tirelessly to control it while the mayor wept like a baby and was incapable of rational behaviour. Everything in the fire's path was consigned to the flames and in desperation the King and the Duke, despite furious opposition, decided to make a fire break and blow up a wall of houses to stop the fire in its tracks. The plan had worked and then the east wind dropped and the air was still. The fires came to a halt in Smithfild and the exhausted monarch returned to his Queen. But he did not rest for long.

Thousands of his subjects were left homeless without food and water. He set an army of men to provide huts and bread and, when the weather became cooler, coals, all provided from his own purse. It was as Clarendon had so often observed, 'It is in adversity that the King reveals his most sterling qualities, which have made him so beloved of his indulgent people.'

During this time the King and Queen were very close. It was to her that he turned for encouragement when his country suffered from one disaster after another.

The Boynton house was spared the flames. Mary sent word to her father and received a reply almost at once. He would not be coming to London to oversee the situation since he could tell that his daughter was 'more than able to decide what to do'. But he had some unexpected news for his Mary.

She received the letter when she had returned to her aunt's

house at Hampton Court for a brief rest. She was seated in the morning room looking towards the river, and the sight of her father's crest made her think of home in Norfolk with a sudden longing. The dramatic events of the past days had left her feeling drained and empty. Only one unexpected emotion flared constantly in the back of her mind, filling her with a mixture of anxiety and excitement. Fernando had begun to occupy her thoughts and she had found herself counting the hours until she saw him and even contriving to meet him on his regular visits to the Queen. They had walked together in the gardens and once his hand had touched hers and he had looked steadfastly and wordlessly into her eyes and she had felt her stomach churn and longed to reach up and touch his handsome cheek and feel his lips on hers. These were feelings quite different from the childhood love she had felt for Anthony. It was obvious that Fernando was a man of experience and could have any woman he chose in the louche sexual world of Whitehall, and yet she knew he was chaste and faithful to his sick wife, about whom he spoke with respectful ambivalence.

She wondered if she were imagining it, but she was sure he saw something special in her, and desired her not just for her youth and looks but something more. Although they came from such different worlds, perhaps they had been drawn together like two ships at sea who find an unexpected port in a storm.

She opened the letter and her happy state of mind shattered as she read the first paragraph. She called out to Judith, who was in the next room arranging flowers. Judith came hurrying in, wiping her hands on the dark green pinafore she wore for her floristry.

'What is the matter?' she asked anxiously, fearing more bad news.

'Father is to be married, and there is more, his Charlotte is to have a child, and we are to go to the wedding which will be in three weeks.'

'I had suspected some such development,' said Judith. 'But a child, well that does come as a surprise.' She raised her eyebrows, a look of concern on her face. Judith looked at Mary but, having been through so many momentous experiences in her life, she had long ago made up her mind to accept what life presented unless there was some obvious reason why she should try to alter the course of events. Thinking quickly about this news from her brother, and mindful of the difficulties he had endured with Harriet, she saw no course of action other than to rejoice in the idea of a union based on mutual affection, which had proved itself over the course of time. Judith knew that Charlotte did not have the breeding of which Harriet had been so proud – by all accounts her family were good solid village people – but Harriet's airs and graces had brought nothing but misery. As she looked at her niece, of whom she became fonder each day, she thanked God that one good thing had come from her brother's marriage.

Mary, on the other hand, was unable to bear the news with quite such sanguinity. She adored her father, and had not allowed her mind to explore the possibility of another woman taking up the reins of Sailing Hall and the fine house she had protected from the fire. And then there was the matter of the child. If it was a boy, what then? Since her arrival at court and her emergence into the harsh reality of the world, since her father had already provided for her sisters, she had begun to consider the possibility of taking up the running of her father's business. Should no suitable husband appear she was sole heir to the family fortunes.

'It's just that I had never thought it through,' she stammered.

'Of course you hadn't, my dear,' said Judith comfortingly, taking her hand and drawing her to a chair in the window. 'You see,' she went on, 'the first thing you must think about is your father, only his happiness, he deserves a kind loving wife,' she said pointedly, knowing that Mary would understand the implication of her remark.

'You are right, Aunt, I am very selfish not to be rejoicing on his behalf, and, besides, another child will be a joy to us all, especially one born from such a happy affair.' As Mary spoke she thought again of the possibility of children, of all the babies she and Anthony had never had, and of her poor Queen whose life was blighted by her inability to experience that simple joy of motherhood, and for a moment she wondered if she too would, in some cruel way, be deprived of that also.

CHAPTER ELEVEN

Mary and Judith made their plans as quickly as they could. The Queen granted Mary leave to return to her father for the wedding, and presented her with a handsome gift of linen for the bride and groom. The imminent departure set Fernando to thinking. He began making enquiries about Sir Miles's business and the King had expressed an interest in this favourable manufacture of hemp, so vital to the navy's safety. There had been a number of cases recently where the safety of vessels had been severely compromised by poor-quality rope and Fernando had seen an opportunity to do some business with Sir Miles and get to know the man better.

Judith had listened to all this with concealed amusement. She noticed the way Fernando looked at Mary. He had clearly fallen in love with her. At first Judith had been alarmed by this development. She knew only too well what a beauty Mary was and it had been her hope that she would attract a suitable husband. But looking around the dissolute and motley crew of available young men at court, all seemingly tainted by the moral turpitude which was endemic at Whitehall, she had to admit that Fernando stood out like a beacon of rectitude and it seemed that his wife in Lisbon might well succumb to an early demise. Fernando was a rich and powerful man and Judith had a wide vision of the world and its expanding horizons. Mary could well have a place in this new brave world. But she decided she must warn her niece to guard her virtue, to sleep with this man would be her undoing. She must conduct a dignified friendship, if only to protect the respect of the Queen who had begun to trust her. She told Mary as much whilst at the same time pragmatically approving of Fernando's company for the trip to Norfolk.

*   *   *

The decision to include Fernando had turned out to be fortuitous. The warm autumn weather, which had helped create the great fire, had suddenly turned unseasonably cold. Equinoxal gales lashed the countryside turning the roads to a muddy quagmire. After Colchester the coach shed a wheel and Fernando took control in a way that two women would have found impossible. He stripped off his fine velvet doublet, rolled up his sleeves and oversaw the repair himself.

The journey resumed in horrendous weather, until the last day, when the sun appeared in glorious splendour, revealing the Norfolk countryside with its pellucid autumn light. And as they approached King's Bircham village, Mary's heart began to race in anticipation, but with more than a slight dampening as she called to mind that there was soon to be another mistress of her family home. It was no longer the refuge to which she had sole claim. She looked at Fernando, so firmly in control, with a shudder of relief that she and her aunt came thus accompanied.

'What a delightful house,' remarked Fernando, as they swept up the long avenue.

The huge front door flew open and there was Thomas, smiling broadly, in what looked like a new livery. 'Miss Mary, and Your Grace,' he said in his best voice, with a low bow in Fernando's direction.

Within seconds, Mary's father was at the door, arms out-stretched, embracing her without a trace of formality. Mary's heart leapt with joy, the sight of her father brought back to her how much she had missed him. As he embraced her, she became aware of Charlotte hovering discretely in the background. She broke away from her father and crossed the floor to greet her and, much to her embarrassment, Charlotte swept her a curtsy. Mary noticed at once that the child was evident in her belly, and spontaneously put both her hands under the woman's elbows and lifted her up.

'Please do not curtsy to me again,' Mary said gently. 'You are soon to be my stepmother, and I only have to look at my father to see how happy he is.'

Mary presented the Duke to her father and observed that Charlotte blushed when introduced to the dashing new comer. Amidst the excitement of the arrival Mary had not noticed that her elder sister, Abigail, whom she had not seen for more than two years, was standing silently in the corner. For one strange moment she thought it was her mother, so alike had the woman become to the departed Harriet. She exuded the same cold censorious disapproval, which pervaded the space around her.

'Mary, my dear, how fine you have become,' she said sourly. 'Not too high for present company,' she said with an obvious glance in Charlotte's direction.

'It is so good to see you,' Mary lied, choosing to ignore her sister's barbed remark, clearly directed towards her future step-mother, who was already aware of the possibility of unpleasantness coming from her sister.

Mary had seen little of either of her sisters as she was growing up, as there was a considerable difference in their ages. The gap had been occupied by her mother's attempts to produce a son, and Mary's eventual arrival had been greeted with disinterest, since in her sisters' view the birth of another daughter merely meant another dowry or jointure which would diminish the family coffers.

Mary's homecoming was a happy event, much more so than she had imagined it would be. Charlotte had already made her mark on the house, and preparations for the marriage filled the house with a festive charm which Mary could never remember in her mother's time.

The great hall was already laid for the wedding breakfast which was to take place the following day, white cloths on a long top table with several tables set against it. 'We have included the village and the workers and we didn't want any below the salt,' explained Charlotte. She had garlanded the cloths with greenery and autumn roses, the top of the tables were threaded with hellebores, obviously grown in Charlotte's glasshouse. The family pewter sparkled and big goblets of deep red crystal sat beside each place. The centrepiece was an elaborate concoction of fruit, even more impressive than some Mary had seen at Whitehall and each guest was to be presented with a horn handled knife on which the date of the wedding had been inscribed.

Her father joined them. 'You see what a marvel my future wife is, she has managed to grow all these wonderful things and the pineapples are the best I have ever tasted,' he said proudly and as Mary looked at her father's happy face, she began to share some of his joy. The whole household had adopted an informal air, so different from the one to which she had become accustomed. She noticed the way Charlotte chatted with the servants and how Thomas smiled warmly at his new mistress. Mary had seen him help her solicitously as she nearly tripped on one of the rugs in the great hall. It was clear that Fernando, too, was willingly entering into the spirit of things at Sailing. He had struck up an animated conversation with Thomas and the two of them were laughing heartily together.

Later, when they had recovered from their journey and the servants had unpacked their things, they all met for the family meal, which, to Mary's surprise, was to take place in the servant's dining area off the great kitchen with its barrelled ceiling and huge open fireplaces, on which the pit boy was turning a haunch of venison wrapped in rosemary and heavily basted in goose fat.

'I hope you will not mind, Your Grace. The great hall is ready for tomorrow,' explained Charlotte, as they assembled in her father's study for a drink of local ale. 'We thought it would be nice to be informal, with the whole household,' she went on. 'They have been working so hard and, as you will see tomorrow, every detail has been attended to before I have even thought of it myself. Why, even the horses have been groomed and their coats brushed till they shine like the copper on the kettles.'

'Madam, it is a great pleasure to be with you for this happy day,' replied Fernando. 'It reminds me of my own home in Portugal. When we have harvested the grapes for our wine, we all celebrate together, and it is a time when servant and master are equal, for both know they depend on the other. It is the observance of this which creates a loyalty which is our country's strength.'

'I only wish our own nobility realised this,' said Miles, who had joined his future wife. Putting an affectionate arm about her shoulders, he continued gravely. 'Some of our own seamen would be as happy to serve a foreign master, and you can hardly blame them. The concept of loyalty is quite gone and our shores are left unguarded. We are well aware of the danger here in Norfolk where we are nearer to the Dutch than out King's court at Whitehall,' Miles said quietly, not wishing to spread alarm. 'All our estate workers are armed,' he continued in a low voice. 'And we have a plan if the Hollanders should come,' he went on. 'The villagers will all come to the big house and we will flood the waterways that surround us and nobody could slip through them unnoticed, as, unless you know the secret channels, they are impassable. We will guard our women and children and our livestock and we have provisions laid down for a long siege if necessary.'

'Father, we must not let this spoil our celebrations,' said Mary quickly, realising such talk would put Fernando in an awkward position. As a diplomat he had to tread carefully and no criticism of the King and his henchman must be attributable to him, although Mary knew only too well what he thought of the King's close confidants.

'Your father is a fine man,' said Fernando when they were alone. They had walked into the garden where a harvest moon was making an appearance in a swiftly darkening night sky. There was the sharp autumn tang of approaching winter and a few birds still fussed in the remaining leaves on the trees around the house.

'How I love the sound of the wind in the trees,' said Mary, as they made their way down the path to Miles's glasshouse.

'We have a saying in our country that the finest saplings are sprung from a good tree. Now I see how you came to be as you are, my little pigeon,' he said softly.

Mary turned and met his fiery dark eyes piercing the fading light. The atmosphere was heavy with dew and she gave a little shiver. It had been many months since he had used the name he had given her on their first meeting. He caught her round her slim waist and gently pulled her towards him, she could feel his warm breath suspended on the evening air and his heart beating through his velvet doublet. He did not need to draw her closer, Mary was driven by a desire she could not control, and he felt it in the soft biddable melding of her body. She felt his warm hand behind her neck as his lips found hers. She closed her eyes, and knew that nothing could be the same between them.

After what seemed like an eternity she pressed her face into his shoulder. With one arm he clasped her as his other hand caressed her tumbling hair. He had dreamed of this moment, but never had it been his intention to let his dreams become a reality, for he knew they were not a natural union as the world would have it. But the dry loveless marriage to his wife Magdalena had shackled his romantic soul and there was a bit of him that knew that somewhere there was a woman waiting for him with fire in her heart and a pilgrim soul, and he knew that, against all the odds, Mary, with her tawny beauty and latent courage, was this woman.

'I love you with all my heart, I want to give you all that is mine, I want your sons and daughters to be my sons and daughters and I vow to you under this harvest moon that I will never harm you. It will not be easy, my darling, for we must both do God's will,' he whispered into her hair.

Mary drew away and looked at him. His gaze was steady, his

face so noble and honest, and there was no doubt that this was a turning point in her life. It was as if she had come of age. But, despite her happiness, in the back of her mind there was more than a frisson of alarm. She remembered her Aunt Judith's warnings, and the more so because she wanted Fernando to make love to her more than anything she had ever desired.

She took his hand and led him to the glasshouse. As they opened the door, the erotic smell of arum lilies wafted around them, mixed with a warm mossy smell of earth. It was as if they were surrounded by fecundity and she wanted him to make love to her there and then. She thought of her father and Charlotte and their coming child, probably conceived in this very place, and for a moment she felt she was flying in the face of nature and all her natural desires. When she looked at Fernando she thought of the child they would have, of its beauty if it were born, of their sighs on this beautiful autumn night under a harvest moon.

Suddenly they heard the noise of barking and, almost without warning, her father's spaniels, Ned and Betty, were pushing through the open door, followed by Thomas, wielding a lantern.

'Miss Mary . . . Your Grace,' he stammered, bowing low and covered in confusion. 'I am so sorry. I thought I heard intruders and you can't be too careful . . . '

'No, my good man, you should not be sorry,' said Fernando lightly. 'Your timing is, as one would say, perfection. Miss Mary and I were just searching for a lamp to take us back to the house. It became dark so suddenly when we were taking some cuttings for me to give to Her Majesty. I have them safely in my kerchief and now you can take us back to the house with your light . . . Sir Miles is fortunate to have a servant like you.'

Thomas's potential embarrassment had been completely assuaged by Fernando's diplomacy, and as they made their way back to the house Mary realised yet again that Fernando was indeed a man worth loving and waiting for.

CHAPTER TWELVE

Mary was woken by a faint knocking at her door. She sat up in bed and reached for her shawl, which lay on the end of the bed. Her first thought was that it was Fernando, and her second that Jayne would be woken by his arrival, and her third one of alarm, for she knew that if he had come to press his advances she would not be able to refuse them. She had been dreaming of him and the sweetness of it still lingered with her. Tentatively she crept to the door and opened it.

To her surprise it was Abigail. 'I had to talk to you,' she said hurriedly, edging past Mary and sitting awkwardly on the bed. Mary saw at once that she was weeping uncontrollably.

'Why, sister, what can be the matter?' Mary asked in alarm. 'Has something happened to Father?'

'No, it's nothing like that. It is too terrible and I think you are the only person in whom I can confide.' Abigail looked appealingly towards Mary who, despite her wariness of her sister, put a tender arm about her shoulders. Abigail's face was red and swollen with tears and Mary noticed she had a large sore on her lip. She registered surprise that she had not noticed it earlier but then realised that her sister had been heavily made up.

'I can see you are looking at the thing on my lip,' Abigail sobbed. 'I must talk to you, I need your help. That blaggard of a husband of mine has infected me with the pox.'

'Oh, my God,' cried Mary, recoiling in horror, wondering if it were her imagination that that her sister exuded a faintly unpleasant odour.

'What am I to do? You know people in high places,' Abigail blurted. 'They say the court is rife with it. The King has given it to all his mistresses . . . there is a cure, the court knows of it and it is my only hope.'

Mary got up and walked to the still-glowing fire, running her hands through her hair. She didn't know what to think. This sister, who had always occupied some strange high moral ground, who had never spoken affectionately to her and never extended the hand of friendship, was sharing this horrible secret with her and at a time when the family should be rejoicing. She felt sullied by the complicity which had been forced upon her, but at the same time she knew full well what Abigail was referring to. There was indeed such an establishment, but she had always regarded such places as representative of the wages of sin and indeed it was one of the prime reasons she had protected her virtue at Whitehall, where the sickly smell of the pox was often in evidence. She thought with revulsion that she smelt it now in her room and her first instinct was to send Abigail away and have nothing to do with it. But, unwisely as Jayne pointed out later, Mary allowed her kind heart to get the better of her.

*　　*　　*

It was, of course, to Jayne that Mary turned, redoubtable Jayne who knew all the court gossip. She found Abigail asleep in Mary's bed the following morning. Mary had risen earlier as the day had dawned bright and fair and she had decided to go to the stables and ride her favourite mare before the family stirred. To her delight she had found Fernando with the same idea and together they had explored the tree-lined banks on the edge of the miles of waterways, sending all manner of wildlife screeching into the fresh morning air. Mary had been amazed at Fernando's skill and elegance on one of her father's old horses. In a trice he had had it lifting its hooves with an eagerness and precision she had never observed before.

It was with a heavy heart that she returned to her chamber, where she knew she would be brought back to earth by the presence of Abigail, who was still asleep in spite of Jayne's busy presence in the room, laying out Mary's gown for the wedding, feeding the fire and bringing in the scented water for Mary's washstand.

Mary took her aside at once and told her the whole story. Jayne's reaction was swift and unequivocal.

'You must have nothing to do with it,' she said firmly.

'But I can't just pretend she hasn't told me, and after all she is my sister,' said Mary.

'That's as maybe,' said Jayne in her most practical tone with no evidence of surprise, since she often knew the family's business before they did themselves. Turning towards the bed where Abigail appeared to be sleeping peacefully, she picked up Mary's gown, which was ready and pressed for the day's festivities, and shook it out noisily.

'I'd like to know where she was when you needed her,' she went on doggedly. 'I didn't notice her full of sisterly love when Mister Anthony died, too fearful of her own skin, I would say. And anyway it was obvious she only married that blockhead of a husband for his money, begging your pardon Miss Mary, you even said as much yourself. And now she has got more than she bargained for,' she shot a venomous look in the direction of the apparently sleeping woman.

'Things are never quite as simple as that. I only wish they were,' said Mary despondently.

Before she could continue, Abigail sat up in the bed, her face contorted furiously.

'I heard your conversation, every word of it. You thought I was asleep, didn't you?' she ranted, her lower lip quivering with emotion. 'How you could permit a servant to speak to you like that is beyond me,' she shrieked at Mary.

'Jayne is my friend, the best I ever had, and if you want my help you will have to treat her as such,' retorted Mary quickly, her voice rising angrily.

'How dare you speak to me like that?' said Abigail, leaping off the bed and starting to flounce dementedly around the room.

'I dare to speak to you the way your behaviour merits, but why couldn't you have waited? Did you have to tell me this today of all days,' replied Mary angrily, thinking of the many times when Abigail had let her down, furious that she had ruined yet another happy family occasion.

'That's typical of you,' fired Abigail sulkily, 'always so perfect. Well, things can't always be like you want them to be, not even in your world.'

Abigail's remarks did nothing to kindle any sisterly love, but despite herself Mary couldn't help feeling sorry for her sister. 'If I am to help you,' she said calmly, 'it is Jayne who will have to be our intermediary, for such matters are things about which I know nothing, and it is Jayne who will have to find out where these places are, where you can have treatment.' She paused for a moment, fixing her sister with a solemn look which left no room for argument, and in a trice Abigail saw the woman her little sister had become: strong, independent and beautiful. She allowed these thoughts with a begrudging kind of admiration and a certain jealousy, for she had already observed the way the handsome Duke had looked at her sister and that Mary was now floating in a universe she herself had never been able to reach.

Abigail looked down, suddenly embarrassed. 'You are right,' she conceded bluntly, looking apprehensively at Jayne, whose mouth was set in a rictus of disapproval. At once Abigail realised that if she were to receive her sister's help, reluctant as she might be to fraternise with servants, she would have to capitulate. 'I will be very grateful for your help . . . that is to say . . . both of your help,' she fumbled, with a semblance of a smile which was not returned by Jayne or her sister.

'Now, Miss Mary, we must get on with the day. After all, this is a happy occasion and . . . ' Jayne said pointedly looking squarely at Abigail.

Abigail relapsed into silence and Mary went about dressing for the wedding, whilst her sister, returned to her chamber where her sulky maid waited with her gown, which she had omitted to press. Within minutes her voice could be heard scolding the girl with all the vigour of a high moral priestess. Jayne tutted violently and shut the door.

*   *   *

Charlotte walked slowly down the centre of the flower-filled church hall to the arms of her future husband. All eyes were happily upon her. The village women had made a tunnel of harvest blooms, thick branches of rosehips and honesty, sumptuous autumn daisies, Pyracantha exploding into masses of colour. Charlotte looked the essence of fecundity and happiness. Her gown of russet red velvet, pleated about her gently rounded stomach, blended with the luscious products of autumn and her hair was massed at the nape of her neck and on her head she wore a circle of bright pink nerines.

'She is a happy woman and your father is a lucky man,' whispered Fernando. Mary sat between him and Abigail, as her father and his bride made their vows according to the Catholic faith to which Charlotte had converted. They had decided to marry in the hall because the local church could not accommodate a Catholic service, and some of the local gentry had stayed away from the ceremony, apprehensive about closely associating with the Church of Rome.

Mary threw Fernando a sideways glance and he gently sought her hand in the folds of her dress, she did not draw it away, and soon she felt his fingers exploring the soft whiteness of her inner wrist. As Charlotte made her vows, Fernando's hand proceeded sensuously up Mary's forearm and, concealed by her hanging sleeve, he probed further into the dip of her waist. She moved nearer to him and closed her eyes as a heady feeling of desire overwhelmed her and she knew that if she were not on her guard it would not be long before she made the journey she had resisted with Anthony.

PART TWO

CHAPTER THIRTEEN

The Palace of Whitehall, Autumn 1666

'You must cover your faces with your hoods,' hissed Jayne as they alighted from the coach. 'Nobody must recognise us, it would be a terrible disgrace,' she warned.

They had travelled to the appointed house in a dubious part of the city; it was raining and a thick autumn fog gave the place a sinister air. The dense smoke from the hundreds of London's domestic fires hung gloomily in the air. As Mary took her sister's arm, she felt her trembling. She had not wanted to accompany Abigail on her grim assignment, but her kind heart had been moved by her sister's anguish, and she had concluded that nobody deserved the awful fate of what was euphemistically called 'the French pox'.

Since becoming involved in her sister's problem, Mary had been forced to learn a good deal about the scourge of syphilis, which was rife not only in England, but in the rest of Europe. It was said to have originated in the East and been transmitted by sailors who had sampled foreign beauties and paid the price. Even babies were being born infected and would die a slow and painful death. The first signs, a sore on the private areas or beside the mouth were often disregarded while the disease lurked in the deepest tissues of the body. Often it went into a dormant state which the victims mistakenly thought was a cure, but when it returned it was fierce and brutal, eating away at the body's extremities and doing its worst in the brain, where madness and dementia finally brought the long drawn out suffering to an end. The stench of the afflicted brought bile to the throat, and, once experienced, was never to be forgotten, and it was that smell, now, which made the women gag and bring out their handkerchiefs.

But the so called cures available offered hope, and it was with this in mind, and thanks to Jayne's clandestine research, that the three women arrived at Mrs Fourcard's establishment. In contrast to the seedy area in which they found themselves, the house was lavishly decorated, and apart from the thick cloying odour, everything was designed to be discreet and reassuring.

A slim woman dressed in the height of fashion introduced herself and showed them to a private room where she enquired which of them was the patient. Abigail fidgeted nervously and seemed unable to articulate.

'This lady,' said Jayne, casting her eye in Abigail's direction with a disdainful sniff, inviting a sharp nudge from Mary who was concerned by the extent of Jayne's resentment.

'Well, Madam, we shall require the payment in advance,' said the woman, looking at Abigail with a slight smirk, 'and, if I recall, your maid inspected the treatment room on your behalf,' she said quickly, consulting some notes in a thick leather book. 'Ah yes,' she said loudly, 'you have selected a course of the mercury bath and not the Gudaic cure which, as you know, is the miracle wood introduced by Spanish sailors.'

Abigail flushed and nodded in silent agreement, handing over a silk purse containing the required money.

Mary was rapidly becoming more and more alarmed, not least by the apparent lack of discretion but also by the lack of information. After all, Abigail was her own flesh and blood and she wanted to know exactly what was in store and to be reassured that these people were not charlatans.

'I should like to see the treatment room,' she said decisively.

'Of course, My Lady; it is only right that you care about your friend,' the woman said in a more kindly tone. She was used to people being overcome with fear as they embarked on the cure, for the side effects were well known: rotting, blackened gums and the teeth falling out, ulcerated cheeks and constant salivating, and the unmistakable stench of mercury, which nothing could disguise. She didn't have much time for the sad array of decadent people who came seeking help but she had a sense that Mary was rather different, a woman of virtue and class. She almost felt she should prevent her from entering, for she knew full well the vision would be very disturbing.

'If you like, My Lady,' she said helpfully, 'I could take the lady myself while you wait here. After all, I am sure that as she is the patient she is capable of making her up her own mind.'

'Thank you but no,' said Mary sharply, 'we shall go together.'

The woman shrugged and led the way, slowly opening one of many doors leading off the panelled hallway. They were assailed by a cloud of pungent steam and Mary reached for her handkerchief. Her eyes were smarting but gradually they accustomed themselves to the dreadful place in which she must leave her sister.

The place was shrouded in white sheets, which also lined a huge bath standing in the middle of the room. In the far corner was a range. There was a kind of copper with a hot plate, on which a large, white-robed man was throwing the liquid contents of an enormous cauldron, creating clouds of acrid steam.

'Oh, my God,' screamed Abigail hysterically, a look of terror flashing across her face. 'I have come to hell. Help me, sister. What am I to do?'

'Wait . . . how does this work? What exactly is it?' Mary asked the woman, momentarily closing her eyes to shut out the distressing vision before her.

'The liquid is a mixture of half brimstone and half mercury. On the hot plate they combine and form a powder which then condenses on the body,' the woman replied unemotionally. But, seeing the distraught patient and realising the fine young woman who was taking such care was none other than her sister, she again felt a certain compassion.

Hearing the commotion, another woman appeared, whom Mary assessed to be the owner of the establishment.

'My dear, I am Mrs Fourcard,' she said, taking Abigail's arm. 'We will look after you. Your friends can leave you in safe hands, and I will give you a glass of wine which will calm your nerves,' she continued soothingly.

'We should go, Miss Mary,' said Jayne, looking nervously about her, rapidly losing patience with Abigail and anxious to remove her mistress from the place with all possible haste.

'How do you feel, Abigail?' asked Mary, trying to keep her voice calm and unemotional while all around her she felt a deep well of fear.

'I don't know,' was the trembling reply.

'It is best you go now, My Lady,' said Mrs Fourcard quietly. 'We will look after the young lady.'

Mary turned to go and said a silent prayer of thanks that she had kept her virtue in the hothouse of the court, thinking that but for the grace of God it might have been her in this unspeakable place.

The woman had an arm about Abigail's shoulder, and before Mary could weaken she found herself being hustled by Jayne towards the door. The woman caught Jayne's eye with a wink. 'The treatment will be for one day only, allowing for the patient to recover and maybe then the mercury can be taken by mouth, so do not worry, the time will soon pass,' she called out, easing Abigail in the direction of a screen in the corner. They left at once, promising to return before dark.

As they made their way outside, towards the waiting coach, there was the clatter of wheels and one of the royal coaches drew up at the door. Jayne hurried Mary into a neighbouring doorway, hastily pulling her shawl over her mistress's head. A heavily veiled woman alighted from the coach and Jayne's stomach lurched as she realised the woman had seen them.

CHAPTER FOURTEEN

'My dear, I must speak with you,' said Judith gravely. They were sitting in an ante-room in the Queen's apartments. It was more than a month since Abigail had completed her treatment and returned to her home. Mary had been gratified when she had thanked her for her help, explaining that Mary was the first person who had shown her such kindness in her life and that she would be for ever grateful. Jayne had been present and given Mary a wry smile, but all the same Mary was glad to have restored some harmony between herself and at least one of her sisters.

'So what is it, Aunt? You look very worried. I hope you are not unwell.'

'No, my dear, but it is you who I understand are afflicted. There are rumours in the court and they have reached the Queen . . . ' she hesitated, looking down in embarrassment and smoothing the satin of her immaculate gown.

'I, why no, I have never been in better health, what do you mean?' Mary asked in genuine bewilderment.

'I will come to the point,' said Judith bluntly. 'It is said you are no longer pure and that you have been receiving treatment for the pox at that villainess Mrs Fourcard's.'

Mary leapt up, her eyes dilated with indignation. 'This is wicked, Aunt. A pack of lies. I will summon my maid Jayne to be my witness as to the truth of the matter.'

As it happened, Jayne was not far away and came with extra-ordinary speed to Mary's aid. 'It was Miss Mary's kindness that has been her undoing, Madam,' she said quietly, slipping Judith a respectful curtsy.

'I cannot think what you mean, girl. Letting go of your virtue is not an act of kindness,' said Judith, raising her eyebrows in amazement.

'Begging your pardon, that is not what I meant. I meant that my mistress was befriending another and taking her to that terrible place . . . and against my advice, because I knew no good would come of it,' explained Jayne in a quiet but determined voice.

'It is true, Aunt,' Mary broke in. 'I cannot tell you who it was; but what I can tell you is that I am as the good Lord made me. It is unbearable that the Queen should have been told such lies about me, and now she will no longer want me as part of her court and I shall be sent away in disgrace, and all because I tried to do the right thing,' Mary's voice was beginning to break, she saw the likelihood of all her life before her in a cloud of disgrace.

Judith got up from her chair with a sigh of relief. 'Thank God,' she said loudly. 'And now we must decide what to do. Things cannot be left as they are. I must warn you, my dear, there is somebody making trouble for you and I think I know who it is. The clever thing will be to use this against her and make her look a laughing stock.'

'There is only one way to deal with this and it may offend Miss Mary and you, My Lady,' said Jayne.

'Well, tell us, I should like to know,' said Judith, with an air of scepticism.

'I know the Queen's physician, Doctor Pearce, for his wife's servant is a friend of mine. Miss Mary will have to undertake an examination which will be proof that she is a maid and is as clean of the fowl pox as the holy Virgin herself,' said Jayne.

'I could never consent to such an indignity,' Mary gasped.

'Hush, girl,' said Judith thoughtfully, pointing an admonitory finger at Mary. 'Your maid has a point, and such things are regarded as normal in court circles. Many Royal marriages only proceed when the bride is proved to be a virgin. But this is a hornet's nest,' she went on. 'We should enlist the wise support of the Chancellor, for he is the sworn enemy of the person who is at the root of all this and, above all, the Queen has learned to trust him.'

'But who is this person who wishes me ill?' asked Mary in bewilderment.

'Why, Lady Castlemaine, of course,' Judith replied unflinchingly. 'She and the Duke of Buckingham are cousins . . . and,' Judith stopped for a moment, unsure whether to continue with the information she had. 'It is said on good authority that there is more than a filial relationship between them,' she went on, forsaking her normal prudence. 'Consequently, as you can imagine, together they are a force to be reckoned with. Some even say the Duke is as powerful as the King himself and that the King dances to his tune. It is certain that Her Ladyship and her cousin are hell bent on destroying the Chancellor, Lord Clarendon, and with him the Queen.'

'But I don't see why they should want to discredit me in this way, what have I to do with all this?' asked Mary innocently.

Judith's face hardened. 'You are loyal to the Queen, and the Chancellor also. But part of the evil plot is to bring down the Queen and the Chancellor, and force the King into another marriage where they can manipulate him,' said Judith.

'But who could take the place of the Queen?' cried Mary, with genuine horror.

'Why Frances Stuart of course,' replied Judith without hesitation. 'She has been the apple of the King's eye for years, and has cleverly never succumbed to the King's ardour, which makes his passion all the greater.'

Mary thought of the myriad of women who occupied the King's bed, and the power that Castlemaine still held over her errant lover, despite the King's obsession with Frances Stuart. Frances was another of the Queen's ladies, a chaste beauty whose family had fallen on hard times, and as she was also a kinswoman of the Duke, she had been educated at court at the King's expense. The King had become infatuated; she was a tempting challenge to a man who did not seem to tire of the chase. But Mary knew enough to be sure that it was still Lady Castlemaine who always got the upper hand. Despite her outrageous behaviour the King always had her back into his bed, and her power within court circles was to be feared as indeed were her henchmen.

As if reading her thoughts, Judith continued unabashed, for she realised that matters had gone beyond fine feelings of decorum.

'This is an evil woman, Mary. As a measure of her depravity it is well know that only recently the Duchess paid some of her ruffians to hunt down a poor man called John Ellis, a minor civil servant who had unwisely boasted of sleeping with her, and would you like to know what they did?' she asked.

'Why yes, I suppose so,' replied Mary nervously.

'They castrated him,' said Judith bluntly.

Mary felt as if she might faint and Jayne drew in a breath, appalled that such a distinguished lady should repeat such things to her young mistress, but then the recollection of the Duke of Buckingham's wild dark eyes flashed before her. Many men had tried to tumble her Mary in the 'merry court' as it was called by the people, but the Duke had been particularly blatant in his advances and Jayne was relieved that her mistress had been particularly virulent in her rebuffs. She had noticed the black look in his eyes on the last occasion, but dismissed it as of no consequence in this hothouse of sexual liberty where dalliances and sexual promiscuity were commonplace.

'You must understand,' said Judith, 'these people are in league with the devil, whose form is many, and Lady Castlemaine is a willing and eager disciple. But we must return to the matter of the Queen and her enemies,' said Judith, moving on swiftly.

'All right then,' said Mary. 'Why would Lady Castlemaine want to replace the Queen with Lady Frances?'

'She mistakenly believes that "La Belle Stuart", as she is known, would be a willing puppet in hers and the Duke's hands,' replied Judith. 'Discrediting the Chancellor and any of the

Queen's loyal servants is part of a terrible plan,' said Judith. 'It is said that there is even a plan to poison the Queen.'

'It is true, Miss Mary, I have heard as much myself – we must all be on our guard,' said Jayne.

'I am beginning to see that however pure you might be, nearly everyone drinks from the poison chalice here at court,' Mary exclaimed dismally.

'My dear, you must not upset yourself too much,' said Judith soothingly. 'We must not lose faith in the power of good over evil. I am going to speak confidentially to the Chancellor and tell him the truth of the matter concerning you. He is an old friend of mine and has a sound head on his shoulders. You have nothing to fear for I know you are speaking the truth.'

The matter was settled for the time being and Judith made a time to meet the Chancellor that same evening. Mary feigned a headache and kept to her quarters, but she felt the dull thud of anxiety whenever she thought of the damage already done and the humiliating things she would have to endure, if she were to clear her name.

CHAPTER FIFTEEN

'I am always at your service, Your Majesty,' said the Chancellor with a low bow.

The King looked at him with more than a trace of annoyance; he could not deny that Clarendon was true and loyal, that he had been, and still was, a wise and pragmatic advisor. But there was something about his humourless sepulchral features which made Charles feel as if he were guilty of frivolous vacuity. The man always gave off a faint air of disapproval and superiority. Charles had always resented his censorious comments. Although most of the time he was right, there was a wily side to Charles's character which was most deceptive: his frivolity concealed a greater understanding of events and the mendacity of man than the Chancellor gave him credit for. He disliked the Chancellor's thin hands, the hands of an aesthete, not those of a man who loved women, as Charles did. It was this love of women which was both his salvation and his undoing. He knew that in his soul and he knew that although the Chancellor would be speaking to him about the war, it would not be long before there was some allusion to the King's private, or not so private, life.

There was also the way the man still observed scrupulous etiquette, always referring to the King as Majesty, and insisting on rigid protocol on all occasions, a thing which caused havoc with the King's various mistresses. But then Charles had to admit that it was the man's sense of this which had kept the King aware of his identity during those long hopeless years of exile. All this contributed to a feeling of guilt, an emotion abhorrent to the King, so whenever possible he sought to avoid the Chancellor, but today he knew things were going from bad to worse. His coffers were empty, his servants unpaid and now resorting to stealing the linen from his closet, so this very morning he had not been able to find a clean shirt.

'Yes, Edward,' the King said provocatively. 'Do please be seated,' he went on, casually indicating a chair on which one of the spaniels lay snoring happily.

The Chancellor awkwardly pushed the dog on to the polished floor; she gave a yelp and scuttled to the King's feet where she looked long and hard at the Chancellor with eyes of bewildered, reproachful innocence.

'Don't pay any attention; we all had a bad night. Her sister whelped in my bed, five perfect puppies and all doing well,' laughed the King.

The Chancellor stroked his immaculate slim moustache and felt slightly sick. He knew Charles mischievously furnished him with such details to rile him, so he turned immediately to the agenda he had prepared.

'With your permission, Majesty, we must discuss your finances and I have here a list of Lady Castlemaine's household expenditure which we should discuss later.'

The King winced and fondled his dogs while the Chancellor set out before him the desperate position in which the country had found itself. The King thought of the seventy thousand citizens dead from the plague, of the loss of businesses and able workers, and then he thought of the horror of the fire, a third of his great city destroyed, and the expense of his plan to rebuild it. 'I know what you are going to say, Edward, that we cannot afford to rebuild our city but we must . . . ' The King rose to his feet and started to pace about the room. 'I know this more certainly than I have ever known anything,' he boomed. 'Mister Wren is a genius sent by God at this time. When will there ever be such an opportunity? It will be the centre of our great nation and will be praised and enjoyed for centuries. Better housing for the population, an end to those plague-ridden hovels. I will do whatever is needed to restore my country to greatness.'

'But, Your Majesty, we must be cautious,' said the Chancellor in a thin voice.

Charles advanced menacingly towards the Chancellor.

'You insult me, sir, if you think I will be dissuaded from my mission. Something worthy must rise from the ashes,' thundered Charles. 'I, as the people's King, have been given this mission. As Rome was not built in a day, our city will be built in a year, and all those who have cheated and robbed our people will be hounded until they pay for their greed . . . I want names, man, do you hear me?' The King was perspiring with emotion and the Chancellor knew only too well how the city had misappropriated vast fortunes of the country's money.

That, the Chancellor thought as he watched the King, is what makes the man so disconcerting. Just when he has played the fop, he emerges as a man of vision and moral commitment. Of course the Chancellor knew the King was right, but from where was this money to come? It was needed at once. And then the Chancellor saw his chance.

'Majesty, it is the war which stands between you and your enterprise,' he said carefully.

'Say your piece,' replied the King irritably.

'You must look for peace, Majesty. This costly war has gained us nothing and all for a dipping of flags. What matters it if the Hollanders do not dip their flag to the British ships, and what of this fallacious attempt to own the trade routes? There is no such thing, Majesty. Diplomacy is the only way. The time is right, and our intelligence tells us that the Dutch have coerced many of our own prisoners whom we have neglected at our peril'. The Chancellor swallowed nervously, he could see the King was in one of his disconcerting silences, which often as not put a person off his stride, but the Chancellor had the floor and he intended to continue. 'Before the summer is out,' he went on stoically, 'the Dutch will attack and we will be unable to defend ourselves. Our men have deserted and our ships lie helpless and unvictualled. You must halt the building, Majesty, eat humble pie with Parliament, and equip the navy. Pay your starving men, and from a position of strength negotiate a peace on favourable terms . . . then,' he finished triumphantly, 'commerce will fill the nation's purse and Parliament will work with you as it used to do before . . . ' the Chancellor paused.

'Before what?' the King broke in fiercely.

'Now I come to the other matters,' said the Chancellor, with an audible sigh.

'Continue,' said the King shortly.

'Majesty, the Duke of Buckingham has brought Parliament into disrepute, he has fought openly with the Marquis of Dorchester on the floor of the house, pulling off the Marquis's wig. You must act, Majesty. This is one act of affront to decent behaviour which has gone too far and if Your Majesty wants the support of the House he must be seen to act. The Tower is the only place for the Duke.'

'Jehovah, *quam multi sunt hostes mei*,' said the King despondently.

'You are right, Majesty, they are increased that trouble you, and I fear Lady Castlemaine is making trouble in the Queen's household, and Her Majesty is very distressed.'

'Oh and how is this?' asked the King.

'Your Majesty will be aware that the Queen has among her women a young lady by the name of Mary Boynton,' said the Chancellor.

'Naturally, I have noticed her, a very pleasing young woman who gives the Queen loyal service. Why do you ask?' the King enquired with genuine interest, his large features brightening for a moment in his dark face as he recalled the pretty girl who had joined the Queen's ladies, who, it was rumoured, had caught the eye of Catherine's most trusted envoy, Fernando, Duke of Almanda.

'I do not quite know how to explain this distasteful business to Your Majesty,' said the Chancellor hesitantly.

'Oh fie, man, I have never taken you for a man who minces words. Out with it,' the King replied impatiently. He was growing tired of the Chancellor's grim news and anxious to go to Birdcage Walk to see some new creatures that had been imported from Africa and some pelicans, a gift from the Russian Ambassador, and he wished to go before the day clouded over.

'I am afraid the matter concerns Lady Castlemaine,' said the Chancellor, noting the King's mouth turning down visibly at the corners and the dark eyes beginning to narrow at the mention of the lady's name.

'Continue,' he said icily.

'Well, Majesty, Lady Castlemaine has, it seems, mounted a campaign to blacken the name of Miss Boynton, a young lady whose modesty is beyond reproach, as I shall demonstrate to you by the letter I have here from Your Majesty's own physician, Sir Theodore Malherne.'

'And how precisely has her Ladyship done this, and why, and what has Sir Theodore got to do with it?' asked the King, in genuine bewilderment.

'I will be brief,' said the Chancellor briskly. 'Lady Castlemaine has been spreading vicious rumours about the young lady, painting her to be a trollop and claiming that she had it on good authority that the girl had the pox and was undergoing all manner of insalubrious treatments, and there was more, but out of deference to Your Majesty, I will not say more . . . ' The Chancellor set to examining his perfectly manicured hands, leaving an opportune silence between himself and the King.

'I understand your concern since this must have upset the Queen. She chooses her ladies with care except . . . ' The King trailed off, recalling the unpleasant scene that had caused the young Queen such grief when he had insisted she had Lady Castlemaine as one of her maids of honour. Of course he regretted that now and the more so because his mistress was beginning to bore him, with her constant scenes and scheming, not to mention her exorbitant demands for money which disrupted his thoughts from more important matters. This was a perfect example.

'This is most regrettable,' the King resumed, 'but how do we know there is not truth in this, although I must confess it all seems unlikely from the little I have seen of the girl.'

'The girl's aunt, Judith Briott, whom we all know to be a woman of utmost propriety, came to hear of this and took matters into her own hands,' replied the Chancellor. 'She had no choice and the poor girl had to submit to an examination by Sir Theodore to clear her name. I have his letter here. The girl is of unblemished character and . . . ' The Chancellor gave an embarrassed cough. 'And untouched,' he added finally.

The King rose from his recumbent position on the gold chair he often shared with some of his dogs and, shooing them out of the way, went to the window and looked out across the gardens where he could see Catherine walking with her ladies. She was dressed as a boy, a fashion she had invented for no other reason, it seemed, than it amused the King to see her thus. The Countess De Palva walked sedately behind the group and the young girl in question, Mary Boynton, laughed at something the Queen had said. The two seemed close, like carefree sisters, and the King knew that his mistress sought to sully this simple friendship and at the same time disrupt the Queen's life in every little way she could. And what better way than to drive all her friends away? He knew he must act, things were out of his control. He had allowed himself to be manipulated. The golden period of the Restoration, a thing beyond his wildest dreams, was being tainted by forces of evil. The sight of his wife in the garden was enough to remind him of the power his mistress had wielded and he was aware of his own weakness, he had banned the woman from court – but already she was wheedling her way back into favour, 'This time, I will be resolute,' he whispered under his breath.

'Do you know, Edward,' he said, without turning round, forcing the Chancellor to come closer in order to hear what he was saying, 'when I came here to wear my father's crown, I vowed to put my country before my God, before the dictates of my innermost convictions. You know of the demons I have fought, how I fell foul of my own mother when I denied the Catholic faith for which she would have gladly died . . . but in doing this I sometimes think God has deserted me and my people, and my poor little Queen without a child to call her own . . . she deserves more. I . . . ' The King hesitated and brushed his face with his hand, almost as if he were brushing away a tear, 'I am grateful to you, Edward,' he finished gruffly, turning around to meet the Chancellor's gaze, the first time he had spoken kindly to the man, his old friend, for many months.

For the Chancellor this was enough. He knew this was the King's way of acknowledging his concerns on all the issues he had raised; he also knew that the King, for all his show of charm and gratitude, had an inherent weakness. He wanted to be loved by all, but as the Chancellor had so often counselled him, to be a strong leader a man must be feared as well as loved. The Chancellor was tired of it all. He knew in his heart that when it came to his own turn, he would not have the stomach to fight the forces determined to destroy him, and what of the man who stood before him, he asked himself? Here was a man whom he had nurtured like his own son. But he was aware that the King was tiring of his cautious advice and fatherly tone. He shivered slightly as he had a premonition that even the King would not stand up and be counted and only history would be the judge.

The Chancellor produced some papers for the King to sign, and as he placed them safely in the leather bag he carried for state papers, his son-in-law, the Duke of York, was announced. The Chancellor bowed as he always did, a thing which constantly irked his daughter, the Duchess, who now found herself in the enviable position of wife to the heir to the throne.

'Father-in-law,' said the Duke, with a cool smile, for he was well aware of the Chancellor's antipathy to the war and that his own credentials depended very much on his prowess at sea and his undoubted skills as a naval administrator. He had acquitted himself bravely and with exceptional skill in his recent battles with the Dutch, but his marriage was troubled. The Chancellor's daughter had become fat and was a spendthrift with debts almost on a par with those of Lady Castlemaine. The Duke regularly left her bed and went straight to one or other of his latest mistresses, but horrifyingly, the most recent scandal involving Lady Denham had descended into high drama. She was said to have been poisoned and was near to death and many pointed the finger at the fat Duchess.

But there was another matter which troubled the Chancellor. It was said that the Duchess was taking instruction in the Catholic faith, a thing guaranteed to put the people even more against her than they already were. Such papist sympathies were getting uncomfortably close to the King.

The Chancellor looked at the two men, in whom he had had such high hopes and who appeared to be so careless of the responsibilities of their rank and unaware of the epiphany which, against all the odds, had delivered them back to their country, and reminded himself of the vital role he had played in their destinies. The Duke he had always known to be less intelligent than the King and excused his behaviour with the knowledge that he was led into his dissolute ways by the example of his elder brother, who in turn was so disastrously influenced by the morally incontinent Duke of Buckingham. In spite of himself he felt a surge of affection for the two men, but it was combined with despair. How, he asked himself, had it come to this? He recalled the thrill of the golden Restoration when they had arrived in England on that dazzling May morning, their hearts full of confidence and joy and the people cheering and scattering flowers in their path. Now all was debauchery and chaos.

Before his voice could betray the disapproval he felt, he did what he had begun to do on these occasions. It was the only way he could remain calm. He set to talking of banalities, the things ordinary people like little Mary Boynton talked about. For these were men over whom he had lost the control that had restored them to potential greatness and they both stood to squander it all.

'How is the young Duke of Cambridge?' he asked the Duke. He was a proud grandfather and held on to that domestic contact as best he could.

'Well enough,' replied the Duke, 'and the new baby, the Duke of Kendall, thrives at the moment, as do Anne and Mary.'

The Chancellor forbore to enquire after his daughter, since the previous week he had riled her by remarking on her increased weight, a matter which was clearly making her unattractive to her husband who had begun yet another affair with a lady of the court.

He feared that the day would come when the King would legitimise his bastard son, The Duke of Monmouth, by acknowledging the rumour that he had married the boy's mother while he was exiled in France. The Chancellor had reasoned that such a move would also dispose of Charles's increasingly unpopular marriage to his Catholic Queen and besides the King loved the handsome boy and had showered him with privileges.

'Why, Edward,' said the King suddenly, as if reading the Chancellor's thoughts, 'you must not be so downhearted. The war is being fought for interest as well as the honour of the nation. The Dutch are the common enemy of all monarchies and it is their wish to establish a universal empire as great as Rome, and the undoubted interest of England is trade. That is the only thing which can make us rich and consequently safe.'

'The King is right,' the Duke broke in hurriedly. 'Without a powerful navy we shall be prey to our enemies and without trade we cannot have seamen or ships. This is a battle we lose at our peril,' he finished passionately.

The Chancellor gave a rare smile and yet again stood corrected in his heart for his sweeping opinions and recalled the words of the Queen, 'You must not be angry with my husband for he has a true heart and many of his actions are a cloak to cover this, for it has been damaged by life and the world. History will judge him well.' He had been silenced by her words, as he was now as he politely withdrew. The King and his brother hardly noticed his leaving. They were already engrossed in a conversation unrelated to the war. He heard them laughing together as he walked down the corridor, and had the awkward feeling that their mirth was at his own expense.

CHAPTER SIXTEEN

Christmas had passed and the New Year brought little relief from the troubles which beset the realm. The Queen had been ill with a fever and confined to her chamber and as usual the court was rife with rumours that she was pregnant, but soon intimate information as to the Queen's most personal affairs was leaked to the gossips and Lady Castlemaine paraded her brood of royal bastards with more than usual smugness.

A break had come with France; the King's uncle Louis was reputed to be disgusted by his nephew's inability to grasp the nettle and put the country's affairs to rights. Louis had observed that Charles was too concerned with the machinations of his various mistresses and the latest scandal involving his passion for one of the Queen's ladies, the supposedly meek Frances Stuart, who continued to refuse the King's advances. The girl had not been seen for some days as she was confined to her bed with an ague which set the tongues wagging with increased fervour. But, despite this, Lady Castlemaine had schemed her way back into the King's favour and was more powerful than ever and the Queen struggled bravely to retain some dignity. Mary had found her weeping the previous day and together they had prayed. The Queen had asked her Lord to smite the cheek of her enemies and as Mary looked sharply at the Queen's gentle face she had no doubt that it was Lady Castlemaine to whom she referred.

This afternoon the women sat quietly contemplating their work, a holy sampler for the Queen's bedchamber. Fernando had asked for an audience and Mary tried to conceal her beating heart. Just as she thought he might not come, Mary felt the cold draft of an open door.

She felt his presence in the room, although her back was towards the door. He had been watching her for several minutes, observing the graceful curve of her neck as she sat with the Queen's ladies; they were sewing and there was the low consistent murmur of conversation, interspersed by gentle laughter. In the far corner of the room a young man played the lute, some intricate songs from his native Portugal. The room was delicately scented with orange flowers and white camellias, the Queen's favourite blooms, which reminded her of home, and some spices which Fernando also recognised, as they put him in mind of some of the all too few pleasant moments of his childhood. Here was an oasis of tranquillity and Fernando thought how the King must derive great comfort from his visits to the Queen, rather as he might a beloved sister, although the Queen's ladies reported that the King still enjoyed his wife as a man should.

It was January and the weather had turned bitterly cold. Mary sat near to the fire, and her cheek was flushed from the warmth as she turned to follow the Queen's eyes as she focused on the arrival of her visitor.

'Fernando, Your Grace, how good to see you, pray be seated here by the fire,' said Catherine warmly. As she put down her work, she noticed the way Mary's eyes lit up when she saw the Duke, and Catherine gave an inward sigh. She watched Mary for a moment, and thought how the poor girl had been so traumatised by the events before Christmas that she had lived the life of a nun, and withdrawn more and more into the tight circle of women who attended the Queen. Catherine was pleased when Fernando made a special point of addressing Mary warmly, enquiring after her family and the health of her stepmother whom, he recalled, must be nearing her confinement.

The group talked comfortably and after a while Catherine suggested tea, as the afternoon was beginning to darken and the candles would soon be lit.

'I come with a request, Your Majesty,' said Fernando eventually.

'Whatever is in my power,' said the Queen.

'I beg leave to return to Portugal,' replied Fernando abruptly. 'My wife's health has deteriorated and I should go home. The estates need attention, the grape harvest was bad this summer and I must travel to select more healthy plants to restock the vineyard this spring. I am afraid the quality of our wines has not improved during my absence.'

Mary heard the news with dismay. She raised her head from her work and found Fernando staring at her intently. Catherine, too, felt a pang of sadness at talk of her beloved homeland. She brushed what might have been tears from her large eyes.

'For how long will you be gone, my dear friend?' she asked.

'Not long I hope, Your Majesty, for there is much to keep me here in England,' replied Fernando slowly, looking long and hard at Mary as he spoke, a fact not lost upon Catherine.

The tea was served and Fernando and the Queen retired to a private corner to speak of matters of state while he produced several documents that she read with care, her forehead furrowed with a deep frown. They talked quietly in Portuguese, for what seemed to Mary to be a lifetime, during which she longed for him to speak to her.

'I must beg leave to withdraw, Your Majesty,' Fernando said at last, gathering up his papers and replacing them carefully in his large dark red case embossed with his magnificent coat of arms.

He did not catch Mary's eye when he left, but pressed a note into her hand as he brushed past her, before giving an elaborate and collective bow to all the Queen's ladies who dipped a curtsy in perfect unison, much as a group of perfectly trained dancers might.

The note asked her to meet him in his private quarters that evening while the Queen was at prayers. He assured her of complete discretion, and insisted that she brought her maid Jayne as chaperone.

*　　*　　*

'You must dress soberly, Miss Mary,' said Jayne as Mary spread out her gowns in the small bedroom they shared. 'This will be perfect, not too bright, and you will not attract attention,' said Jayne.

They chose a black velvet gown with long sleeves edged with pearls. She wore her hair swept from her face but loose down her back behind a little velvet band which stood up like a tiara, again discretely sown with matching pearls. The dress had a cloak and hood of the same fabric, lined with white satin, a present from the Queen. Mary admired herself in the long mirror and thought how much older the formal dress made her look. She felt a surge of confidence. Here was no simpering maid but a woman in charge of her destiny.

Mary and Jayne made their way at the appointed time. The long passages at Whitehall were bitterly cold and badly lit. It was incumbent upon people to provide their own light and Jayne held an ornate brass lantern low, in order to avoid the frequent reminders of bodily functions, both human and canine.

Fernando's servant replied to their discreet knock. The room was instantly welcoming, the warmth from a huge fire enveloping them as they entered. He was at his desk, working on a mound of papers, but rose at once as they came through the door.

'My dearest Mary,' he said, as he strode towards them. He took Mary's hand almost reverentially and raised it towards his face. His lips finding her skin under the velvet sleeve, he held still for what seemed to Mary like blissful eternity, whilst his eyes held her own in a gaze of passionate intensity. His servant took the cloak that Jayne had removed from her mistress's shoulders and stood back as the couple made their way instinctively towards the fire.

The servant touched Jayne's arm as he had been asked to do and together they withdrew to an ante-room, leaving Mary and Fernando alone.

'I am so sorry about everything you have suffered at the hands of that despicable woman,' said Fernando, referring to Lady Castlemaine.

'It is of no matter, now my name has been cleared,' said Mary hesitantly. 'My great concern, Sir,' she went on boldly, 'was that such tales would come to your ears and you would think me a slut like so many of the women here at court.'

'I could never have done that, Mary, for I am a good judge of character. My silence of late has been unconnected. I have many problems at home and it is they which mean that I must leave so soon,' said Fernando, taking her hand again and pressing it between his own. The message was clear to Mary: the feeling of attraction was mutual. The tone of his voice, the look in his eyes, the nearness of his breath, made her feel dizzy with expectation, and yet he was telling her that they would soon be parted.

Her heart lifted as she realised that he had not, for one moment, believed the vicious stories circulating about her; the reason for his lack of attention lay elsewhere. But her relief was tempered with the fear of parting. As she looked into his dark handsome face, gently lit by the many candles in the room, she knew she loved him and that her guard was down.

But for Fernando the connection between them lay uneasily with his cautionary nature. He recognised beyond doubt that he had grown to love this young woman. She represented fecundity, the possibility of the kind of fulsome love he had never had with his wife Magdalena.

'What I love most about you,' he blurted suddenly, taking her by surprise, 'is the way you revel in your youth.'

'They sometimes say that youth is wasted on the young,' she said quickly.

'But not you, Mary, not you,' he said urgently, his voice dropping low as he closed the gap between them. 'It is your smile. When I see it, the world lights up.'

She could hardly believe he was saying these things to her, but she took the mood and let her hand brush his. His eyes did not flicker as he went on. 'It is your fresh enthusiasm for life. I saw it when I went with you to your family. That is what the Queen loves about you. I watched you the other day, running in the garden, both dressed like boys, as carefree as two young lads might be.'

'The Queen is very kind to me. I am always mindful of the

honour she bestows on me when she treats me as such a friend,' said Mary gravely, 'but I would never take advantage of that. It is when she feels like a young girl again that she is at her happiest,' Mary continued carefully. 'Perhaps that is the same way with you, maybe I remind you of something in your past?'

'I do not want to think of you in the light of something in my past, Mary,' he shot back. 'You are the present and the future,' he said, lifting her hand to his lips and caressing her fingers with his mouth. The gesture was both immediate and sensual and she hastily pulled away.

'My father says, that the past is history, tomorrow is a mystery and today is a gift, which is why it is called the present,' said Mary solemnly.

'Your father is a wise man,' said Fernando.

'Fernando,' she said seriously, 'talking of the past, the time has come when I feel I must ask you more about your wife. You have never talked about her. How can we let our friendship go further if I do not know the truth about you? I do not know why I have never pressed you on the matter before.'

'I married young, hardly more than a boy,' he answered frankly. 'You have no conception of the repressed life high-born Portuguese females must endure, they are the product of years of imprinting.' He paused for a moment, unsure about his next remark, but he made it all the same, 'Do you know, Mary, I have never seen my wife unclothed.'

'I do not understand, do you mean you never . . . ' Mary stopped, at a loss as to how to continue.

'No, it is not as it sounds,' he said with a hint of embarrassment. 'She allowed me to make love to her because it was her duty, no more that that. We were promised to each other when we were children. It was an advantageous match, which had brought together two great estates.'

'I see,' said Mary, almost relieved at the dispassionate way Fernando could at last discuss the hitherto vague explanation of his marriage.

'The union has at least produced a celebrated wine,' he said ironically.

'But, I know enough about you, Fernando, to know that you must have loved her just a bit,' Mary probed.

'Of course I grew to love her in a way, but as a brother might love a respected sister,' he replied.

'I still do not understand where that leaves us,' said Mary despondently, imagining that she would never be anything but a secret affair, waiting for a few crumbs to fall from the marital table.

'I do not quite know how to say this,' he answered haltingly. 'Magdalena is mortally sick. Please do not ask me any more, divine providence has our lives in its hands, but while she lives I must support her come what may.'

'I see,' said Mary softly, her mind racing as she took the meaning of his words. There was silence as their eyes held and many unspoken thoughts were expressed in a long lingering look.

'My little pigeon,' he said eventually. 'I would rather lose my life than dishonour you. My feelings for you are above a brief love affair. I will put our future in the hands of God. He is merciful and we must obey his laws.'

'I have not seen a very merciful God recently,' Mary rounded, pulling away from him, her cheeks fiery with frustrated desire. 'I held back from love with Anthony, and when he died I realised that the grave is not a noble thing, and much as the behaviour of some people here at court disgusts me, I do not want so-called purity to go with me to the grave – a sad old maid who has missed her life waiting for what could never be. I would rather live now that not at all.'

Mary shocked herself as she uttered the things; these were sentiments that should never be uttered by any self respecting girl of breeding. A look of amusement flickered across Fernando's features as he formulated a response. But then he abandoned it and took Mary in his arms again and whispered in her hair.

'I will be back, Mary, I have my duty to attend to; I owe a debt of care to my wife, she is gravely ill, she has a sickness of the lungs, she suffers much and only God knows how long she can endure it. She is a good woman, and I . . . ' he hesitated, 'have not always been the most attentive husband.'

He pushed Mary away, putting her at arm's length and looking at her with a fierce intensity. 'When I take the woman I love to Portugal she will take my arm with pride, and I will never have Magdalena's unhappiness on my conscience. I will be to her all that a husband should be, if it cannot be with honour then our love would for ever be tainted,' he said steadily, indicating the chairs by the fire where they sat down opposite each other.

For Mary there was no possibility of misunderstanding. In that moment Fernando had made his feelings clear.

'I am sure your wife deserves no less, Fernando,' said Mary, 'and your loyalty is a measure of what any woman should expect from you in the future,' she finished in a voice rich with emotion.

'Now, my little pigeon,' he said quickly. 'Let us talk of things which are possible at this very moment. I have a plan. Before I go back to Portugal I would like to visit your father again. There are matters I need to finalise with him following our conversations. As you know,' he continued briskly, 'your father's business is doing well, and I want you to understand what we are discussing. Your family are Catholics and there is much anti-Catholic feeling at the moment. England is not a safe place for a Catholic heart. Your father's business interests need protecting, who knows what the future will bring but these are troubled times for England and for my Queen . . . ' he paused, waiting for Mary to acknowledge the gravity of his words. She nodded thoughtfully as he continued. 'Perhaps you should know, my dear, your father is not the simple country squire he would have the world believe.'

'What do you mean, Sir,' cried Mary indignantly, leaping to her feet. 'I will have nothing said against my father; I love and admire him more than any man living.'

'Of course not,' Fernando assured her. 'I share your admiration of your father, but it is a matter of faith, my dear. It seems a man cannot pursue his beliefs with freedom in your country. Your father is one of many who have become embroiled in this. It is high politics, and the repercussions of it have far reaching consequences for your King and his consort, and,' he added, 'the succession, should God in his wisdom grant them a child.'

'I understand; the act of exclusion has ruined many Catholic families,' said Mary, 'but I thought my father had circumnavigated that. You hint at something far more important and I don't know what you can mean,' she ventured in genuine bewilderment.

'My dearest love,' said Fernando solemnly. 'I feel it is my duty, before I leave you to go back to Portugal, to treat you with the respect you deserve. It is wrong that neither your aunt nor your father has told you certain things which from my perspective you are well able to understand, and, more to the point, you need to know for your own protection.'

'Please tell me everything,' said Mary firmly. 'I can assure you that my few months at court have inured me to shock. Nothing would surprise me, and I have often wondered just how my aunt secured me such an advantageous position. At first I used to think that the King might have had plans for me like those he has for Frances Stuart. But he has always behaved with utmost courtesy towards me.'

'That is only part of the story,' said Fernando mysteriously. 'You must know that all the ladies sell secrets. Lady Castlemaine, for example; the new French Ambassador Colbert de Croissy provides the lady with one of the main sources of her income. King Louis pays well for the latest news of the factions at court, you are but a fledgling, my dear, in this maelstrom of vultures, but I fear . . . you have been a disappointment,' he added with a wry smile.

'How so?' Mary rounded indignantly.

'You are apparently incorruptible, and loyal to the Queen, that has been clear from the start, and . . . ' Fernando broke off, not altogether sure if he should say what was in his mind. 'My regard for you has been noted. This has protected you. Where my loved ones are concerned, I take no prisoners.'

Mary looked at him sharply. To be encompassed in his collective mention of his 'loved ones' was profoundly reassuring; it imbued her with a feeling of security and happiness. 'Thank you, Fernando,' she said, smiling warmly as she used his given name for almost the first time. It slipped out before she realised it and he shot her an affirming glance.

'I think I am going to leave your father to explain to you just how he is implicated in the web that is continually woven in your country's troubled situation. I think you know that in his heart the King is Catholic but he must keep his cards close to his chest. He knows he would lose his Crown if he declared his soul in this, and mark my words one day this war with the Dutch will end and it is anybody's guess which way the wind will blow. Your father is well placed, my dear, with his secret waterways and closeness to Holland. He receives many visitors under the cloak of night . . . but he will tell you and we shall be there together and maybe to celebrate the birth of your half-brother or half-sister.'

Mary thought of home, of the child that was soon to be born, of the happiness that would bring and had a sudden urge to be away from the tedium of duplicitous scheming at court. A vision of walking with Fernando, in the fresh clean Norfolk air and of her father and stepmother holding their baby, the time for its arrival was no more than a week away. She imagined Fernando brushing snow off her cloak in the way her father had done on countless occasions. She saw them returning to the house to warm themselves in front of the fire, enjoying a rapturous greeting from the dogs, Ned and Betty, and she thought how good it would be to see Thomas again and hear his wise pontifications on life. Her face flushed with excitement, she turned to Fernando and gripped his hands, 'When shall we leave, we must go as soon as possible,' she cried excitedly.

'I hoped you would be pleased with the plan,' he replied with satisfaction. 'We will take one of the Queen's coaches and her driver, and my three menservants will ride postillion.'

'Surely we do not need so many attendants,' Mary said in surprise.

'I fear it is necessary,' said Fernando with finality. 'There have been many incidents of robbery on the road to Norfolk recently. I will send word to your family to expect us within a few days.'

It seemed to Mary that Fernando had planned everything and later, when she told Jayne, the girl gave her a strange, knowing look and drew her mistress to the far corner of their bedchamber.

'Miss Mary, please forgive me, but I love you as a sister and I have been watching you and His Grace for a long time now,' said Jayne falteringly.

'Oh yes,' replied Mary quizzically, with more than an inkling of what was to follow.

'There is no doubt that His Grace is in love with you and he is a fine man,' Jayne persevered staunchly. She noted how Mary's head inclined sharply towards her, as if she didn't want to miss a single word. 'And if you will pardon me, Miss, you are only flesh and blood and from the way you look at His Grace it is plain for all to see that you care for him deeply.'

'Oh, Jayne, you are right,' Mary interrupted breathlessly. 'I love him and I sometimes think I am wasting my life, waiting for the impossible, a man I can love and marry and have children with,' she stopped abruptly and started to cry silently. Large uncontrollable tears poured down her cheeks on to her folded hands.

Jayne pulled a lavender scented handkerchief out of her own pocket and handed it to her mistress. The mention of children had given her the chance to proceed with what she wanted to say. 'It is that which I must talk to you about, Miss Mary. I have served you for years now and I know you well. You still know nothing of the ways of the world. I am fearful that you will give way to your desires and be ill prepared,' Jayne continued unabashed. 'There are ways . . . a woman can make herself safe from disgrace, and not be got with child. How do you think the great ladies at court carry on their intrigues as they do? If they didn't know some tricks there would be babies all over the place,' Jayne laughed on a lighter note.

'Go on,' said Mary, blushing profusely, realising that Jayne had pre-empted her own thoughts. Recently the court had been rocked by the scandal of one of the ladies dropping a baby in the midst of a ball. Combined with the joy at the prospect of visiting her home with Fernando was the fear that she would take him to her bed and be got with child. She had seen the many amorous assignments at court and wondered, herself, at the witchery which had prevented the ultimate disgrace so feared among young unmarried women.

'There is a French woman who can tell you everything,' replied Jayne forthrightly, relieved that she had indeed been able to speak frankly to her beloved mistress on such matters.

'Do not be embarrassed, Jayne. I need to know these things. It is a sad fact that I have neither sister nor mother who can guide me. I only have you, dearest Jayne,' she said gratefully, looking directly into Jayne's wide honest face.

'Very well then,' Jayne persevered. 'She will give you some sponges soaked in special oils to place in the private place, but first of all there is nature's own prevention, and you should not let a man near you unless it is just after or just before your courses. And should you be careless and the worst should happen the woman is so skilled she can rid you of the child by massaging your belly.'

Mary listened unabashed. She had come to the conclusion that she could no longer remain an ingénue and would have to accept the world in which she had encountered Fernando. Although he was so principled, he was never the less a man, and something told her that the time had come to consummate their love. She knew that he would not take the gift of her maidenhood lightly, for him this would be an unbreakable bond.

CHAPTER SEVENTEEN

It was evening at Sailing. The candles had been lit and Thomas had stoked up the great fires. A smell of applewood and rich winter shrubs came from the carved stone mantle above the fireplace in what was now an intimate family parlour created by Charlotte from the seldom used morning room on the south side of the house. She had created a floral edifice of cotoneaster, daphne and hellebores and exotic heavily fragrant winter vibernum. All about them were the sure touches of Charlotte's hand. Thick damask curtains kept out the freezing damp of encroaching night as the wind howled outside the windows and twigs from the creepers surrounding the house tapped on the windows like a lost traveller wanting to join them.

Charlotte sat away from the fire, as her advanced state of pregnancy was making her increasingly hot. Sir Miles fussed about her like a young lover and she received his attentions with a sweet and obvious contentment. Mary had noticed at once after their arrival the previous day that Charlotte had truly become a swan. She looked radiant as only a woman about to give birth can do. This evening she wore a rich brown velvet gown, gathered just below the breast, which hung in a fan of pleats over her expanding waist. About her neck was a thick rope of pearls which Mary recognised as a family piece rejected by her own mother as too simple for a lady of quality.

Sir Miles had prepared his wife's chair with care, piling it with cushions to support her back, for the child was large, and although he had not shared this with anyone, much less his wife, he was filled with anxiety about the forthcoming birth. He had experience with his hunting dogs that a maiden bitch of mature years would be sure to deliver slowly, and Charlotte was not young to bear her first child. For this reason he had engaged the most experienced and respected midwife in the county, not for his Charlotte the filthy village slut who delivered the local women. The woman had already warned him that the child had not turned and that she might have to manipulate it when his Lady's time came.

But for now such concerns were dimmed by a surfeit of excellent food and Fernando's most prized wines. He had brought a selection in a hamper conveyed by his manservant with as much reverence as if they had been the crown jewels. They had eaten a dish called Portuguese Oglio, a recipe secured by Charlotte in Fernando's honour. Some pages of music lay resting on an ornate music stand. Charlotte was surprisingly competent on a small wind instrument, a flageolet, to which she had added some keys. She was very proud of the innovation, and they planned to make some music together, and to Fernando's delight Sir Miles had produced Mary's guitar which she had not played since her mother died.

The ambiance of the household produced an air of relaxed harmony, so much so that Fernando had given up all pretence of hiding his feelings for Mary. Her father had made no comment when they chose to sit together on a small embroidered love seat which Harriet had banished as inelegant and now took pride of place in front of the fire. Mary had concluded that it was the favourite place for her father and Charlotte to spend their evenings, but tonight Charlotte's condition had pointed to a larger chair and her father directed Mary and Fernando to the place without demur.

'My Lady Boynton, that was a splendid dinner,' said Fernando appreciatively. 'I have not had that dish since I was in Portugal. Tell me exactly how you made it,' he asked.

'I can tell you exactly,' said Sir Miles proudly. 'We killed our best pig and the mixture of that and pigeon breast, mutton and two of our pullets was cooked very slowly with ginger, nutmeg and cloves. The broth it made was served on the side of beef, and such a concoction it was but my wife is a genius in all things domestic, as in all else. There was never a man so blessed.' Sir Miles looked lovingly at his wife, who met his gaze with a quiet confidence which touched Fernando's heart. He took Mary's hand and held it tightly in his own, as if he to would like such a life as this.

Eventually Charlotte complained of tiredness and the decision was made to retire. Thomas had been sitting outside the door, listening to the music. At the sound of his master's voice he responded at once, embarking on the nightly ritual of preparing the household for the hours of darkness. Ned and Betty leapt up in anticipation of their nightly prowl about the grounds, the shutters were secured, fires dampened and guarded, candles carefully extinguished, and, finally, the doors were secured and the hall boy took his seat for his night's vigil in the domed chair at the bottom of the great stairs. Ned and Betty settled beside him with a contented sigh.

'Now don't you drop off, lad; there is trouble abroad tonight. I could tell by the screech of that old owl and the moon being full. It's as daylight for the ruffians on the waterways, so be on your guard – though much good it would do us all,' cautioned Thomas, giving the boy an affectionate cuff about the head.

The family made their way upstairs, preceded by the servant girls carrying the lights for the chambers, each with their own flint ready in case of necessity. A formal good-night was said and the chamber doors shut. Eventually Charlotte eased herself gratefully into her soft bed and as a precaution Sir Miles sent the maid to fetch the midwife, from the adjacent room.

'Just to be sure, my dear, for you look fatigued,' said Sir Miles as the woman came respectfully to the bedside. Sir Miles withdrew, and heard the murmur of women's voices behind the thick bed curtains. 'It will not be tonight, but Her Ladyship is near her time and should she complain of anything, your Lordship must call me at once,' said the woman as she emerged into the room.

For some reason which he never quite understood, Sir Miles did not remove his day clothes but lay quietly beside his wife until he heard the sound of her breathing and saw the peaceful rise and fall of her breast as she fell asleep.

* * *

Jayne had laid out a new nightgown for her mistress; one that had been acquired for Harriet from the bleaching fields in Holland. There was nothing so fine could be obtained, since the war had prevented the import of such exquisitely white linen. It had never been worn and had been stored in a lavender-scented chest along with many other items which Charlotte had forborne to use, keeping them for her stepdaughters. The room was warm and heavily fragrant with early narcissi which Jayne had picked from the glasshouse. The bed hangings on the ancient four-poster bed had recently been replaced with an opulent dark red silk, embroidered with garlanded lilies. A flickering light from an ornate candelabra on the dressing stand picked up the glistening silk and the silver dressing set on a heavily laden table by the fire. As Jayne brushed her mistress's hair to a burnished gold, she sighed enviously at the thought of what would inevitably follow on this cold moonlit night in the intimate opulence of the room. She knew that Fernando would come to his love, and that for all the dissembling, he would not leave her chamber and her arms until he had made love to her. The two women were silent, the atmosphere in the room in the old house charged with a thousand stories of love and consummation. Words were superfluous.

As Mary slipped from her chemise and into the nightgown, she shivered slightly as if aware of the irrevocable path she was about to take. Jayne went to a chair before the fire and fetched a dark green velvet wrap bordered with white ermine and slipped it about her mistress's slim shoulders.

Without a word, she left the room and stood for a moment hugging her arms about her in the bitter cold of the passage outside. Her heart gave a lurch of something like envy, as she remembered the humble cottage room where she had celebrated her wedding night. But for all that, it remained in her mind as if it were yesterday, a link with a past which fate had snatched from her. Loving her mistress as she did, grateful to her and Sir Miles for rescuing her and enfolding her as a friend, a member of the family, she recognised that Mary's future was her future. She hurriedly crossed herself and said a silent prayer for the mistress in whom she had invested so much care and devotion.

Fernando watched her leave and make her way down the passage, to an adjoining chamber. He walked tentatively to Mary's door, knocking softly. Almost at once she was there. The sudden impact of her beauty and a waft of warm scented air overcame him with desire; for so many years he had saved himself for the sterile bed of his God given wife. Now this wondrous young woman stood before him in all her innocent glory, and he could tell by the soft look in her eyes that she longed for him as he did her. He took her in his arms. Her hair fell about her shoulders. They moved as one towards the bed, the velvet wrap slipping to the floor like rippling water. He supported himself on his hands as he leant above her on the bed and slowly lowered his mouth to hers. His hands explored under the white nightgown and found her hard eager breasts. She sighed with desire, his tongue slid between her lips and he could taste the wine they had drunk earlier. He felt he must take her with a savage passion of which he didn't know himself capable.

'No, Fernando,' he heard her cry out as he began to pull at the lacings in his breeches.

'I ask your pardon, my dearest,' he breathed huskily into the arch of her neck.

'I don't know,' she stammered. 'Is this right? I wanted you so much but suddenly I am afraid . . . what if . . . ' she didn't finish the sentence.

'What if I got you with child? That is what you mean, isn't it?' he whispered.

'Yes, that is it,' she said weakly.

He did not answer her immediately, neither did he pull away. 'I will caress you, my darling,' he said in a quiet voice. 'I will not take that which you are guarding. Give yourself to me and to love. We will pleasure each other but I will keep you safe.'

Should Jayne have heard her mistress cry out at that moment, she would have known the cry for what it was: not the cry of a coy virgin but one of ecstasy. These were the rapturous sighs and the combined sound of a man and a woman who have achieved perfect harmony.

Jayne thanked God that her mistress had just finished her courses, and hoped she had noticed the small ormolu box she had placed on the bed table.

Jayne tiptoed towards the bed, to make sure that Mary was alone before she pulled aside the hangings on the windows. It was a crisp morning and a fresh fall of snow gave the light outside a sparkling brilliance. Having assured herself that Fernando had gone, she swept the bed curtains aside. Mary lay sound asleep beside the deep indentation where her lover had stayed for most of the night. She gradually opened her eyes and gave Jayne a satisfied smile that said all that was needed about the previous night.

'I know you will not ask,' said Mary eventually when she had drunk the posset of milk, honey and nutmeg that Jayne had brought her. 'I will tell you anyway,' she said dreamily. 'I love him, Jayne. I didn't know such things could be with a man and woman.'

Mary stopped, her face clouding as she considered the fact that Fernando would soon be gone, although he had assured her that he would be back. He had told her that his wife was sick to death but all the same she thought, to bank her hopes of happiness on the death of another woman lay badly with all she knew and believed – and yet that is what had been understood but never spoken between them.

She got up out of the bed, gathering the crumpled nightdress about her, and Jayne noticed at once the tell-tale stain on the white sheet. While Mary went to the washstand where Jayne had left hot perfumed water scattered with jasmine flowers, she hummed a tune from last night's music. Jayne heard the immemorial Dowland words, 'Now, oh now, I needs must part, joy once fled can once return.'

Jayne quickly reached for the ormolu box beside the bed and opened it. The contents were still there, untouched, and she felt a flutter of anxiety.

When Mary had dressed, she went at once to her step-mother's chamber, anxious about the imminent arrival of the baby. Charlotte looked flushed and agitated. She was pacing the room, ringing her hands, clearly agitated.

'My dear what is the matter? Is it the child?' Mary asked solicitously.

'No, not yet, although my back is aching most horribly,' said Charlotte. 'Come to the window, I must speak with you,' she went on, her voice dropping to a whisper. 'It's your father. We had a visitor in the night, it is not unusual, but this time your father has not returned, and I am so worried.'

'What do you mean, what kind of a visitor?' asked Mary in alarm.

'There has been a lot going on, you should have been told, it was wrong not to confide in you. There are plots to murder the King, and the Queen for that matter; your father receives intelligence from Holland, from Catholics who infiltrate into the Protestant stronghold,' she stopped, gripping her stomach and grabbing the bedpost. 'Sometimes they are discovered and then they come here. It is their only escape. Your father finds them a new life, a new identity and, more often than not, there are secret messages, but of those I cannot tell you,' Charlotte gasped.

Suddenly everything became clear to Mary, the mysterious comings and goings she had witnessed in the waterways behind the house during her last visit, the Dutchmen who came and went under the pretext of helping the locals dredge and drain the land for hemp. And that was when she saw in a sudden flash exactly what Fernando had been trying to tell her. 'But where do you think he could be?' she asked, her heart beginning to pound.

'I don't know. Anything could have happened,' said Charlotte miserably. 'But I do know my time has come, and I do so want to find him. It means so much to him to be here for the birth and I need him so very much, Mary,' she cried desperately.

'Can we ask Thomas, does he know any of this?' asked Mary.

'We cannot ask him for he is with your father. He knows every inch of that water, even in the dark, for last night there was no moonshine, as the weather changed suddenly,' replied Charlotte. 'I would trust Thomas with my life, at least I know that . . . but there was something in the urgency of the man who came last night, and your father went so quickly. He had not got into his night shirt, as if he were expecting something to happen in the night.' Charlotte stopped speaking abruptly and held on to her stomach, bent double with a terrible cry of pain.

The midwife appeared as if by magic, putting a strong arm about Charlotte's shoulders. 'It is your time, My Lady; we must go to the bed and call the women. All is prepared,' she said confidently.

Charlotte allowed herself to be led to the great curtained bed and sank down on the pillows groaning in another spasm of pain.

'Send for the women,' the midwife ordered Mary firmly, it being the custom to surround the labouring woman with as many local female matrons as possible.

CHAPTER EIGHTEEN

Bess had been promoted to housekeeper by Charlotte, something which had caused Sir Miles a good deal of concern as he was not convinced the girl was up to the responsibility of the role, but, as Charlotte had pointed out, he had married a country woman who liked to take an active role in running the house, and she was confident that the girl would learn well and prove to be a devoted servant. Charlotte had been proved right and Bess had a knack of finding the right people for the job so Sailing was well served, in a manner which caused envy among the local gentry, who consistently found fault with their own servants and bemoaned the frequent departures which resulted.

It was Bess who now produced the birthing stool the midwife had brought with her, and the birthing sheets from the family chest. They had been boiled and bleached over the years and had seen the arrival of all the Boynton babies, with the exception of Harriet's, for she had refused to use them. Bess ordered the stoking of the fires in the chamber and water to be held ready in the kitchens, the wooden rocker was brought to the fire, the swaddling bands neatly folded on its little pillow.

Mary had never attended a birth before, and felt a keen reluctance to see her new stepmother in such an intimate way. She was about to withdraw when Jayne intervened. 'Surely you will want to be with My Lady. She trusts you and I am fearful that the midwife is the interfering sort. I saw her with her bag of spiked thimbles, she intends breaking the fluid around the child to speed the delivery,' she hissed disapprovingly.

'What do you mean?' asked Mary in horror, half anticipating the reply.

'I need not describe it but it's a thing that should never be done, the babe will come in its own time and does not need to be cruelly hurried into the world,' said Jayne.

Mary looked towards the bed where Charlotte lay quietly waiting for the next spasm, her mother bathing her brow with a linen cloth soaked in rose water.

Charlotte let out a long strangled cry, and without hesitation Mary was at her side, she took her stepmother's outstretched hand. 'Where is your father?' cried Charlotte.

'Fie, My Lady, we can have no men in the birthing chamber, it brings bad luck,' said the midwife disapprovingly. The woman had a kind face and her voice was strong and reassuring. Mary did not know what to think, Jayne had been present at many a birth and indeed had delivered a few babies herself, and her disapproval of the midwife had been evident from the start.

'Do not worry, we have word Father is on his way,' Mary lied. 'I am sure the midwife is right,' she added nervously, 'and you have everyone here to encourage you,' she said, regarding the gaggle of excited women gathered round the bed.

'Tell My Lady to push as if her bowels were moving,' called one, while another urged caution, regaling the company with details of one of her own births.

As Charlotte's labour progressed, she clung to Mary's hand and arm so strongly that she felt her fingers numbing. Mary was becoming increasingly horrified by the brutality of the scene. The crowd of women moved aside when Charlotte eventually made her way to the birthing stool. With as much modesty as was possible, her night shift was pulled up and the midwife sat on a stool at Charlotte's feet, revealing the sinister contents of her bag which now lay on a clean cloth, mercifully out of Charlotte's view.

As the hours passed, and Charlotte's pain increased without any sign of the child, Mary became desperately anxious. Charlotte appeared to be relapsing into a lethargic state, and Mary noticed the midwife's expression becoming concerned. Her face was perspiring and the room had been heated to an inferno by Bess, as was the custom for a lying-in.

'I think the child is finding it difficult to pass through the birth canal,' the midwife said eventually. As Charlotte seemed to be too exhausted to understand what was going on, the woman turned to Jayne.

'Her Ladyship is getting tired,' the midwife confided in a low voice. 'I am not one of the breed of butchering midwives who interfere with the natural process of birth, which is why his Lordship found me . . . but I think I should use the thimble and release the fluid to encourage the child, but I am in some difficulty for his Lordship wanted to be consulted. He was most insistent, as he had heard so many tales. What do you think I should do?' the woman pressed, turning back towards the bed as Charlotte gave a feeble cry.

'Would you permit me to look. Without doing so I cannot give you an opinion,' said Jayne, much encouraged by the midwife's circumspection, 'and let's hope you will not have need of the birthing hook, for I have never yet seen a mother or child survive it,' she whispered to Mary.

The midwife heard the aside and interceded quickly, 'I do not carry one and have never had cause to use it, so let us pray we do not have to send for one in the village.'

Charlotte seemed oblivious to their deliberation and to everyone's relief had begun to strain. Her cries had become strangled screams. There was an ominous silence in the room full of women and all eyes were upon Jayne and the midwife.

'I can see the head, the Lord be praised,' cried Jayne suddenly, just as Mary had said a Hail Mary and prayed never to be given a child.

The next scream coincided with a commotion in the doorway, all heads turned towards the doorway as the dishevelled figure of Sir Miles bounded through the door, pushing past the cordon of women. In an instant he was at his wife's side, and even in her pain she managed to smile at him. He took her hand as the next pain came and with a great triumphant cry she pushed out his fourth daughter.

Bess came bustling through the gang of gawping women, her white starched apron and wimples cracking as she moved. On her arm she carried a white sheet to receive the baby. She took her to a copper bath filled with cold water scented with rose petals and plunged her in without ado. The child screamed vigorously and the room applauded unanimously. Bess gently wrapped her in another clean sheet and handed her to her mother. Sir Miles lent over his wife and daughter with an expression of joy that Mary would never forget. As Charlotte looked up at her husband with equal delight, all the pain and horror of birth was forgotten. Sir Miles tenderly stroked the child's head, which, with the benefit of washing, was revealed to have a shock of fiery red curls.

At once the mood of the room changed from anxiety to celebration. 'Come, Mary,' said Sir Miles, looking toward Mary, who was standing at a discreet distance. 'See, you have a sister exactly like yourself when you were born. You had the same hair and the same cry.'

Mary came forward and her father handed her the child. She cradled her for a moment while the women attended to Charlotte and moved her back to her bed. Bess took charge and the linen was swiftly gathered up and fresh herbs sprinkled on the floor.

As Mary held the child and inhaled the soft smell of her tender skin and hair, she was overwhelmed with feelings she could hardly identify. It was as if she had a vision of something sublime, the reason for her life, the love of a mother for a child, the consummation of the mother's love for the father and she saw in her mind's eye a wishful peephole into the future as real as if it were happening now. She saw herself holding Fernando's child. She felt cocooned in an ark of happiness, in a place where the sun always shone and a tiny tear trickled down her cheek as the beauty of the moment disappeared, as does a dream on waking.

She was holding her stepmother's baby in her arms. Her own happiness could not be attained in this simple way, for the man who would enable it would soon be gone and the future was an unwritten book whose contents she could only imagine.

There were so many imponderables. She would soon return to the careless world of the court, to serve a woman whom she had grown to love, a woman whom God in his wisdom had deprived of the very thing Mary now saw was the reason for her being.

She was about to hand her sister to Bess, who was to wrap her in swathing bands, when the women in the room dipped in a respectful curtsy; the reason being the arrival of Fernando. He stood hesitantly in the doorway. Charlotte's mother beckoned him in, for now Charlotte lay in her clean bed and the room was in pristine order and it was customary for the mother to receive a visitor if she wished.

Fernando stood very still, for a moment he did not look towards the new mother but to Mary sitting in the corner, cradling the child so tenderly, her own hair catching the light as it always did and the small head of the child so like her sister, and his heart gave a lurch. This should be her child, his child, and he wished for a second that he might gather this glorious woman in his arms and take her to a place where they might drop the heavy mantle of obligation and service for which he had been groomed since childhood. So, what value are the affairs of state, he asked himself, when the affairs of the heart are left untended and unresolved. He went to Mary and as he approached she looked up and smiled at him. He caught her eye and their thoughts engaged in silent communion. The women were around the bed and for a minute they were left in their own private world.

'What a beautiful child, she will be like her sister,' Fernando said, peeking at the downy head and holding the tiny outstretched hand in his own. 'One day this will be you,' he said in a whisper.

Mary did not reply. She let his words hang in the air in the contentment of the room, as if leaving them there they would be safe and one day her wish would be a reality.

CHAPTER NINETEEN

'There is no doubt we will have to decide what to do. It is beginning to show,' said Jayne, looking balefully at Mary's expanding belly.

The discovery that she was with child had struck at the very foundations of Mary's soul. At first she had refused to believe it and had lulled herself into a state of denial.

It was now early summer and the weather was unseasonably hot. Mary had begun to feel the need for her fan as her entire body seemed to be consumed with the vital force which both terrified and thrilled her.

She looked down at her tightly strapped waist and as she did so she felt the child move, a sudden flutter as if it were telling her to have courage, like a little bird in a cage, reluctant to emerge into a strange world of predators, and that was just how Mary sometimes felt herself. She longed for the peace of the countryside, perhaps the strong steady arm of her father, the man who had always supported her. But now just how would he feel? A child born out of wedlock, the father far away in Portugal – a man who was deeply committed to his responsibilities, a man who had told her of his obligations to his sick wife, obligations which Mary knew were at the very core of his being. For that reason, despite many urgings from Jayne, she had not told him of her pregnancy.

The time had come, she knew, when she would have to tell the Queen, something she dreaded. The Queen was so pure and deserving of the child that Mary now carried in her womb, the child that must be born in the shadows to Mary knew not what. But then, as she looked out at the bright June day and heard the merry chirpings of the birds in the Privy Gardens, she felt a sudden surge of optimism. After all, Fernando would return of this, she was confident. He had written to her, letters of discreet friendship, for spies were everywhere, with an under-current of passion that only she could detect. She had replied regularly but curiously received no indication that he had read her accounts of events at court and news of her family and she had even sensed a cooling in his responses, which troubled her.

'I have decided,' Mary announced. 'I will write to my father and ask if I may have the child at Sailing and you will go as his nurse, and I shall keep it from the court, for I intend to return to the Queen if she will have me. After all, many women of rank have borne children they cannot bring up . . . ' Mary stopped, feeling sick at the enormity of what she had just said. To bear a child for the man she loved, and then for him, for she knew without doubt she carried a boy, to be wrenched from her arms, never to feel his little mouth on her breast, not to see him grow and take his first steps. She bowed her head, racked with sobs, great tears coursing down her cheeks on to her gown.

'I know why you weep, Miss Mary,' said Jayne, putting an arm about Mary's shoulders, 'but just think,' she went on staunchly, 'His Grace loves you, of that I am sure. When God takes his wife, after a period of mourning he will return to you and to the child. Who can tell, it may be only a matter of weeks, though God alone knows why you do not tell him.'

'We have been through that,' replied Mary testily. 'When he returns to me I want it to be because he adores me and wants to spend his life with me, not out of a sense of duty, and, besides, think of the strain it would put upon him when he is trying to support his dying wife. It is my fault, Jayne. He did not want to sleep with me. I made him do it.'

Jayne's disapproval was palpable. It floated on a bed of silence. Her life's experience had left her with a very low opinion of the male sex, and, despite her assurances to her mistress, she was not entirely confident that the Duke would stand by her.

'Well, what is done is done,' she said briskly. 'We must think of the child, of the Duke's child,' she emphasised.

*   *   *

More than two weeks elapsed before Mary received a response from her father. He did not mention the matter directly, aware that his daughter's correspondence was subject to many prying eyes. Mary read the words, 'This is your home whenever you need it.' He went on, 'Everything you need will be here and your stepmother sends you her support and her greetings.' He described her half-sister, and told her of news in the village. Mary felt a wave of relief; at least her father and stepmother were able to receive her news without condemnation.

Mary was in a hurry to attend the Queen at prayers, and had just shown the letter to Jayne. She had made up her mind that she would not, after all, confide her news to Catherine. It would embarrass the Queen to have such information and put her in a difficult position with the Duke.

At first Jayne had encouraged Mary to tell the Queen but she had been persuaded that discretion was the best choice . . . she had, after all, known of many women who had borne children in secret. Jayne was aware of the nature of Sir Miles's relationship with Charlotte and the arrival of their child so soon after Lady Harriet's death. This boded well for a sympathetic response to Mary's dilemma, besides which, she was heartily sick of life at court, and, much as she loved her mistress, the idea of caring for the Duke's baby was not unattractive.

The child would be loved and welcomed, and, who knows, if Jayne had her way Mary would not return to court but wait quietly at Sailing for the return of the child's father. As for prattling neighbours and scandal, well, Sir Miles was much loved in the neighbourhood . . . a husband could well be invented in the unfortunate event that the Duke did not return.

The chapel bell peeled the angelus as Mary was pulling her cloak about her in the palace corridor when she was assailed by the sharp and almost sickly smell of a perfume. She at once recognised it to be that of Lady Castlemaine, even in the dim light of the corridor she exuded an air of voluptuousness. She wore a dark green velvet gown trimmed with some kind of exotic white fur, the bodice low cut to reveal her rounded breasts, with what the Queen referred to as shameless immodesty.

'So, little Miss Virgin Mary, your step is not quite so agile as one might expect. Is it perhaps because you have acquired a little weight well disguised under that charming gown?' crowed Lady Castlemaine, blocking Mary's path.

'I do not know what you mean, My Lady,' replied Mary aghast. The meaning of Her Ladyship's remark was perfectly plain, but in an instant Mary decided to play the innocent while her mind raced. Why would Lady Castlemaine have taken it upon herself to take an interest in the affairs of one of the Queen's junior ladies? And then Mary thought about how the older woman had spread a false scandal about her and been reprimanded by the King. Lady Castlemaine was an enemy and a clever one at that. She clearly saw a way to put Mary's secret to good use.

'You are with child, my dear,' she said cunningly, 'and it will, I must say, give me pleasure to see you recognised for the minx you are. But the question is, who is the father? Is one to suppose that you have confined your appetites to the handsome Duke Fernando and, if so, why is he not at your side?'

Lady Castlemaine's finely plucked eyebrows were raised in her flawless brow and Mary could see by the flickering light of the candles they each held that the corners of her mouth twitched viciously in barely suppressed amusement as she toyed with Mary like a cat with a mouse.

'The Duke is with his wife in Portugal, Her Grace is unwell,' said Mary evenly, without any detectable trace of emotion, although her stomach churned with a combination of almost visceral dislike and fear. She intended to be scrupulously polite, sensing that by her being so Lady Castlemaine would be provoked into one of her famous outbursts.

'Just listen to the girl. Why,' shot Lady Castlemaine, her magnificent bosoms beginning to heave with indignation, 'I do declare, you have the impudence of a low trollop. Hardly surprising since one must remember that you are sprung from some ordinary country buffoon, from whom one would expect as much. How dare you respond to me in such a way?'

Mary thought for a moment that the woman was going to strike her, but instead she produced a delicate lace handkerchief and held it to her nose in a gesture of undisguised rudeness, as if to be in Mary's presence had become odorously offensive to her.

'I do not propose to discuss my private life with you, My Lady,' Mary persevered, with a spirit which surprised not only Lady Castlemaine, but herself as well, 'and say what you like about me,' she continued quickly while she had the advantage, 'I don't suppose from what I have observed that many people will be in the least interested in what you have to say, but, be sure, I will convey your remarks to the Duke.'

'Oh, so you think your fine lover will come back to avenge you, do you?' said Lady Castlemaine, with an air of smugness carried on a raft of insult. 'I rather think not,' she continued, enunciating her words with dreadful intensity. 'He comes from a country where they do not even have the courage to kill the bull that they fight, and you, my dear, come very low in the pecking order. If my suspicions are correct, your fine Duke has long forgotten you and the sly girl you are. You will dispose of the fruits of your little dalliance with a gentleman way above your station, and retire to obscurity which is where you belong.'

Just as Mary began to feel she might succumb to the tears she had so far concealed from the vengeful and terrifying Lady Castlemaine, for whom Mary knew she was no real match, the figure of Jayne emerged in a great flurry.

'You must come quickly, Miss Mary, or you will be late for Her Majesty,' she announced with disarming calm, almost pushing Lady Castlemaine out of the way and fussing over the train on Mary's dress.

'How convenient, your servant intervening at this precise moment, one might almost think she was listening,' said Lady Castlemaine sarcastically. She pulled her fan from a little ribbon at her waist and noisily clacked it open in front of her face, turned on her satin heel and made to walk back in the direction of the King's apartments.

'I bid you good-night then,' said Mary, lowering herself in an obeisant curtsy to the disappearing back.

'Oh, before I forget, the French consul will be visiting Portugal next week. He will be seeing his Grace. I will be sure to send news of you,' Castlemaine retorted with a little silver laugh.

* * *

The following day the Queen's chambers were in a state of delight, the Queen had been spared 'those' for the second time and hopes were high that she might at last be with child. Amidst the excitement Mary almost forgot about her own predicament, but then Jayne reminded her that she was to take tea with her Aunt Judith while the Queen was visiting her mother-in-law, Queen Henrietta Maria, in her newly refurbished apartments at Somerset House, no doubt to tell her the good news.

The prospect of Judith's arrival brought Mary back to reality, and she knew that Judith must be told the truth. She dreaded her aunt's reaction, she would have every right to feel that Mary had let her down and would cause terrible embarrassment for Judith, who was trusted and respected, and had been responsible for plucking Mary from obscurity. Now she would have to retire to the country in disgrace.

Mary told her the facts without dissemination; it was all she could do. Her aunt sat stony faced and expressionless before rising and standing by the window. She looked out at the lengthening shadows of the winter afternoon. The long avenues and formal walks were busy with promenading ladies and gentlemen, chattering and flirting. The following week a banquet had been planned by the King in an attempt to lift the pall of gloom that hung about after the plague and the great fire and, not least, the twenty-two thousand deaths of the sailors who had perished fighting the ever increasingly futile war with the Dutch. Judith had come with plans for a new gown for her niece and words of encouragement about the absence of the Duke, whom she was confident, if Mary played her cards correctly, would return and renew a respectable courtship.

The two women remained silent, eventually Judith retuned to her chair opposite her niece, who sat with bowed head, absent-mindedly twisting Harriet's engagement ring that she wore on her right hand.

All Judith's hopes had been focused on this beautiful girl, her brother's daughter, who had enchanted the court with her innocent loveliness and, above all, given the Queen devoted and loyal service.

'The ring should have been on your left hand,' said Judith plainly, in a lowered voice. She felt like weeping. Something heavy in her chest, like a dead weight, encased her heart. Her first reaction was anger, but despite the fact that she wanted to rail at the girl, tell her of the opportunity she had thrown away, she kept silent. She loved Mary as a daughter and she had seen in the girl's unblemished youth, when her brother had entrusted her with her care, all the golden romance she had never had herself as a young woman, and yes, there had been a bit of her which looked forward to the rewards her niece's life would bring. She had loved the King's brother and sister and cared for them as if they were her own children but they were both dead. She had wept bitter tears for them, and then her only daughter had married a Frenchman, a relation of her husband's and gone to live in France. She had felt very much alone and then along came Mary, and she had hoped she would be the bridge on which she could contemplate her future. And now what?

Mary looked up suddenly and broke the silence. 'I am so sorry, Aunt, but I love him with all my heart, and the world is so full of misery; he was . . . we were so happy. Charlotte and Father, they . . . ' she hesitated. 'I can't quite describe it, but the house was so full of love and I felt it was the natural thing. Something told me to love him and in a way I am not sorry. That is the awful thing; I should feel ashamed, but I do not.'

Still Judith said nothing, but then Mary got up and knelt by her chair and took her hand in her own.

'Aunt, it will be all right . . . I have written to Father. The child, Fernando's child, will be a splendid boy and even if I never come back to court I will have something, won't I, Aunt?'

'Well, we will have to make sure of that, won't we, my dear,' said Judith absently. Her mind was racing as she formulated a plan which would save her niece from disaster. With a dull thud she recalled the dual standards operated at court. Lady Castlemaine had just thrown her pretty servant Wilson, who had served her faithfully for many years, into the street without a penny because she was pregnant. The same attitude would no doubt prevail where Mary was concerned.

Her strategy formed unequivocally. Mary must go to her father and have the child. It would be safe and cared for, but Mary would have to do what many had done before her, her life had gone too far for her to think she could retire like a simple maid to the country. She must not tell the Duke, in that she was correct. When, or more to the point, if, he returned, he could be told the truth. But by then Mary would have recovered her status and fulfilled the destiny which had taken her to the highest circles in the land.

The girl was only vaguely aware of the things which were about to be expected of her. Nothing must be allowed to wrench this opportunity from her niece. The Queen needed her more than ever and Sir Miles had been secretly corresponding with Judith. A plan had already been made for Mary to go to Sailing and return to the court as an important messenger with matters which affected the very security of the throne.

Judith just prayed that the good opinion of those who had

been carefully watching Mary would be able to be held intact. But first Mary must allay all suspicions and Judith knew that the perfect opportunity would be at the great banquet.

She explained all this to her niece, only hinting at the challenges for which she had been chosen, and Mary listened with a mixture of sadness and relief, knowing in her heart that Judith was right.

* * *

St George's Day and the night of the banquet arrived. The Banqueting House looked resplendent in the light of a thousand candles. The King and the Knights of the Garter wore their robes and insignias. Charles was seated by himself on the dais.

As Mary entered the room, following the Queen who had temporarily come out of mourning for her mother and wore a golden gown studded with pearls and her magnificent hair interwoven with diamonds and white camellias, her favourite flowers, she lowered herself in a deep curtsy, along with the other court ladies, as the King rose to a fanfare of music to denote the arrival of his Queen. Mary was profoundly moved by the sight of the country's great monarch standing in front of a sideboard groaning with rich golden plate catching the light of the candles, the long lines of richly laden tables, set for the knights and their ladies and the heady mellifluous sounds coming from the court musicians at the back of the hall echoed by trumpets, kettledrums and wind instruments from the minstrels' gallery.

Catherine did not join the King but stood at Charles's left to watch the meal, as the knights devoured forty different dishes before assigning the remnants to the lower orders, who set upon them with a coarseness which shocked the little Queen. She was about to leave when Lady Castlemaine arrived, arrogantly sweeping past Mary and the other ladies with no more than a cursory dip to the Queen. She was attended by her black page, her latest novelty. Dressed in an exotic costume, he swaggered arrogantly behind his mistress and, to everyone's delight, tripped on one of the King's errant dogs. As he righted himself, he swore at the animal and Mary could hardly believe her ears when, to the astonishment of all, he cried, 'A pox on the dog.' There was a stunned silence and the King looked down thunderously at Castlemaine, who stood, with an equal display of disrespect, below the platform on which the King stood. Mary observed the King's normally benign features harden with undisguised anger. His ample cheeks were visibly shaking.

'What on earth is the matter with Lady Castlemaine? She must have taken leave of her senses,' Mary asked the Duchess of Panalva, behind her fan.

'So many things, my dear,' the Duchess replied curtly, with undisguised disgust, 'things from which a young lady such as yourself should disassociate herself. I say to Her Majesty, as the sun rises in the morning and shines through your open windows so God will also do, but Her Ladyship does not open her soul to God but to the devil. Today she comes to make a scene with the King and she will pursue her quarrel unashamedly like the slattern she is.'

'We must withdraw,' said the Queen suddenly. 'I have no wish to be present at what must surely follow.' Her face was ashen white and her hands trembled as she picked up her skirt to curtsy to the King, who didn't notice her departure.

Lord Clarendon had approached the dais and whispered to the King some words that had caught the attention of the Duke and Duchess of York.

As Catherine's party departed back to her apartments, Jayne tapped Mary on the shoulder, 'Come back with me for a moment, Miss Mary,' she hissed excitedly. 'There is a fine spectacle about to take place in the ante-room as the guns have fired from the Tower and the King is repairing to another place with Lady Castlemaine in hot pursuit.'

'Do I really want to see this?' asked Mary, becoming bored with the Duchess's antics.

'Of course you do, and besides, the Duchess Panalva needs

someone to observe and report back to her,' Jayne retorted quickly.

Mary glanced towards the Duchess who gave her a conspiratorial nod and as Mary slipped in at the back of the gaping throng she could hear Lady Castlemaine's voice, shrill and out of control like a low fish-wife from the streets. 'You have betrayed your friend. A man who was like a brother, the man your own father took as his own. You are a fool,' she screamed.

The King faced her, his body shaking with anger, 'Madam, if you were a man I would send you to the tower, along with your treacherous cousin Buckingham. To cast the horoscope of the King is an act of treason, and for you to defend him tars you with the same brush.'

'You are still a fool, and if you were not, you would not suffer your business to be carried out by fools who do not understand it, while you send those best able to serve you to the Tower,' Lady Castlemaine shrieked.

The room fell into a shocked silence and two of the King's guards pressed through the crowd. Lady Castlemaine hardly noticed their arrival, so intoxicated was she with her perception of her own power, which every person in the room knew she had dissipated in a single moment.

The question of power was not lost on Mary, for recently she had become aware that some of the courtiers had begun to acknowledge her in a way they had never done before. Her first months at court had given her the feeling that she was almost invisible except for the odd attempt at a tumble from the Duke of Buckingham and his ilk; but these random attentions carried with them an implicit kind of insult, as if she were a person of no account whom they could treat like any common servant girl. But now the same men would bow to her and greet her with some form of polite enquiry and even the ladies had begun to invite her to join them for walks in the gardens or even rides in the park. But Mary had declined all these advances and remained quietly in attendance on the Queen. She had no wish to join the chattering throng who surrounded the King. Even as she was perusing these things in her mind the group in which she was standing suddenly became silent as the King approached. Mary's heart almost stopped when it was not one of the people standing near her whom he addressed, but herself.

'Mary Boynton,' he announced, 'you look most handsome in that gown, I noticed it earlier. I am sorry that Her Majesty has retired; although in the circumstances perhaps it were better so.' He waited a moment and nobody dared to break the silence. His face assumed an almost quizzical air, the anger he had felt a moment before soothed by the beautiful unspoilt face of his wife's servant. 'Tell Her Majesty that I shall spend the night in her chamber . . . I shall be no more than a little while as I have some unfinished business, that is to say I must leave no room for doubt in the mind of Mrs Villiers.' He laughed and turned, his eye running past the group as if to make his point clear as indeed it was. 'And by the way,' he threw over his shoulder, 'remember me to your father, Sir Miles.'

All eyes were upon her as Mary held her curtsy; she felt the beam of attention as if she were surrounded by sunlight. It was a heady moment. The King had, in his indomitable way, singled her out from obscurity. He had complimented her and entrusted her with a personal message for the Queen, which in itself highlighted the rift with Lady Castlemaine, whom the King had referred to derisively as Mrs Villiers, and in the same breath he had made his intentions to visit the Queen clear for all to hear. But, most of all, he had mentioned Mary's father. Mary was astounded; she had no idea that the King had an acquaintance with her father.

As if echoing her thoughts, she heard the quiet voice of her aunt. 'Do not be surprised, my dear. I have often hinted to you of the many pools in which your father swims and the explanation for the ease with which we secured you a position at court, and that is why we must leave now for you to resume your duties with the Queen and tomorrow you must beg leave of absence to attend to your family affairs.'

Judith's meaning was plain and Mary reluctantly addressed her mind to her predicament. As she looked about the dancing figures in the room, basking as she was in the King's attentions, which had in no way been lascivious, she had a glimpse of a wide arena where she could have a significant role and in a flash she knew that her aunt was right. She would give birth to her child and leave him in safe hands while she pursued her destiny.

*   *   *

A week later the news came that Fernando's wife had died. Mary received the information during tea with the Queen; Jayne shot her mistress a beady look, as she fussed over the huge basket of embroidery silks. Jayne had assumed responsibility for this task as it gave her the perfect opportunity to eavesdrop on the latest court news. Mary caught her eye from across the room and Jayne inclined her head towards the door, indicating that Mary should absent herself at once.

Mary duly whispered an excuse, and left the room with apparent composure. As soon as they were outside Jayne hustled her into a quiet corner. 'May the Lord forgive me, but this is good news indeed, Miss Mary. Now the way is clear, you must write to His Grace immediately and tell him your news. There is nothing standing on your way now,' said Jayne excitedly.

'Give me a moment . . . Yes, you are right,' replied Mary, her heart beginning to lift, 'I will write at once, dearest Jayne.' She paused a moment and clasped her hands together in front of her face. 'I cannot believe it, Jayne; perhaps at last all will come well.'

The two women fell into each others arms, and Jayne looked out of the window over Mary's shoulders to see a darkening sky. For some reason she felt a slight shiver as if in foreboding. A warning voice in the back of her mind asked why her mistress had not received the news from the Duke himself, but had to hear of it through the chatter of the Queen's waiting women.

CHAPTER TWENTY

Fernando had been awaiting his messenger to convey another letter to Mary when the emissary from London was announced. The weather had been unseasonably cold for early summer but today the sun had appeared and the brilliance of the day was at odds with the sadness he felt in his heart. Magdalena had died the previous day. Her passing had not been easy; a slow death from consumption was not a pretty way to join your maker. Fernando had been an attentive husband at the last, never leaving her side, but his concern was not shared by everyone. Even whilst she was still living, his mother had been negotiating Magdalena's replacement.

'A fine match will combine two great estates and at last provide an heir to the family fortunes, two noble houses should combine splendidly,' she announced the day before Magdalena died.

Fernando had long observed a cold selectivity where his mother was concerned, one of the reasons he had decided to accompany the Queen to London, and, truth to tell, Magdalena, with her characteristic wisdom, had encouraged him to break the bond with his overbearing mother, the dowager Duchess Consuelo.

Now, recovering from the previous day, he allowed himself to consider the proposal his mother seemed to think was a foregone conclusion. He recalled the girl in question and remembered that she had a fine down of dark hair on her upper lip and her figure already showed signs of dumpiness, rather as if everything had sunk to the lower half of her body, a fact she endeavoured to conceal under the huge skirts favoured by aristocratic Portuguese ladies, a fashion the Queen had soon abandoned in London in favour of the naturally flowing lines which left less to the imagination.

Not unnaturally, he suddenly thought of Mary and her peaches and cream complexion, her willowy limbs and her soft voice, and he felt a shudder of excitement; he was free, he could do as he pleased, this time he would marry for love. He would write to Mary at once. Despite all the evidence to the contrary, he still felt so sure of her, and confident that her recent silence had some obvious explanation, and he had to admit that for the past few weeks, even months, there had been too much on his mind for him to communicate the feelings adequately. Now at last he felt able to do so but, just as he began to compose the words in his mind, his faithful servant announced an important diplomatic visitor. He brought news of the Queen and more besides.

Lord Cottenham came directly from London. His journey had coincided with the inclement weather, and he had been violently sick for most of the crossing. He was a small man, tending to a large paunch, and his sallow complexion had been accentuated by the journey. He felt an immediate dislike for Fernando, with his tall confident looks and his magnificent palace and faithful servants. As a young man Lord Cottenham had had ambitions, but his family fortunes had never been restored after the Restoration and women had never found him attractive. He nursed a dark and slightly perverted obsession for Barbara Villiers, who knew just how to play him. A waft of sexual promise always accompanied the assignments she gave him, and the financial rewards were helping him put away a tidy sum for his retirement. The King's men seemed also to trust him and the Duke of Buckingham, with whom he also had a duplicitous kind of friendship, worked well with the King's mistress, suggesting him for diplomatic missions such as the one upon which he was now embarked.

Ably abetted by his supreme skill as a forger, and the boast that he had even carried documents to the King of France from Barbara and her henchmen, he prepared his thoughts for the important diplomatic matters he was to discuss with the Duke. But all the while in the back of his mind was a salacious anticipation of his other mission. Barbara Villiers' demonic obsession with the destruction of the Queen's little waiting woman, Mary Boynton. It was well known that anyone who crossed her Ladyship's path in the way the ill advised girl had done, opening Barbara to ridicule in front of the court, was foolhardy in the extreme. This girl would be just one of many who had crossed her Ladyship and regretted it, and naturally Barbara continually undermined anyone or anything to do with the Queen and Lord Clarendon.

But even this was not quite enough to explain the trouble Barbara had taken to exert her revenge. Forging letters in the girl's hand had not been easy and neither had it come cheap. There was obviously more to it than simple female jealousy, although it was rumoured that Barbara had raised her skirts in the direction of the handsome Duke and received a fulsome rebuff. This had not sat well with her, she prided herself on the infallible powers of her own sexuality, and a rebuff was a reminder perhaps that her powers were waning.

His Lordship thought smugly, as he kissed Fernando's patrician hand, how well it would sit upon him to ruin the man's hopes of love with the ravishing Mary Boynton. The Duke was a man so supremely confident of his own place in the world and why should he enjoy an affair with one of the Queen's prettiest waiting women and hope for a happy ending? He had once made overtures to the girl himself and her rebuff had annoyed him and he was a man who, like Barbara Castlemaine, harboured a grudge with all-consuming obsession. It was this dark side to his nature which enabled him to recognise the paranoia which Barbara Villiers harboured about Mary Boynton. It was irrational, but then this woman had not kept her place in the King's bed through rationale.

'Firstly, Her Majesty sends her greetings,' he said roundly, 'but, as you will appreciate, when I left England we knew nothing of the sad loss you were to suffer and I offer you my deepest condolences,' he finished with an affected bow.

Fernando acknowledged the remarks with a barely detectable nod.

'I have many documents,' his Lordship continued blithely, satisfied that he had dispensed with the matter of the Duchess's death, and thinking delightedly of the sum of money Lady Castlemaine had given him to deliver the information which was the real purpose of his visit. Fernando felt at once that he was a devious man but was entirely deceived by his excellent credentials and the apparent importance of his visit, as notified in advance by the diplomatic pouch. These matters were dealt with quickly and with what seemed to Fernando admirable efficiency. Fernando called for wine and whilst his servant left the room to fetch it, Lord Cottenham took a dive into the dangerous and dark waters in which he felt so at home. 'I have news which is of a most delicate nature, Your Grace,' His Lordship confided.

'Well out with it, man,' urged Fernando, feeling a trifle irritated by the man's egregious tone.

'Well, firstly Her Majesty's condition is not as was hoped last month, and much sadness is felt,' said Lord Cottenham with what appeared to be genuine sympathy. 'But there is another matter of a similar nature which it is felt should be of interest to, Your Grace,' he went on in a confidential tone.

'And what is that?' Fernando enquired guardedly.

'It is the Mary Boynton affair,' said Lord Cottenham triumphantly.

'Pray, sir, what can you mean? How dare you use such words,' replied Fernando, leaping to his feet indignantly.

'The young lady has retired to the country to give birth to a child and I have here some letters which have been intercepted. They are a correspondence between her and the father, who is a married man, and leave no doubt as to the parentage of the unfortunate infant. We felt that it was in Your Grace's best interests to give you this news, since you have been shall we say . . . and . . . ' Lord Cottenham introduced a masterly use of the pause. Observing a stunned silence from the Duke, he pressed on. 'Well, shall we say it was noted that Your Grace had more than a brotherly interest in the girl . . . er hem these letters may distress you, My Lord Duke.'

Fernando did not reply at once but stared at the package Lord Cottenham had produced from the ornate embossed document pouch he had brought with him. He observed the offering with disgust, much as if it had contained a venomous snake. Thoughts raced through his head. Firstly he thought of refusing to look at the contents, but then the practical side of his nature took over. After all, he thought quickly, if the letters were genuine it was a serious matter, one which would change the course of his whole life, shattering a happiness that had just been born after his wife's death, a happiness for which he had waited for so long, only to be snatched away from him before he had even had time to fully comprehend it. But then if the letters were a forgery, as they surely must be, then the blaggard who had written them must be found and punished.

With a steady hand he took the letters. 'I would ask your indulgence while I take the letters and examine them. My servant will bring you some wine and I will return shortly,' said Fernando with as much calm as he could muster.

He withdrew to a small library next to the reception room on the first floor of the castle where the views of the surrounding vineyards and the distant hills of Cintra glistened in the spring sunshine. In the last few days the beauty of the castle and the surrounding estates, one of the largest in Portugal, had taken on a new significance. He recalled his wife's last prayer. Pious to the end, she expired as it had suffused her lips. She departed this life free of the sins which were claimed to be elucidated in the letters he held in a shaking hand. Again and again she had repeated the prayer as if it would ease her journey, '*Santa Maria,*

Madre di Dio, prega per noi peccatori, adesso e nell'ora della nostra morte.' The words echoed in his head as he opened the package and the letters fell out on the blood red velvet cloth on an ornate lacquer table by the window. He tentatively looked at one of the envelopes addressed in Mary's distinctive hand writing. He had often admired it, for it was at variance with the forward sloping regular italic script of the time.

As he took out the first letter, a lock of her red hair fell out and fluttered to the table and he began to read.

Eventually he sank to a chair beside the table, letting the last letter drop to the ornate tiled floor. He placed his head in his hands and, for the first time in years, he wept. The explicit contents of the letters, the sensual lust articulated to the father of the child she had conceived long before she was seducing him under her father's roof. It made his blood run cold. And then he thought in horror of the convincing signs of her virginity when he had made love to her. He had heard of such things; how women used a pig's bladder full of blood to fain the event. He was filled with disgust, not only towards her, but also towards himself for being thus deluded. In the blinking of an eye the love he had felt for this fresh English rose turned to contempt: she was no longer a fragrant flower but a poison ivy that still clung to his heart, suffocating him with misery which quickly turned to anger.

In a flash he put up the only defence he could. He would meet with the bride suggested by his mother. Not for him ever again the seductive valleys of love. He would do as the families wished and make an heir without love, for of what benefit was that or had it been? Never again would he lower his guard.

With fained indifference he returned to the room where Lord Cottenham waited; he spoke firstly of practical diplomatic matters, assuring His Lordship, he informed him that he would be returning to London for a spell when certain family matters had been attended to. They spoke briefly of the sorry state of the British navy and the war with Holland, and Lord Cottenham discussed the King's concerns about the Spanish Netherlands, one of the thorns in the sides of the Dutch.

'It is suggested that the King's cousin Louis might well declare war on the Spanish,' said His Lordship. 'It is my guess that we shall be forced into an alliance with Holland and Sweden before the year is out, and no doubt,' he announced with an air of importance.

'I see,' said Fernando, vaguely in reality, his thoughts being far from the room.

'As Your Grace will be aware, the Earl of Clarendon will be the scapegoat of this affair,' His Lordship persevered with evident pleasure.

'It would seem that this Dutch affair might be the King's nemesis,' said Fernando. He wanted more than anything to be alone, to be able to think, and he was not in a mood to consider the serious consequences of the war with Holland or the various fickle European alliances to which Lord Cottenham had alluded.

As for His Lordship, he was anxious to take his leave and return to England as soon as possible and when he noticed Fernando's strained face and preoccupied manner he felt confident that his mission was accomplished. He felt particularly smug that he they had been able to avoid naming the fictitious lover, although they had of course a plan if it were necessary. The girl was well advanced in her pregnancy and he fondly assumed that she would retire to obscurity and, anyway, his attentions were already committed to another matter with which to destabilise the Queen and her power base.

'Before you depart, you may take news back to London of overtures which have been made to Portugal by the Spanish,' said Fernando perfunctorarily, rising to his feet as if echoing His Lordship's thoughts. 'I will be preparing some intelligence before my return to London,' Fernando concluded, determined to terminate the interview on an official note.

He hardly noticed as Lord Cottenham left the room and made his way along the long gallery to a wide circular staircase which lead to the lower level of the castle. Liveried footmen bowed to him at intervals and he found himself passing the entrance to the Dowager Duchess's state rooms. The double doors were open and as he walked past he cast a glance inside. The Duchess Consuelo stood silhouetted against the windows. She wore her customary enormous farthingale and tall mantilla. He could not see her expression but she acknowledged his presence with a deliberate, approving, nod putting one gloved forefinger to her lips, in a gesture advocating silence, and turned her back.

As she heard Lord Cottenham's footsteps disappearing into the distance the Duchess indicated to one of the servants for the door to be closed. When she was alone, she carefully went to a heavily carved chest, took a key from the many hanging from her waist ribbon and took out a stack of letters. Slowly and deliberately, she approached the fireplace where some slow embers smouldered from the night before; even in summer the castle could be cold in the evening. She knelt down and scattered the letters in the embers and taking the long blow pipe which stood by the grate she blew the paper into flames.

As they reached up into the vast chimney, she smiled inwardly and felt she had done her duty. Of course she had been young once and her own heart had been fired with love. But her parents had opposed the match and she had done her duty and married Fernando's father; the history of her stifled soul was written on her long features and her downturned mouth and immobile unsmiling eyes, through which a faint glimmer of the beauty which had been hers in her youth still emerged.

When her guard was down she forgot for a moment that life should not be all about duty but sometimes about spontaneous pleasure. The one glimmer of light for her was the anticipation of a grandchild, someone to ratify the sacrifice she had made to her birth and its obligations and now Magdalena had died, Fernando must make a suitable match.

The fact that he had got a child by an English girl of no great breeding, a nonentity in Consuelo's terms, was neither here nor there, but even so she could not help but feel a spark of admiration for the girl. Nowhere in the letters did she mention the pregnancy, and although Consuelo's spies had been confident that the child would indeed be her son's, she was unmoved by the prospect and determined that Fernando must be protected from any foolish notion of claiming it for his own. 'Yes,' she said quietly to herself, 'that is the last of Mary Boynton and her bastard child.'

CHAPTER TWENTY-ONE

September 1667

Jayne pulled aside the heavy curtains on the long windows in Sir Miles's study and looked out on the gardens, so at peace with the world. She seemed a long way from the dire news which filtered from London. She was glad to be away from it all here in Norfolk, awaiting the arrival of her mistress's child. Each day she prayed that the father would appear but as the days turned into weeks and the weeks into months she began to think it a vain hope. But Jayne was a pragmatic woman and as Thomas constantly reminded her, their own personal troubles were as nothing compared to those of the nation. In June the Dutch had, with the help of renegade English sailors, sailed up the Medway and destroyed the ineffectual chain placed there by Lord Albermarle to protect the neglected and unmanned English fleet. The rout had been ignominious even to the extent of heeling over the pride of the navy the *Royal Charles*, the very vessel on which Charles returned to claim his Kingdom, low tide skilfully towing it back to Holland on a low tied, where it stood as an insult to all Englishmen. A peace had been negotiated from the wreck of the navy, but economically the effect on the country was a disaster, with properties being sold off for a pittance to ruthless speculators and many people falling into irrevocable debt.

There were many signs of this even in Norfolk, but Jayne and the rest of the servants were grateful that despite the dismal and continuing bad news from London, life at Sailing continued with all the delightful domestic calm that Charlotte managed with such ease, even to the extent of treating Mary's pregnancy with such delicacy that it was more or less accepted that Mary had contracted a secret marriage to a high ranking diplomat who would emerge in due course. But that, of course, was far from the truth and on this day of all days Fernando's silence was all the more poignant.

A sharp cry interrupted Jayne's thoughts. It was Bess who came running through the door, her apron strings flying and her cap askew.

'It's Mrs Mary. Her time has come,' she cried. 'You must come at once, Jayne.'

'I think the child is coming,' Mary gasped as Jayne rushed into the room. And yet another wave of excruciating pain consumed her body.

'I will summon the midwife at once,' said Jayne, quickly taking a look at Mary's ashen face.

Soon Charlotte came hurrying into the room. She bustled about, ordering the maids to light a fire and bring in the cradle that her daughter Emily had already outgrown. The birthing chair was produced and sweet herbs were spread on the floor, and Mary began the business of bringing Fernando's child into the world.

'I wish Fernando was here, I cannot go through this on my own,' Mary moaned as the hours wore on and the bright morning sun gave way to the golden tones of evening.

'You must not worry, he will come,' Jayne reassured her, as she bathed Mary's head with lavender water. She did not for a moment believe what she said but any lie was excusable if it would help her mistress.

'I am sure he has written,' she assured Mary. 'No letters are getting through. After the catastrophe with the Dutch the whole country is in turmoil. At least we have some news, and the death of his wife must weigh heavily upon him.'

'But why, if we can get that news through the Queen's messengers, why do I not hear from him?' Mary sighed.

'You must not distress yourself,' said Jayne quickly. 'The most important thing is for you to produce a fine baby.'

Another hour passed and the women knew that the baby was about to come, they were amazed by Mary's strength, especially Charlotte who was vicariously reliving the birth of her own baby. She caught the midwife's eye as Mary's pain reached a crescendo.

'For a first baby she is doing well and it will not be much longer now,' the woman responded. And then, in the determined manner which was to characterise his life, with one gigantic push from his mother Fernando's son slid into her capable pair of waiting hands.

The child was plunged into cold water at once and his vigorous cries filled the room. He was quickly wrapped and handed to Mary. Despite her exhaustion, the love she felt for this tiny bundle temporarily overwhelmed her. She could find no words to express herself and was oblivious to the flushed and expectant faces of Charlotte, Jayne and the midwife. She felt their breath on her face as she capped the little head with her hand and smoothed his shock of thick black hair.

'You have a fine boy, My Lady,' said the midwife.

'I knew it was a boy,' whispered Mary.

The midwife was pleased with her work. The child was big and the mother was not obviously built for child bearing, but the girl had a strength and determination which the midwife did not often see in the gentry, who tended to make more fuss than the village women. She had not questioned the absence of the father but the child was dark, and the vague story about the mysterious husband did not convince her, but with such a united family, the girl would find a way, and the child would be loved. As the woman set about the task of setting the room to rights, the girl's father came tentatively into the doorway.

'May I see my grandson?' he asked with undisguised delight.

'Father, take him into your arms, he can be like the son you never had,' said Mary emotionally.

Sir Miles took the child and gazed intently into his face; there was no questioning the likeness to Fernando, and he felt a wave of resentment towards the absent father. He was angry with life in general, that his beautiful daughter should be giving birth without a father for his grandson; this was what happened to village girls, but in their case the father would be sought and forced into wedlock. If that were not possible often the girl would be disowned by the family and abandoned to her fate. Sir Miles had often observed these terrible dramas unfolding and been tempted to take the girls in with their infants, but Charlotte had warned him it was the way country folk implemented some sort of order in the community. Fear of pregnancy kept a girl pure for her wedding night and only then did she submit.

Sir Miles pondered these things momentarily and considered the possibility which he had done for many months of calling Fernando out. Only recently the women had let him know that the Duke's wife had died and whilst he knew the man would be observing a decent period of mourning, he could not for the life of him understand the man's silence. But when he had broached the subject with Mary her response had been ferociously independent. She would not even tell him if she had told the Duke of her pregnancy. She had made him swear on the family Bible that he would not interfere.

The child stretched a tiny hand and Sir Miles put a finger in the delicate fist, which closed with surprising strength. He felt a wave of joy at the arrival of a new life in the family, vowing that he would protect the little boy and guide him through childhood if his own father could not do so. At the same time he tried to stop himself hating Fernando for what had happened and then he looked at Mary, lying back on the clean white pillows, her voluptuous red hair framing her pale face and was again reminded of her striking beauty. She looked calm and composed as he handed back her baby.

'It will be all right, Father,' she said weakly, breaking the tension she felt when she saw her father's face. His feelings had always been transparent to her and she knew full well the confusion he felt at her predicament. Her father handed back the child and she held him to her breast and nuzzled his sweet smelling head and she made herself believe that God had a purpose for the way her life had turned out. Her father had imbued her with a fierce pride. She would not go crawling to any man, she would make a life of her own and her son would be proud of her. The King had an enlightened attitude to independently minded women; there would be a role for her at court. Even now she knew that she could not remain at Sailing once she had recovered from the birth.

'You must think of a name for him,' said Sir Miles practically.

'I shall call him Phillip,' she replied.

* * *

Mary decided to nurse her baby for the first few weeks, a fact which disturbed Sir Miles since he was concerned that his daughter would bond too closely with the child she must leave when she considered the challenge with which he was about to acquaint her.

Today the fires had been lit early in the day, since autumn had come with a vengeance; a cold wind blew from the north, denuding the trees of their last reluctant leaves, silencing the song birds as they sought shelter in the hedgerows and sending their migratory friends on their way. The cattle began to huddle by the gates, waiting for the summer hay to be spread around their mud-caked feet, and the business of preparing for the bitter Norfolk winter began in earnest.

Soon the regular visitors who came up the secret swirls of water behind the house would become fewer as the journey from Holland became less inviting; in the long grey winter, the North Sea was greedy and claimed many an experienced sailor. The spies who came with intelligence for Sir Miles would spend more time infiltrating their sources in Antwerp and Amsterdam now the weather had turned, but for now there was work to be done and Sir Miles had decided that the secrets of Sailing Hall must at last be revealed to his daughter. The birth of her child had given her a maturity which had become clearly apparent during the last few weeks, and she had handed her son to a wet nurse and lost the weight she had put on during her pregnancy. No word had come from the child's father but a coach had come from London with letters which Sir Miles did not doubt would change the course of his daughter's life.

When Thomas had lit the lamps and pulled the thick curtains against the gathering darkness, Sir Miles was sure that the usual busy daily activity in the household had quietened down. Family prayers concluded his domestic obligations; he awaited his daughter in his study. The room was warm and welcoming; there was a smell of leather and tobacco and the rich aroma of burning pine from the fire. Here was complete privacy and not a soul was allowed to enter it without Sir Miles, except for the trusted Thomas, who knew of and kept its many secrets with a devotion born of deep admiration for his master. He knew he was not an ordinary squire; he played a significant and courageous role in the affairs of the country. But his courage did not have a witness, and the man was adamant that it should remain so, for the benign mantle of disinterested country squire was his strength.

'Phillip is asleep,' said Mary quietly as she entered the room.

'And what of my little daughter?' enquired Sir Miles, smiling indulgently.

'She also is fast asleep. She had a busy day, Father, and we all went to the village while you were working. We took baskets of food to Nan in the cottage by the lodge whose husband left her with no money except for the pathetic little they had saved,' said Mary, her brow furrowed in concern. 'Bess and Charlotte took some of our hens so at least she will have fresh eggs for the children.'

Nan's husband had been conscripted for the Dutch war and never returned. No details had been given to the wives and families but Sir Miles knew he had probably been burned to death in his ship, along with many thousands of others. No provision had been made for the widows and children except for the infamous tickets which both women had taken to London. They had been sent away with nothing.

'That was good of you, my dear. We cannot let them starve, and I have waived the rent. Nan's husband was a good man who served me loyally, and I can tell you this,' he assured her, 'we have formed our own vigilantes and no men will be taken from this village again,' Sir Miles boomed for all the house to hear if it had a mind, for he was disgusted with the way anonymous men from London played God with the lives of his villagers and he was determined to protect them, if necessary by a little carefully applied force.

'Oh, Father,' cried Mary, 'it breaks my heart to hear how the men were taken and not even being allowed to say goodbye to their children.'

'I know, my child, but we can't change the whole world so we must do what we can when the chance arises and that is why I want to talk to you,' said Sir Miles solemnly.

He gestured to a large table near the fire on which he had spread a number of papers and documents, indicating a chair.

'Now, my dear, I know I can trust you completely for the welfare of many depends on matters I would like to share with you,' he said gravely.

Mary saw out of the corner of her eye the King's cipher on the broken seals on some of the papers and her heart began to race. She had been trying to piece together many things in her mind since her return, particularly the King's references to her father before she left court. And then there were all the comings and goings at the Hall and Thomas's severe face as he stood guard outside Sir Miles's study.

At last she understood exactly what was going on. Her father was receiving intelligence for the King. He was, she realised, perfectly situated. The village had always known that spies from Holland regularly landed on the coast and slipped unnoticed on to the inland waterways.

'I expect you must have guessed what goes on here,' said her father, as if reading her thoughts.

'I have, Father,' she said tentatively. 'But I don't understand who these people are and what they tell you which is of so much interest to the King.'

'There are many Republicans who fled when the King returned to the throne,' Sir Miles explained. 'They were sufficiently bigoted not to accept the amnesty offered to them, except of course for the regicides, who were hunted down without mercy,' he added, his eyes flashing as he recalled the betrayal these men had perpetrated, and the just revenge they had received.

'And I suppose these men conspire to harm the King and Her Majesty,' said Mary thoughtfully.

'Yes,' replied Sir Miles, shaking his head and picking up one of the documents and waving it towards his daughter. 'Thanks to these brave men and . . . ' he paused, 'women, for often they are the best at obtaining information without arousing suspicion. If their identity were known there would be a price on their heads. Yes, because of these brave people we have been able to foil a number of serious plots, and it is not only the republican issue that absorbs them. They are vehemently anti-Catholic and the Duke of York is also at risk.'

'Of course he is,' Mary conceded. 'Why, Father, do you think he has been so unwise as to declare himself so provocatively? Surely he should have taken a leaf out of the King's book and been a little more circumspect. After all, look what happened to his father because he could not play a more subtle game.'

'You are very wise, my dear,' said Sir Miles, nodding approvingly. 'I can see you have learned some diplomacy at court. The Duke should never have openly declared himself a Catholic. In fact, by doing so he has endangered the succession and there is much to fear. The King spends a great deal of money on intelligence, though not enough in my opinion; Cromwell spent five times the sum and nothing escaped him.'

'But what have I got to do with this?' asked Mary nervously.

'It is simple, my dear,' her father replied briskly.

'I receive information here and of course it is in code. Some- one has to convey it to the King; a person who will not arouse suspicion and knows the cipher, that messenger must be able to decipher the documents directly to the King. Naturally we have to change it quite frequently but the basic principal is quite simple once you begin to understand it.'

Her father looked steadily at his daughter while she silently digested his words. He continued watching her carefully. He knew his daughter well; he knew she was of above average intelligence. If only she had been a boy, he speculated, as he often did, she would have taken over the running of his business by now, but because she was a girl she had landed in the position she now found herself. He did not condemn her, as many fathers would do, because the circumstances of his life had made him into a worldly and tolerant man; after all, he himself had lived in sin. It was a mixture of extreme caution and luck which had prevented the situation that now confronted his daughter. He knew Fernando's wife was dead and why the man had not come to claim his daughter remained a mystery. Sir Miles sensed that there were many factions at work, but he also knew that his daughter was proud and he admired her for that. She was no simpering country girl who would go begging, she would climb the mountain and wait for Fernando to come to her, and here was the ladder she needed.

'Father, I could not have imagined my life as it has turned out,' Mary said suddenly. 'I thought I would fall in love and marry and live a normal life without complications. I knew nothing about the life at court or about the world outside our own secure existence. But events took control, so many things have happened. I could not go back to that ordinary life now.'

'Well, my child, ordinary people, ordinary fates, extraordinary people, extraordinary fates. You have become extraordinary,' said Sir Miles with obvious pride. 'You have such an air of confidence about you. I believe you have been fortunate to have this opportunity to do something worthwhile. I have always thought intelligent women are wasted. One thing we owe the King is his enlightened attitude to women.'

'You are right, Father,' said Mary, taking her father's hand affectionately. 'And you have that in common with the King, you have always supported me, so let us begin at once . . . teach me the code,' she said resolutely.

'Very well,' Sir Miles agreed, 'but first let me ask you, when do you think you will be able to return to court, where of course nothing is known of the birth of your child. I know Her Majesty has missed you and your position awaits you . . . ' Sir Miles asked.

'Whenever you think it appropriate,' Mary replied. 'I shall leave Jayne here to care for Phillip. No child could have a more devoted nurse, she has been like my right hand and I will find it hard to survive at court without her wise council but, I will have to stand on my own two feet,' said Mary steadily.

'No, my dear, you will need a servant, and one has been found for you, a girl who has served one of the King's most trusted women informers. The woman has gone to Antwerp and the girl, like yourself, receives information from her former employer which is of great value to the King. His Majesty will pay her wages, and although I know you will be reluctant to accept this, you will be handsomely rewarded by His Majesty. Indeed I am already instructed that you should not return to court in anything but the finest gowns.'

Mary's first reaction was one of horror. 'I cannot take money for serving my country and protecting my Queen, who has been so good to me. Why, that would make me nothing more than a form of harlot,' she cried indignantly.

'Child, that is ridiculous,' Sir Miles rounded, both surprised and vexed by Mary's coyness. 'Soldiers do not go to war in shabby uniforms, and if you are to circulate in the echelons which surround the King's most intimate circle, you must not be derided as a country bumpkin and, besides, there is another thing of which you should be aware,' said Sir Miles, looking uncomfortably at his daughter's honest face.

'And what is that?' Mary asked sharply.

'You will have to accept that as you are to spend time alone with His Majesty it will be assumed that you are his mistress.'

'Are you mad, Father?' Mary gasped furiously. 'I cannot believe you are saying this to me. I still love the father of my child and I know in the bottom of my heart that one day he will come to me.' Mary could not go on. She burst into a torrent of sobs and laid her head on the table, her tears falling like rain on the King's letters.

Sir Miles observed this decline with surprise, and then he had to remind himself that he was dealing with a young woman about to be separated from her baby, and one who was, in his opinion, unlikely to experience the happy outcome to her present circumstances that she so touchingly expected. Even considering his unfashionably progressive attitude towards women, he still had an element of doubt about the role of women in the predominantly masculine world of politics and intrigue.

'My dear,' he said gently, 'look at me. I am your father. I love you more than anything in the world and I want nothing but the best for you, but it has to be said that the birth of a child outside wedlock is a thing to be avoided. Without the protection your family can give you things would be very different.'

'But, Father,' Mary interjected, lifting her tear-stained face.

'No, Mary, you must listen to me,' said Sir Miles, lifting an admonitory finger. 'You cannot stay here. There is nothing for you. Much as I would like to have you with me, when you fell in love with a Portuguese aristocrat and allowed him into your bed the die was cast. You chose to enter that world, the world into which Fernando was born; you caught the eye of the King, not because he wishes to bed you along with his many other mistresses. He noticed you because you served his Queen and made her life happier, and because he knew you were my daughter. How do you think I have managed to keep the estate going and look after the village and sustain our London house? It is because I have worked untiringly for the King's protection, and, yes, the family business has flourished because of His Majesty's patronage.'

'I hadn't realised any of this, Father. I feel so stupid,' said Mary. 'When I see how many families like ours have lost everything. I should have guessed we were not surviving as we have without more than just a family business.'

'Well, now you do know how much we owe to His Majesty,' said Sir Miles emphatically. 'It is time to acknowledge the debt but you must not be alarmed, you will not be compromised, the King is, despite his prelidiction for beautiful women, a man of honour. He does not know of the birth of your child, or if he does he has probably been told a pack of lies by the people who wish to undermine the Queen's power base. After all, what better way to damage her than to cause mayhem amongst her court. No, my dear, let the world think what it will, the truth will always triumph in the end. The King will not take advantage of you and who knows you could have no better friend.'

When Sir Miles had finished speaking Mary felt calm and resolute. She went to her father and embraced him, thinking once again how he was the rock of her life and, it would seem, the brave protector of many more. She would do as she was bidden, but she had one question to ask her father.

'Father, who is the woman whose servant I am to have?' she asked evenly.

'Her name is Mrs Aphra Behn,' said Sir Miles. 'She is a talented writer and when she returns to England she will be a woman who will be one of the first to make a living from her pen. She is a thing rare among her sex and you, my dear, are of her like. Your life, Mary, is only just beginning.'

'Well, father,' said Mary without hesitation, 'where is this code? Let us have a look at it.' Mary drew her chair nearer to the table and Sir Miles could barely suppress his look of extreme pleasure. He could see by the flush on his daughter's cheeks that her interest was aroused and he knew her well. She was no ordinary girl and once her mind had been engaged there would be no stopping her.

He got up and went to the corner of the room and lifted the heavy tapestry that Mary had admired since childhood. To her amazement he pressed the top of the panelling which had been previously hidden and an area the size of a door opened. Mary sat completely still. He returned to the table and took a candle.

'Come, child, it is time you saw something,' he said with a sideways look.

She followed him and as he lifted the candle and the interior of the space was illuminated she saw a small room just big enough for a man to lie down in. There was a table on which appeared to be some wine and a jar of what looked like ship's biscuits. There was a candle and a flint and a pile of bedding in the corner and a large sea chest with an iron lock.

Mary gasped in amazement, following her father into the space, dipping her head slightly as there was not quite enough room for her to stand completely upright. The first thing she noticed was the powerful damp smell of the marsh water she knew so well. While her eyes were adjusting to the gloom her father took her arm. 'There is more,' he said, lifting the candle to the far corner. Again he pressed something in the wall and with a heavy groaning noise the wall opened with a cold, damp rush of air, revealing what looked like a passage.

'It leads directly to the waterway at the back of the house,' said Sir Miles. 'But not the one we use normally. There is another tributary, well hidden, which goes straight to the river and then to the coast. There is always a small boat waiting,' he added, shutting the heavy door.

Mary felt a slight shiver; she wanted to get back to the warmth of her father's study and he, as if sensing her feelings, took her arm and gestured for her to return to the room.

'It is important for you to know this,' he said, when he had replaced the tapestry and put the candle on the table. 'I make the journey down the tunnel often to receive the intelligence which is delivered at great risk, for at least half of the people who profess to work for the King are double agents, and if I am to continue to help him I must never be identified as the source. And this is where you, my dear, will fill such an important role. Once I have taught you the code, the letters will be delivered to the office at the London house; they will appear to be part of the normal transactions for the sale of our hemp. It is for you to collect them and then take them to the King and decipher them, and the beauty of it is that nothing will ever be written down.'

'Father, this is all so bewildering. Why didn't I guess at some of this, I feel such a fool?' Mary blurted as they sat down.

'That is the whole point; I would have been very bad at my job if you had. The time was not right. Although your aunt was sure, I felt you were not mature enough, but I see now that you will be of great service to the King and to our country at this troubled time,' he said passionately.

'Oh I will, Father,' said Mary. 'We all have a duty to fight for what we believe in. The King and Parliament and the right to worship as we please; it is fundamental to each and every human being, and the King's enemies would deprive us of that right.'

Sir Miles wasted no time, giving Mary paper and pen he set out a number of letters in front of her. 'Now, is there anything you notice?' he asked.

'Yes, Father, of course. Some of the letters have Greek derivations.'

'You are right, my dear,' said Sir Miles, smiling indulgently. 'But it is a complex cipher which was used by the late King and constantly changed during the Civil War. It was invented by Captain Firebrace who was one of the King's attendants during his captivity on the Isle of Wight.'

'This is wonderful, Father,' cried Mary. 'Of course I have always appreciated my knowledge of Latin but I hated Greek even though you made me learn it, and now for the first time that knowledge can be put to use. I already see some of the words and how they repeat. Surely it is the order which is the key,' Mary could feel her heart racing.

'Now, let us begin while the house is quiet,' said Sir Miles with satisfaction, 'we have much to do in a short time because you will be returning to London armed with dangerous tools, my dear,' he warned darkly. 'And although the court, with its half-hearted friendships, professional poets and affairs of the heart, seems a low place at times, one must remember that the excesses of life are a distorted view of the experimentation of life.'

'But, Father, the Restoration brought back civilisation, arts, painting and poetry and drama, and dissimulation returned to England,' cried Mary.

'Yes, I agree and you must learn to be part of that,' said Sir Miles. 'The Queen will know well that her little maid comes back in different clothes but with a soul as true as it ever was.'

CHAPTER TWENTY-TWO

A fierce storm awoke Mary during the night. She had been dreaming of many things, mostly a blurred melange of life back at court. The Chancellor, Lord Clarendon, had featured significantly. She had been with him in a boat, her baby had been there, and the sea had got up, the boat had overturned and Fernando was standing with the King on a distant shore and then her father came, he was not alone. Mary had seen them all, and she had jumped out of the boat into the raging sea to go to her father, but the waves began to overcome her. She awoke pouring with sweat, her heart racing.

Her breast felt swollen and uncomfortable, it had been several days since she had fed her baby. The wet nurse had taken over. The girl had been allowed to bring her own child, now a bonny two year old, to the Hall so the nursery was well occupied.

Mary slipped out of bed. She had a compelling desire to see Phillip. Despite all the bravado she managed in front of her father, she cried herself to sleep each night when she thought of the leaving her child. She tiptoed along the freezing passage to the children's room. As she opened the door, a waft of comforting warm air welcomed her. There was a dim rosy light from the fire which was kept burning all night. She could hear the soft breathing of the wet nurse, and she quietly approached Phillip's cradle. As if he sensed her presence the child awoke as she leant over him, his little face broke into a broad smile at the sight of his mother and he lifted his little hands towards her, quivering with excitement. She had forbidden the customary habit of binding babies tightly from birth and Phillip had learned to wave his arms vigorously at an early age, a habit he would retain throughout his long life.

Mary's heart missed a beat as she took her child and held him tightly to her. He nuzzled for her breast. Spontaneously she lowered her nightgown and he sought her nipple. She fed him for what she knew was the last time, her tears came fast and furiously in an unstoppable stream which landed on his head, dampening his hair.

'My darling little boy, I leave you with my heart, soon I will come for you, and until then your grandfather will love you and care for you as one day I know you will care for him,' she whispered softly in the silence of the room.

But they were not alone. Mary's thoughts went to Jayne. She would be able to put things in perspective. Mary knew that Jayne had been the one stable thing in her life for so many years and soon she would have to part from her as well. Jayne crept towards her mistress and the child and she enfolded them both in her capable arms.

'Do not fret, Miss Mary, I will guard him with my life, and I know it will not be long before we are all together. It is for the best,' she said in a low voice.

'I know, Jayne, but it is the hardest thing I have ever had to do,' said Mary, stifling a sob.

Almost at once they were aware of footsteps proceeding stealthily in the passage outside. They became silent, listening with all senses pricked, until Jayne carefully opened the door a crack and saw Sir Miles's back view descending down the wide curved stairway.

'It's the master, dressed for rough weather. It's best you take no notice, this is man's work,' whispered Jayne.

'Here, take the baby,' said Mary having no intention of ignoring her father's activities. She had a sudden desire to see for herself exactly what these dangerous missions entailed. Instinctively, she knew that there was no going back, for she had committed herself to the King's service and to her country. If she were to survive unscathed she must know everything there was to know. It was a case of all or nothing. She ran past

Jayne and down the stairs; the moon was bright despite the storm and it chose that moment to appear with amazing effect from behind the scudding storm clouds, brightly illuminating the stairs through the enormous window. In the corner of the great hall she saw her father and Thomas struggling into cloaks and boots from the chest by the oak front door.

'Wait, Father, I am coming with you,' she cried out impetuously.

Both men turned round, their reactions alerted by the task ahead of them. 'What are you doing here, Mary? Go back to bed at once. We don't want the house alerted,' hissed Sir Miles angrily.

'No, Father, if you want me to be part of this, I have to come with you,' shot Mary. 'I must see for myself what manner of things have been occupying my own father in the service of the King. That is my final word on it. You take me with you or I want no part of it.'

Sir Miles and Thomas stood in stunned silence, Sir Miles was unaccustomed to such determined and forthright words from his daughter, but he could see by the defiant tilt of her head that she meant what she said, and he thought quickly.

'Very well,' he said abruptly, aware of Thomas gloomily shaking his head in the background, 'but you say nothing,' he went on gruffly. 'So go get yourself some warm boots. There is no time to lose. Thomas will find you a thick cape and some breeches for I will have no petticoats on this expedition.'

Mary did not hesitate, and within a matter of minutes she had returned, to find Thomas holding breeches and cape. They went quickly to her father's study, the door carefully locked behind them as Thomas held a lantern while her father opened the panelling.

CHAPTER TWENTY-THREE

There is no manner of affliction which renders a man more insensible than sea sickness and as the great ship began to roll Rupert Willoughby felt the first dizzying pangs.

'It's going to be rough, but no more than this lady can weather,' announced the Spanish Captain ominously. The men could hardly hear him as the sea got up into a yellowish scum, the darkening sky reflected in the swirling waters with ever increasing force. 'This wind is dead foul,' the Captain bellowed to his passengers. 'Best go below or you'll be lost over the side.'

Waves began to pound the creaking ship, the sailors' shouting reached a crescendo, as the noise of the pumps and the cries of the men jangled in a dreadful confusion. Soon Rupert heard the ship's bell and a cry to bring her to, and ride out the worst of it, but Rupert was prostrate on the floor of the Captain's cabin, heaving into a filthy bucket which had the acid stench of previous vomit.

'My God, will ever a man be more happy to put his feet on dry land?' he gasped, staggering up the narrow steps to the deck, praying that the freezing air might subdue the tempest in his stomach and sure that he had nothing left to bring up but a grey mucous. The wind had risen to storm force, so furious that the rain came in torrential sheets. The ship had to shorten sail to a mere mizzen and bare poles and suddenly the urgent cries of the men assumed a different sound. 'Man overboard,' came the frantic scream, the words all sailors dread, since all knew there was no prospect of survival.

In an instant Rupert would never forget, he saw the lad go over the side as the ship, plunging up and down like a wild animal in the foaming seas. For a brief flash the boy was there, all limbs desperately flailing as he tried to grab the rope hanging from the side. Even in his misery Rupert recognised the lad's courage as he climbed the mast to let down the sail; he had not tied himself on as the captain had told him and although he had held on stoically as the mast practically lay flat on the water, one giant wave took him. One minute he was there and the next he was gone.

Rupert's companion, Jan de Lauden, enjoyed nothing more than a good storm and never once had he doubted the resilience of the *Castel*. The boat had been built by a rich Spanish diplomat the Marquis Castel Rodrigo, Governor Plenitentiary of the Netherlands. It normally took spies to Bruges from Gravesend, but this trip to the North coast had been a vital alteration, since the route had become known and lives had been put at risk. The chain of command had to be guarded at all costs.

After an hour or two, the storm subsided enough to hoist some sail and as evening approached they could see the English coast; with a following sea they finally discerned what Rupert prayed for, the dim lights of the port, and soon the blessed relief of the mouth of the river.

From then on the men knew that speed and concealment were paramount, they slipped off the ship as secretly as they had embarked. Jan knew the routine well, for he had made this journey many times. The men travelled light, with just their papers, the most important of which were concealed in Rupert's vest, and a brief change of linen.

Sir Miles and his servant would be waiting in the usual place, in a sheltered clump of trees behind the inn. There was a winding path through the trees and by moonshine it was easy to find. Rupert followed intently as he knew that he would have to remember the route for future occasions, though with the memory of the horrific sea crossing, he had a mind to linger as long as possible in England, perhaps until the spring when the North Sea had relaxed its angry fight.

'Tread carefully,' warned Jan, 'the ground is slippery after the storm.'

Rupert was not sure if his imagination was playing tricks on him, his senses being heightened by the journey, but a distinct cracking sound alerted him. He stopped in his tracks immediately and touched Jan's shoulder, urging silence with a cautionary finger to his lips. Both men stood very still listening, and there it was again, as if footsteps were breaking twigs in the undergrowth.

'It's probably nothing, just foxes,' said Jan after a few moments.

They continued on their way, but Rupert could not suppress his feelings of alarm. He had an instinct that they were not alone. Soon they saw a distant light moving rhythmically and in the moonshine the vague silhouette of three figures, what looked like two men and a boy.

'There they are,' whispered Jan, increasing his speed. It had begun to rain again and a thick bank of cloud obscured the light. Rupert tripped and as he was attempting to regain his balance, there was a crashing in the undergrowth. Within a split second a figure appeared from nowhere. Rupert saw the flash of a knife and heard a gurgling sound, the clouds scudded passed and in the light he saw Jan, a torrent of blood spurting from his throat, his body supported by his assailant's arm which held him by the throat. As the man released his hold, Jan flopped to the ground like a rag doll and the man leapt towards Rupert with all the ferocity of a raging bull.

Rupert knew he was at a disadvantage, for he was beneath the man on the slope and the velocity of the man's body would fell him to the ground with ease. In vain he reached for his sword, knowing that the man would be upon him before he could extend the blade. His entire life flashed before him as he prepared to fight. But, thinking quickly, he sidestepped the man, throwing himself into the undergrowth. As he had anticipated, the man came down, but with a blood-curdling scream which echoed through the night with horrible intensity. There followed an unexpected and sinister silence.

'I got the bastard, Sir Miles, he won't be troubling us again,' came a voice, and three figures came hurrying down the slope.

Rupert was not taking any chances and remained concealed until he heard the familiar voice of Sir Miles calling his name.

As Rupert revealed himself, he saw the figures bending over Jan's body; the boy had his head in his lap and was desperately trying to bind the gash in his neck with some sort of scarf.

'It's no good, Miss Mary.'

Rupert recognised it was Sir Miles's faithful servant Thomas who was speaking.

'The brute must have followed you,' said Sir Miles as he greeted Rupert breathlessly.

'I must make sure he was alone. Let me look at those tracks,' said Thomas, raising his lantern in the direction from which the man had sprung.

Rupert kneeled down, looking at the empty staring eyes of his friend and companion Jan, the head lolling in the boy's lap. He felt a low sob ominously gathering in the back of his throat. Jan had been a man of bravery and courage, a man who had suffered many dangerous missions for the cause in which he believed. He had a wife and two small children. As Rupert looked at his dead vacant face he wondered if the King of England would be aware of the sacrifice this man had made, of the suffering it would bring to his family, who like himself had been convinced of the man's invincibility, and then he heard the soft voice of the boy who cradled Jan's head.

'*In paradisum deducant te Angeli: in tuo adventu suscipiant te Martyres, et perducant te in civitatem sanctam, Jerusalem.*'

'*Chorus Angelorum te suscipiat, et cum Lazaro quondam paupere aeternam habeas requiem.*'* Rupert finished, as he gazed into the wide blue eyes of a girl of extraordinary beauty.

---

* May the Angels lead you into paradise:
    may the Martyrs come to welcome you,
    and take you to the holy city, Jerusalem.
May choirs of Angels welcome you,
    and with Lazarus who is poor no longer
    may you have eternal rest.

'Madam,' said Rupert softly, 'my friend was a fine man, a good Catholic, and could not have wished for a better passing to heaven, I will be for ever grateful to you.'

Mary felt she might be sick. She had never seen a dead person before, not even her mother, who had been decently contained in her coffin before Mary had been able to get home. The man was large with a good strong face that even in death showed signs of the kind of man he must have been. Instead of the hideous look of terror she would have expected, he seemed peaceful and resigned. It was the suddenness of it all that made Mary shake uncontrollably, the thought that death altered everything in an instant, just as Anthony's death had changed her life. It was his death which had pushed her into the path on which she found herself in a tangled web of betrayal and murder. What dark force had driven the person who had killed the man whose head she had in her lap?

'Was he married?' she asked of Rupert, looking up at his clearly distraught face.

'A wife and two children,' Rupert faltered. 'I have no wife, it should have been me. He has always protected me . . . I . . . ' Rupert stopped, gripped between anger and a feeling of guilt that he could have done more to fight off his friend's murderer.

'The man died bravely,' said Sir Miles briskly. 'We are all soldiers, even you, daughter, we must have fortitude. Anything less would belittle the fight for which we all take such risks. We must be practical and thank God that Thomas with his sure aim was able to project his knife at this man in time to save at least one of you. He knew they must get back to the house with all speed. 'Rats seldom travel alone,' he said urgently. 'We must be gone from this place as fast as we can. Together we will carry our man to the house. We must give him a decent burial. Let us conceal the other man in the undergrowth and when daylight comes, Thomas will return with one of our men and cast the body into the sea by the cove where the tide will carry it away.'

Rupert obeyed at once, responding to the military precision

of Sir Miles's instructions, and pondering why this beautiful daughter of his should be present in a man's world. Even in the faint light and the intermittent illumination of Thomas's lantern, he could not fail but notice that the girl was a beauty.

'I have been forgetting myself, Thomas. You saved my life,' said Rupert suddenly, taking the man's arm and clasping it with genuine camaraderie.

'It was all in the line of duty, Sir,' said Thomas.

Together they began to lift Jan's body, Rupert being astonished at how heavy he was. Despite his weight, his friend had always been surprisingly agile and moved like a panther. It was these qualities which had often got them both out of trouble. Rupert felt very much alone as they struggled up the slippery incline to the entrance to the tunnel.

CHAPTER TWENTY-FOUR

Rupert Willoughby's grief at the loss of his friend hit him hard. Although he was from a military background, his father having served the late King bravely, his family had fled with so many others and eked out a kind of twilight existence in the shadows of the impoverished heir apparent in exile. They had spent five years in Bruges with Charles and both he and his father had served in the token rag bag of a Royalist army which followed the King in waiting. The restoration had left him perfectly placed to be one of the King's most valuable intelligence connections, his perfect knowledge of the many different dialects and languages and a fluency in French were just some of his excellent credentials. This visit was both as courier and the beginning of a period planned in London where he was to circulate amongst the King's most intimate circle, where it was suspected some pernicious forces were using their positions to feed information to dissidents abroad. All this he was to explain to Mary in the next few days, during a period at Sailing Hall.

The following morning, after a good night's rest, Rupert was bidden to Sir Miles's study; he had just returned from a delightful walk in the gardens accompanied by Sir Miles's dogs, Ned and Betty.

'May I pour you some chocolate?' enquired Mary as she presided over a huge silver tray on a table by the fireside.

Rupert accepted gratefully, it had been bitterly cold outside. One of the first snowfalls of the winter had covered the landscape and the brightness from the sun reflected into the room through the tall leaded windows. This was the first time he had seen her in woman's clothes, as after the previous night's events they had all retired to their rooms. Jan's body now lay in the private chapel, waiting for the local priest, a trusted Catholic, to come and assist with a secret burial that night. Rupert was piquantly aware of the contrast between the living and the dead as he took pleasure in watching Mary's graceful figure bent over the chocolate jug, her breasts tantalisingly revealed amidst the ruff of her bodice. He was more than ever overcome by her beauty, but he detected something hesitant about her as if she had something to hide.

'So you have served Her Majesty for nearly two years. How did you find the court?' he enquired casually.

'Indeed, Sir,' she replied, glancing towards her father, who gave a brief nod of ascent indicating that she should answer the question freely. 'I have,' she continued, 'and to answer your question, in Her Majesty's service I did not circulate freely in court circles. Her Majesty does not care for some of His Majesty's close friends.'

Rupert could not fail to recognise the inference in her reply, or to see that this reference to Lady Castlemaine, and presumably her dastardly cousin the Duke of Buckingham was a test to see how he would react; he also knew that much depended on his response.

'Ah yes,' he said at once. 'I suppose you mean Lady Castlemaine, or Mrs Villiers as she is sometimes called.'

'I do,' replied Mary bluntly.

'In that case I may as well be frank,' said Rupert. 'The woman has destroyed a man who has done more for His Majesty than any other living person.'

'Do you mean Lord Clarendon?' asked Mary, with a feeling of dread.

'Yes, we do have some bad news for you, my dear. Since I know only too well how both you and your Aunt Judith trusted the man, and I too have always held him in high regard,' said Sir Miles.

'Is he dead?' Mary asked.

'No, he is not dead,' Rupert responded quickly. 'But treated in such a way as he might wish he were. Lady Castlemaine has long made it her life's work to get rid of the man and successfully drummed up supporters among the King's most dissolute and despicable hangers on.'

'I suppose we include the Duke of Buckingham; he is most surely the worst of them,' said Sir Miles.

'Perhaps not quite the worst. There is his close friend, Lord Rochester. He is equally low, a man who kidnapped and compromised that poor young woman Elizabeth Mallet to get his hands on her fortune.'

'These men are animals,' said Sir Miles furiously.

'True,' agreed Rupert, 'and they are just some of the signatories to Lord Clarendon's impeachment, and if the poor man is found guilty the punishment could be death.'

'This is shocking,' Sir Miles expostulated. 'Rochester's mother was a good woman and, more than that, Lord Clarendon was Master of Oxford and welcomed the fourteen-year-old Rochester as a Bachelor of Arts. He was no more than a penniless lad and he protected and nurtured the boy and this is how he repays him.'

'The fact is the Chancellor has been made a scapegoat. He has already handed in his great seal and there is no saving him,' said Rupert despondently.

'But this is iniquitous,' cried Mary despairingly. 'It is almost impossible to understand the web of betrayal and lack of honour which surrounds the poor Queen.'

'Yes,' added Sir Miles, 'and let us not forget he was the one man who was not only against the war, but even forecast the invasion of the Spanish Netherlands by the French – and nobody listened to him.'

'He was the only one who spoke sense,' Mary interjected. 'I heard him telling the Queen that we should let the French and Spanish do the fighting while we watched and waited to take our pick of the victors with our navy intact. Just think how many lives would have been saved if his wise words had been listened to.'

'Madam, all those who truly love and serve our King are fearful of the forces which surround him and the loss of so great a man as Lord Clarendon is beyond words . . . ' Rupert looked downcast for a second and then looked up with a slight smile on his face.

'Why do you smile?' asked Mary sharply. 'I wish I could think of something to smile about in all this.'

'This might comfort you just a little, Madam,' Rupert replied. 'As Lord Clarendon rode in his carriage to deliver his seal he passed Lady Castlemaine's apartments. She ran out into the Privy Gardens in her night shift, jeering at His Lordship like a wonton gutter woman, and he called to her for all to hear, "Madam, may I remind you that one day you will be old," and all who heard it admired His Lordship and a few cheered him and called insults at Her Ladyship, with names I could not repeat in your company.'

'Even so, it is a horrible story,' said Mary, stifling a laugh. 'It is a sad day for England when the King stands by and allows his old friend to be treated in this way. How do you explain it?'

'You have to understand, my dear,' said Sir Miles. 'The King is juggling so many things at once, France, Holland, Parliament and the fight to protect freedom of religion; and, even more remarkable, despite his barren wife, he is determined to hand the succession to his Catholic brother the Duke of York, something Parliament is determined to prevent. Lord Clarendon is an old man; he has been at the King's side since His Majesty was a boy. The King probably thinks in a misguided way that he should make way for a younger man.'

'I am surprised that the King is not a better judge of character,' said Rupert. 'I keep asking myself why he has decided to dispense with so good a man.'

'The sad fact is that times have changed,' sighed Sir Miles. 'Clarendon no longer has the tools to fight the devils which beset this country and perhaps the King knows it. He has fallen foul of Parliament. Corrupt as it is, it would have been wiser to play the King's game and find a middle way. It is probably fair to say that with age he has lost the ability to bend like a branch which does not obey the winds of change and so must snap. That is the way it is with the Chancellor,' he finished ruefully.

'You are right, Sir Miles. But I am sorry for the man,' said Rupert. 'He loved the King as a son and indeed when he pleaded his case to His Majesty, he said those very words and His Majesty is reputed to have replied, "I have but one father," and everyone who heard it knew the Chancellor's days were over.'

The three of them remained still for a while, as if in respect for the old man who had served the King so loyally whilst they considered, although they did not share the thought, that there was a lesson to be learnt.

'A man must anticipate the coming of old age,' said Sir Miles 'and withdraw before all dignity is lost. Now, Rupert,' he continued briskly, 'will it please you to tell Mary a few things about these factions at court.'

'Of course,' Rupert agreed and reeled off some names. 'Let us start with Lord Arlington who will be your paymaster, Madam. Your father will have known him as Sir Henry Bennett before the King ennobled him. He has recently petitioned the King for more money for intelligence. They say he has acquired over two thousand pounds alone for his own services this year. I have my reservations about the man, for he is married to a very rich Dutch woman, and is most certainly anti-Catholic so you must be on your guard. And last but by no means least,' he finished with a flourish. 'There is Mrs Aphra Behn, whose maid you are to employ. She is a very clever and beautiful woman, but sails close to the wind. She had a relationship with a notorious double agent called William Scott, the son of one of the supporters of the Regicide, who was executed.'

'So where is this Scot man now?' asked Mary.

'The King pardoned him despite his early involvement with

his enemies and rewarded him handsomely to spy on dissidents in The Hague,' said Rupert. 'But Scott became a double agent in league with de Witt the Stadhalter of Holland and for a thousand pounds a year betrayed his fellow agents Oudert and Thomas Corney who died in a Dutch prison. The damage the man had done is incalculable.'

'The man should be punished, it is iniquitous that he can get away with it,' said Sir Miles.

'There is worse,' Rupert went on. 'The King issued a proclamation last year ordering disaffected Englishmen to return to England and face fare trial for treason. Twelve of them did so, among them your father's old friend Colonel John Desborough who held power in the army of the united provinces. Some of the men were executed, but as your father knows Desborough has been in the Tower for a year.'

'It is a shocking thing when a man is punished for behaving with honour,' said Sir Miles.

'Ah yes,' said Rupert. 'But there is good news. Lord Besborough has just been released and will be allowed to live quietly in the country.'

'Well, that at least is splendid news,' Sir Mile agreed with genuine pleasure.

'Yes indeed so,' said Rupert. 'But what is astonishing, and leads me to warn your daughter about Lord Arlington, is that the two-faced Scott managed to negotiate a deal with his Lordship and he has complete immunity and continues working as a spy in Holland.'

'And are you saying that this blaggard Scott, who is clearly a double agent, has been romantically involved with Mrs Behn?' asked Sir Miles.

'I am afraid so. It is a friendship of long standing,' said Rupert carefully, not wishing to elaborate, for fear of offending Mary. 'They met when Mrs Behn was a girl living with her father in Surinam, and most unfortunately again in Antwerp where, as you know, Mrs Behn has been a most effective and trustworthy informer for the King. But happily Mrs Behn is too clever a woman to be hoodwinked for long. She is well aware of the man's duplicity. Although there is no longer a romantic attachment she uses the man most cleverly.'

'If you lie down with dogs you will get up with fleas,' Sir Miles remarked. 'The man will come to a bad end.'

'This woman Aphra sounds extraordinary,' said Mary. 'I would like to meet her. Do you think that would be possible?'

'I know she will be in London in the next few weeks,' said Rupert. 'And yes, she is most unusual. But I should warn you, Mary, this woman's life is not easy. She has risked a great deal with her work and I have it that she is in severe financial difficulties. But there is quite another aspect to her. She is a playwright, and one whose work I admire. The purpose of her next visit is to negotiate the production of one of her plays at The King's Theatre.'

'Well, it is certain that we live in extraordinary times,' observed Sir Miles. 'She will be the first woman I have ever heard of who is able to earn money by writing. This is why we must be aware of the enlightened influence His Majesty has brought with him.'

'I fully acknowledge that,' said Rupert. 'But if His Majesty has a failing, it is to grasp the financial responsibilities owing to people who work for him. With the exception of his mistresses,' he added wryly.

'Before we go any further,' said Mary, 'I must know if the Queen knows exactly what I am doing?'

'She has already given her blessing,' Rupert assured her. 'She knows that there are threats to her own safety and she was at first reluctant to concede to your involvement, since she feels responsible for you.'

'Curiously, I feel well protected by you all,' said Mary. 'The Queen is a wonderful person and if she approves I am much encouraged.'

'Well, then, let us proceed,' said Rupert perfunctorily, anxious to get down to business.

'Yes, please,' said Mary with a trace of impatience.

'The first thing you will have to do,' Rupert began, 'is to venture out of the sanctity of the Queen's close knit circle. For example, you must visit the theatre and get in the swim, for there you will pick up a great deal of gossip.'

'So far, the work does not sound very onerous,' laughed Sir Miles.

'No Sir, I expect Mary will take to it very well, especially visiting the milliner's in Hackney where the owner is a brave woman who receives information. You will be expected to order some splendid creations.'

'But how will I pay for such luxuries?' cried Mary in alarm.

'Funds will be provided, do not worry,' said Rupert.

'And what other avenues must I pursue?' asked Mary.

'There are the schools kept by matrons for young women,' said Rupert. 'Many of these are a ruse and a secret meeting place for agents. The Queen will appoint you as her representative to take an interest in these places, for what will appear to be philanthropic reasons.'

Mary had begun to get quite excited about the prospect of her new life, but all the time a small part of her felt torn between her love for her child, from whom she did not wish to be parted. In reality, though, she knew she really did not have a choice. As if echoing her concerns, there was a tapping at the door. Sir Miles got up and opened it a chink. Thomas was standing on the threshold.

'Begging your pardon, Sir Miles,' he said anxiously. 'Little Phillip has a fever and Jayne asks for Mrs Mary to attend.'

'I told you we are not to be disturbed,' snapped Sir Miles through the crack.

'There, what did I tell you,' shot Thomas to someone the other side of the door.

'I don't mind what you told me; the baby needs his mother,' said a woman's voice.

Mary leapt to her feet unhesitatingly, a look of terror on her face. Knocking over a mug of chocolate, she gave the men no more than a token curtsy and fled the room.

Rupert knew at once, despite Sir Miles's attempt to cover up by pretending the child referred to was his own, that Mary had a baby and that she was not married. There was a mystery, something the family wished to keep secret. He quickly concluded that perhaps this was another reason why she would prove to be a worthy servant to the King.

'So, Sir Miles,' he observed quietly. 'One thing is sure; those who have secrets are the best at keeping them.'

*   *   *

'Oh Jayne he is burning up,' cried Mary, as she held Phillip's head next to her cheek.

'He has been very distressed,' said Jayne. 'He has cried so much he has worn himself out. All he wants to do now is to sleep.'

Mary's brow furrowed as she thought about what best to do. 'Come, Jayne, we must get his fever down. Lay him on the bed. Send to the ice house. We will make some compresses, we have no time to lose,' Mary commanded.

As she unwrapped her baby, and looked at his fat little limbs and angelic face, she felt totally overwhelmed with love for him and asked herself how she could even be considering the possibility of leaving him.

Meanwhile, Jayne was running as fast as her feet could carry her to the ice house. The semi-underground store was by the water at the back of the house, where ice cut in deepest winter still remained under a cover of sacking and straw. Throwing open the door, she set to with the little silver axe kept for the purpose. She hacked away like a woman possessed. Her feelings for the child were the strongest she had ever felt since the death of her own baby.

'He will be all right, please God he must be,' she prayed frantically as she worked.

She was soon back at the house, flying through the door, past Sir Miles's study and up the stairs.

'Here we are, Mrs Mary. I brought as much as I could carry,' she panted, and Mary saw her face distraught with worry and fear and was comforted by the knowledge that Jayne, her friend, would in fact guard her baby with her life. Together the women set to wrapping the ice in clean linen cloths. All through the night, they bathed and swaddled him. Slowly his head cooled and his eyes began to open. Miraculously, by the morning, he delivered a smile which practically wrought his face in two, and he began to cough.

'It's good. He needed to cough to get up the mucous in his chest,' said Jayne with relief. 'If you will permit me, Mrs Mary,' she went on, 'we should try the onion remedy to kill the infection. I cut an onion in half and stand it in a plate of sugar, the juice from the onion seeps into the sugar and we will spoon it down his little throat and he will recover, Mrs Mary, you will see.'

Two days later Phillip had recovered completely and Mary's boxes were ready in the great hall. A period in Mary's life had passed and now she was to return to the reality of life at court. She knew she had but one chance to recover her position and fight for her son's future.

She had said her private goodbye to Phillip. It had been an emotional farewell as Jayne delightedly showed her that he was cutting his first tooth. Mary took him in her arms for what she knew would be the last time for many weeks. He moved his small fists in excitement and gurgled with delight. Mary's whole chest felt it might explode.

'I leave with a heavy heart, dear Jayne,' she said, as the two women embraced. She turned and hugged her father and Charlotte. Rupert tactfully turned his back and spoke to the driver until Sir Miles gave him a quick nod and then he opened the carriage door and helped Mary up. As they swept out of the lodge gates Rupert lent towards her and quietly took her hand.

PART THREE

CHAPTER TWENTY-FIVE

Whitehall Palace, November 1667

Mary's return to the palace passed relatively unnoticed. The Queen was preoccupied with a strange turn of events about which Mary was quickly to find out. Entering the Queen's chamber for the first time since her return, she quickly drew back into the ornate hangings in front of the door. An extraordinary scene was taking place before her eyes and hers were not the only ones; the Queen's other ladies stood at the other side of the room, their backs tactfully turned, but clearly able and eager to hear what was going on.

The beautiful Frances Stuart lay prostrate at the Queen's feet. 'Oh Your Majesty, how can you ever forgive me,' she sobbed wretchedly. 'I never meant the King to think I was anything more than a flirtation, I have never, before God, lost my purity. Madam, how can you ever forgive me?' Frances raised a face bathed in tears to the Queen. 'It is my vanity and love of admiration which has brought this about and it is my only sin,' she cried.

'My dear,' said the Queen sympathetically, raising Frances to her feet. 'I believe you implicitly. I will offer you my protection and you must never leave my side until this matter is resolved. You know as well as I do, the King loves beautiful women, but in reality, it is my enemies who have brought this about, and those of the Chancellor.'

'Oh the poor man – he is to leave the country for ever, and after all he has done. He has been the truest friend the King ever had,' wept Frances.

The Countess Panalva beckoned to Mary from across the room, indicating that she should approach the Queen and present herself. Mary thought for a moment, reluctant to impose on such a dramatic event. But the Queen saw her out of the corner of her eye and nodded, smiling and lifting her hand. Mary approached and curtsied. She thought the Queen looked tired, there were dark shadows under her eyes and she had lost weight, but when she saw Mary her face brightened.

'I have missed you, Mary, and much has happened since you went away,' said the Queen, gazing despondently at her folded hands, in which she grasped her crucifix.

'We are all the worse for it,' she continued in a low voice and then suddenly speaking loudly and with resolve, as if to the whole room. 'Lady Frances will now be under my protection and let us hope we can all recover some dignity and peace of mind . . .' the Queen hesitated a moment and looked away quickly, as if once again the things to which she was referring caused her pain.

'Oh, Madam,' cried Frances. 'I am so grateful to you and may I present the Duke of Richmond to you, for I must recover my good name and he wishes to press his suit to me.'

'Why, my dear, this is wonderful news. You should have told me this,' said the Queen with genuine delight.

'I did not tell you at once, Madam, for I knew that if Lady Castlemaine and the Duke of Buckingham get to hear of it they will do everything in their power to stop me. It is as if they are all dedicated to ruining anyone who wishes to serve Your Majesty loyally, as I know you, Mary, have done,' she said, taking Mary's hand in a gesture of solidarity.

'Now, you two ladies must go and talk,' said the Queen finally. 'Your secret is safe with us all and Mary is a loyal servant and true friend who has been abused by this faction just as much as you, my dear,' she said confidentially to Frances.

Later, when she had had a brief conversation with Lady Frances, Mary felt the encounter had been very providential. Understanding what unhappiness Lady Frances's vanity had brought her; she had been seduced by the aura of the King and flattered by his attentions. Mary was all the more aware of the careful path she would have to take if she were to be in close contact with the King. There was no doubt that he would charm her as he charmed all women, but her love of the Queen and the indelible vision of Lady Frances prostrate at the Queen's feet would be forever etched in her mind. As she was leaving the Queen's apartments to meet her new maid, she saw that Rupert had been waiting for her.

'Mary, I hoped you would not be too long for I am come to bid you attend the King before he takes his dinner.' He was smiling admiringly at Mary. The pleasure he felt whenever he was in her presence was as if each encounter was the first.

'And what is the occasion?' Mary asked.

'Well, today, as you know, His Majesty is to dine with the Queen in view of the general public, an affair their Majesties both dislike. I for my part find it a ridiculous custom since neither the Queen nor any of her ladies consume any food on these occasions and all is for show, but then . . . ' Rupert broke off and then, with a dismissive gesture, continued, 'The King must dissemble. It is an essential ingredient for survival in these troubled times, an art which the King has perfected and all who serve him must adhere to his example . . . ' he hesitated, fixing Mary with a look. 'Except in one respect of course,' he finished, leaving a question in the air.

'Sir, I know exactly what you mean,' said Mary at once, 'but the sight of Lady Frances broken with remorse and throwing herself on her knees before our good and noble Queen, who has the quality of mercy and forgiveness, is a salutary experience.'

Mary found herself examining Rupert with renewed interest, for now, in the Palace of Whitehall, he had adopted a completely different persona. He was as dashing as any of the court blades wearing the latest fashion of slashed doublet and tight breeches which showed off his tall slim build. His hair, which had been scruffy and unkempt after his harrowing journey to Sailing Hall, had been cut and his beard carefully trimmed in the pointed style favoured by the Portuguese diplomats. She had been struck by his fine profile, strong jawline and full lips, and his eyes, a piercing blue grey, complimented by a healthy skin darkened by the weather and the sea.

Having been so long in the shadows of sexual attraction, all her emotions tied up with the birth of her baby and the ignominious circumstances of her pregnancy, Mary had forgotten the powerful forces that her femininity could evoke, Rupert's look was lingering and spoke a language without need of words. She felt herself responding and, to her surprise, enjoying the feeling of vibrant communication and acknowledging that she belonged in the turbulent world of high politics with its undertones of physical attraction.

'Will you permit me to compliment you on your gown, Mary, you look beautiful; and so very different from when I first saw you in boy's breeches,' Rupert laughed.

'Thank you,' said Mary, nodding graciously. 'It was ready for me when I arrived; my Aunt Judith commissioned it from the Queen's dressmaker. It is my favourite colour, but I find the style rather too revealing for my taste,' replied Mary, blushing slightly as she saw Rupert's eyes travelling to the low-cut bodice.

Mrs Behn's maid, Julia, had arrived the previous day and Mary had submitted to her expert crimping and styling and her red hair had been tamed into tightly bunched braids either side of her face, wound tightly and interwoven with dark green ribbons which set off the deep red of her dress. It was the bareness of her neck which made her feel almost more naked than the gown, the curve of her neck and the faintest glimpse of the cleft in the top of her white shoulders which particularly affected Rupert and he edged closer to her. To his delight she did not move away and for some reason the ante-room outside the Queens apartments was unusually empty. He felt Mary's answering gaze and an expectant stillness, a body language which did not speak of a shy coy girl, but of voluptuous womanly invitation. He closed the space between them and when he put an arm firmly about her slim waist, he felt her hips arch towards him. She lifted her face and slowly he pressed his lips to hers. They remained so, neither wanting to pull apart, until they heard the sound of approaching footsteps; they drew quickly away from each other, Mary trembling slightly.

'This is only the beginning, you cannot deny the passion I feel for you, meet me again tonight,' he whispered under his breath.

'For now, I will follow you to His Majesty,' she said with an enigmatic smile, and swept Rupert a deep curtsy. Rupert was by no means inexperienced; he had enjoyed the attentions of many women, but had always felt a strange kind of reticence. The unashamed wanton attainability of the women who circulated in the twilight world of expatriates in Holland had imbued him with an almost fastidious reluctance to allow his emotions to come into play. In fact he had sometimes wondered if he really liked women at all. Now for the first time in his life, he felt overwhelmed, as if his entire soul had been wrapped up in a glorious shining sun of happiness; he had fallen in love.

He felt his legs tremble as he led the way to the King. The faint perfume from Mary's neck remained on his face, he wanted to turn round as he heard the silky rustle of her skirts, to take her in his arms again, but in spite of his ardour something told him to hold back. Here was a woman who would not be easy. There was still something unfathomable about her, even now after their embrace which had simmered with promise, that deceptive smile played about her lips. And then there was the downward glance she had a habit of giving after she had spoken, as if to break the dialogue before it progressed to a stage of mutual intimacy.

There was also her disconcertingly flashing intelligence, born of a boyish confidence not usually found in women. But most intriguing of all was the knowledge that she was a mother. That, at least, he had ascertained, despite the tight-lipped granite loyalty of her father's servants. And what, he asked himself, of the mysterious child? He had seen it once in the nursemaid's arms, a fat cherubic dark baby, nothing like his mother. The nursemaid had pulled an elaborate lace bonnet over its head and hurried off and he had known not to ask any questions. It was only in the last few days since they had arrived at Whitehall that little ripples of rumour had begun to make waves in the back of his mind.

*   *   *

After the public dining, Mary had been informed that she must accompany Rupert to the King's private apartments. The first thing she noticed on entering the King's rooms was the fusty aroma of dog combined with a slight whiff of what she could only describe as a mixture of leather, tobacco, wine and the unmistakable waft of body. This was the King without the carapace of formality with which Mary had become acquainted. At first she hardly recognised the man who rose to his feet from a comfortable chair. His periwig was perched on the back of a stand by his desk, revealing the fact that his own hair was cut close to his hair and completely white. Mary remembered now that it had turned so during his wife's illness four years previously, a measure of his deep affection for the woman whom so many had sought to devalue.

Half a dozen spaniels lay about the room and one occupied a pile of cushions on which she suckled a squirming mass of tiny puppies. As Mary approached, she jumped involuntarily at a chorus of striking clocks which set off a confusion of yapping dogs.

'Welcome,' said the King delightedly. 'Come and see my latest acquisition,' he added, beckoning Mary towards a magnificent clock of a type Mary had never seen before. It stood above the height of a man in an elegant mahogany case, elaborately inlaid with a motif of flowers on the top of intricately silvered face were two magnificent brass finials.

'This clock is the first of its kind,' said the King, following Mary's gaze. 'It is made by Thomas Tompion from Bedford and I have another commissioned from Daniel Quare. We must invite your father to see them, Mary. Did you note the sweet sound of the strike so gentle and true? The bell is unique.'

Mary would come to realise the King had a gift for putting people at ease. He would launch into a subject far removed from the matter in hand and establish a feeling of intimacy which gave way to a frank and productive dialogue. It worked like a charm upon Mary who shared her own father's interest in clocks. She forgot she was speaking to the King of England.

'Oh, Sir, my father would be fascinated,' cried Mary enthusiastically, clapping her hands together like an exited child.

'I am delighted you are interested in my collection,' said the King looking at her indulgently. He was delighted to find a woman of such beauty who displayed a genuine interest in one of the many passions in his life.

'Oh yes Your Majesty,' said Mary undeterred. 'I have always shared my father's love of clocks. I have never seen the like, and to get all of them to strike at the same second, it is perfect. I have spent many hours with my father while he tried to achieve it, and do you know, he has an idea for a clock which will make a tune on the hour?'

'Well, that is extraordinary because it is the very thing on which we are working,' said the King with genuine interest. 'You see, Mary, I feel it is my duty to advance all these skills as much as I can. The Royal Society for instance, did you know we took the blood from a dog and replaced it with another dog's and the animal flourishes? It is my duty to do all I can to enhance human life and the secret of it all is knowledge and the courage to use it.'

Rupert had been absorbing the scene between Mary and the King with pleasure and surprise. Although most of his meetings with the King had taken place in these informal circumstances he had never been taken into the royal confidence in such a way. To see the King enthusing with Mary about these other dimensions of his royal duties was intriguing. Knowing the King quite well, he knew that he was a man of whom it was prudent to consider his actions, not in the light of the reason given, but more the real reason, and he was treating Mary in the way he would a man. There was no sexual innuendo, none of the elaborate dance of verbal semantics, just manly talk, to which Mary was responding with admirable candour. And then Rupert realised that it was the King's clever way of creating the uncluttered trust which would be essential for future dealings between him and Mary.

'Now let us sit down around the table,' said the King briskly, as if reading Rupert's thoughts, sweeping aside a pile of papers. Rupert quickly pulled forward a carved gilt chair for Mary. As she sat, he let his hand briefly lie on her shoulder, and she turned her head and flashed him an almost imperceptible look. The King, from whom very little escaped notice, saw the exchange and saw at once that it was an indication of intimacy between them. He caught Rupert's eye, as if to acknowledge the boundary established.

'Now, we must get down to work. Rupert do you have the papers?' he asked.

Rupert undid his coat, revealing what appeared to be bulky waistcoat. He deftly removed it and spread it on the table, inside were all the relevant documents he had brought with him on the traumatic journey from Antwerp.

'Splendid. Now let us get to work at once,' said the King. 'Mary, will you translate for us?' he asked.

Mary began to decode the papers, occasionally resorting to pencil and paper, while the King nodded.

'As I thought,' he said eventually, 'the blaggard Scott is as despicable as ever. Well, little does he know how devious a monkey he has in his zoo. He must remain in ignorance of the fact that we know he is the very devil who would sell his own mother to the highest bidder. And we must listen more to Mrs Behn and speak at once to Lord Arlington. God alone knows why he leaves Mrs Behn unable to pay her bills. Will you convey our concern to his Lordship, Rupert, and see that the matter is dealt with promptly, for I fear we shall have to recall Mrs Behn before long and she must be given every mark of our appreciation for her bravery and courage.'

'I will indeed, Sir,' replied Rupert gravely, relieved that the King had volunteered the comment because he had been determined to raise the matter himself, had the King not preempted him.

'I propose that you take this and other matters to His Lordship at once,' said the King, looking sharply at Rupert. The message was clear; he wished to be alone with Mary. Rupert responded at once.

'And the other matters, Sir?' he asked quizzically.

'Why, the matters we discussed yesterday,' said the King with a slight trace of irritation.

Soon Mary was alone with the King. 'Let us sit by the fire,' he said, rising from his chair and indicating some low stools near the hearth. 'Now that we are alone, I need to establish some facts about you, Mary, if you will forgive me,' he continued gently. 'You have served Her Majesty and it is her welfare which must be my primary concern and in this I am satisfied, but . . .'

The King placed his hands in a cathedral shape and peered above them, while an awkward silence ensued. He saw Mary's bosom begin to heave nervously.

'But what, Your Majesty?' she blurted.

'It is your private life which appears to be of interest and therefore regrettably of use to the people who would seek to undermine the Queen,' he explained ominously.

'I have tried to be discreet about my private life, Your Majesty,' Mary retorted defensively. 'It is the conduct of others one cannot control, individuals from whom one would look for more.'

'Look for more by all means, but the question is will you find it?' said the King philosophically. 'Personally I have found it wise to assume the worst in so far as the conduct of others is concerned, and then events can produce a pleasant surprise when you least expect it, ' he broke off momentarily. 'You, my dear, are just such a surprise,' he finished with a flourish of his hand.

'Sir, you honour me,' Mary stammered, blushing furiously, and heaving an inward sigh of relief, fondly imagining that the question of her private life had been dealt with.

'Yes,' said the King abruptly. 'Honour! I like the word and naturally it is synonymous with truth. You can have no secrets from either the Queen or myself. Now, what about this child of yours?'

'I know. Of course, Your Majesty,' Mary began tremulously, knowing she had to make a decision. She must tell the King everything or nothing. If she were to tell him everything, she would have to believe for whatever reason that he was her friend. She must also establish whether or not the Queen knew about her child and if she did why she, who had the highest standards, had accepted Mary back into her inner sanctum. 'Yes, Sir, I have a child. He is the most important thing in my life,' gulped Mary.

'That is as it should be,' said the King quietly. 'But there are stories about the court and they are naturally regarding the parenthood of your child. I think we must know the truth of it,' the King persevered.

'The father of my child is the only man who could have been,' said Mary evasively, darting the King a look.

'And by that I take it you mean the only man to have shared your bed,' said the King.

'Yes, Sir, and the man with whom I had expected to share my life,' replied Mary.

'You must of course be referring to His Grace, the Duke Fernando,' said the King, quietly casting her a look with his cool dark eyes. Mary met his gaze for a fleeting second and then looked down to her hands nervously folded in her lap. The King was not wearing his customary cravat and she had noticed his dark skin under his shirt, and felt the frisson of his famous sexual attraction. She knew, had circumstances been other then these, she would have responded with a message which would have taken her to the King's bed. Charles noticed this, and, having long ago recognised that the way to a woman's heart was both through the mind and the body, the former undoubtedly being the way to the latter, he considered the change that had come about with Mary.

He had first remarked upon her when she had tripped on her gown when she was presented to the Queen. He recalled that it had been the Duke Fernando who had saved her from falling and saw the irony that if he was correct it was the Duke who was responsible for the awkward circumstances in which the girl now found herself. But one thing puzzled him, why had the Duke not returned. His wife had been dead for some months and the Queen needed him. Added to which, Charles, who had a highly developed sense of responsibility towards all his children, would have expected him to take some interest in his child. But, observing Mary, he saw in her a dramatic change, gone was the inexperienced girl who had come to serve the Queen, here was a beautiful confident woman, intelligent and alive to the ways of the world and more than a match for the bitchy court beauties who had begun to notice this rival in their midst.

It was this new Mary who made his pulse race more than he could remember of late. Admittedly his affair with a pretty little actress who now, thanks to his patronage, was the most famous of his mistresses, had made him feel giddy with excitement. Although he loved her in his way, her coarse bawdy humour had already begun to bore him. Mary Boynton had the makings of a seriously powerful woman, but she also had what was to the King an almost unnerving quality of goodness, an obvious moral probity which Charles found challengingly exciting. But for all that he would not trespass into the bedroom of one of his Queen's most respected diplomats. He made a mental note that he would enquire more closely into the Duke's plans.

'Yes, Sir, His Grace has a son, for I cannot tell you of all people a lie, but we had an understanding and,' Mary faltered slightly, going on to explain how Fernando's silence had both puzzled and then devastated her.

'I am glad you are telling me this,' said the King nodding gravely.

'I am trying to make the best of it,' said Mary in an unexpectedly lighter tone, aware that the King must not think that her personal circumstances might come between her and her new commitment. 'I have a chance to prove myself as an independent woman, and do something valuable for my country. You will not regret the trust you have placed in me.'

Charles noticed there was something peeping from the fold in her gown and realised it was a rosary. He was, despite all his love of women and the sins of the flesh, a man of firm religious beliefs. His mantra was one of freedom to worship and freedom to love. Had poor Catherine been able to give him the child she craved he often thought he could have been monogamous, but as it was he found it hard to resist the tilt of a pretty chin just as Mary's tilted now. Despite the girl's enthusiasm for the path she was so eager to follow, he still had doubts about her suitability. She was not cut from the same cloth as women like Mrs Behn who were basically of humble origins, only too glad to grasp at anything which might advance them, women who were not reared into a solid well-bred family where the role of wife and mother was the only path considered for them.

But then he thought about the Mary's father, Sir Miles. He remembered the man saying once that he had wished his younger daughter had been a boy because she had a man's brain. He had gone on to say that the stifling of women's brains had been a sad loss to the world. The King had always remembered the conversation because it had so exactly mirrored his own feelings on the subject.

'My dear,' he said in an avuncular tone, 'you are no ordinary woman. Whatever life has in store for you I am sure it will be a delightful surprise for us all. But for now, you are doing very well and whatever happens I note that there are others who would be glad to fill the vacancy left by the errant Duke,' he went on quickly, clearly referring to Rupert, 'and you must not worry about the Queen, she knows of your situation.'

Then he quite perfunctorily indicated that interview was at an end, and Mary smiled and dipped a low curtsy of acknowledgement. With immaculate timing a footman tapped on the door to announce another visitor.

Charles had forgotten that Lady Castlemaine had demanded an audience with him that afternoon. He looked apprehensively at the clock as she swept through the door, her face a picture of serenity until she recognised Mary, who swept her an exaggerated curtsy.

Lady Castlemaine's expression had changed into what seemed to Charles to be almost a grimace; her features were as if frozen. As Mary rose silently from her obeisance she assumed a seraphic smile, and seeing the amused twitch of Charles generous lips she decided to let Lady Castlemaine break the silence, aware that she would most probably utter a less than dignified greeting.

'So, little Miss Mary is back!' she proclaimed with a sneer. 'You have lost weight and you look mighty pale,' she paused, attempting a coy if not conspiratorial look in Charles's direction, which to her chagrin he chose to ignore. Flicking her fan impatiently, and with theatrical concern she ploughed on. 'Was the Norfolk air not quite to your liking? Ah, but maybe it is the colour of your gown that makes you look so out of sorts. Had you not heard that red is so very last season?'

'Regrettably, Madam,' the King shot at Lady Castlemaine with barely concealed contempt, his hand at the same time staying any response from Mary, 'your visit is at an end. I must make ready for an important meeting with an envoy from Spain.'

Mary managed to retain immaculate composure and Lady Castlemaine had no choice but ignominiously to turn around and start to leave the room.

'Do not close the door,' the King said to the footman, 'Her

Ladyship is just leaving, and Madam,' he called after her, 'your manners are low, we expect more from those who seek the King's favour. It is not birth that makes a lady, Madam, you would do well to remember that.'

The footman caught Mary's eye, his face wreathed in satisfied smiles.

CHAPTER TWENTY-SIX

'It is time you behaved as your rank demands,' said the Duchess Consuelo, staring coldly at her son.

It was spring and many months had passed since the death of her daughter-in-law, and although the Duchess still demanded full mourning in the castle, her heart had moved on. In fact she could hardly remember what Magdalena even looked like, but as human nature filters the memory, so it had done with Consuelo. She did not well remember the many hours of tears and weeping her son's loveless marriage had occasioned in her son's wife, and it never occurred to her that this might be a matter of regret to anyone, let alone herself who had been largely responsible for the ill starred union. After all, it had merely been a re-enactment of her own marriage, a condition which survived only on a grim endurance; the rigid humourless exchanges which had been the currency of her own marriage were to her no more or less than the norm.

And now her thoughts were solely preoccupied with the urgency of finding a new wife for Fernando, but her attempts to find a suitable replacement bride had been rudely thwarted by his undisguised indifference to the match that had been suggested. After a few contrived meetings, which had not blossomed beyond the most formal of courtesies, Fernando announced his intention to return again to Lisbon as soon as possible to take instructions from the Queen Regent.

'I have news of the greatest importance,' he explained to his mother. 'My Lord Sandwich has managed to achieve peace with Spain. I hope to be recalled to London to the Queen Catherine's service as soon as possible,' he went on, lifting a hand to arrest her interruption. 'There are new alliances in the wings and the Queen will need advice, and besides, Your Grace,' he said, using the formal mode of address she had always demanded, 'I must not remain here when I can be of use in the world.'

'Has it not occurred to you, Fernando, that you have duty to put your own house in order before you try to set the world to rights? You have an obligation to provide an heir for the great house which in turn has provided so many illustrious men to serve our great country.'

'And what of my own happiness?' he replied sharply. 'The brides you have so kindly suggested for me would be no more than brood mares. I could feel nothing for any of them. I did my duty, as you call it, with Magdalena and even though I tried to love her and respect her it was the love to be found between brother and sister, a mean thing for a marriage, which caused us both great anguish,' he shuddered as if someone were walking over his grave. 'She suffered,' he said pointedly, 'and I believe it destroyed her.'

The Duchess felt the blood drain from her face; to be addressed in this way, by a grown man, her own son, and the allusion to things best left unsaid, it was unthinkable, shocking, self-indulgent, the kind of talk to be expected from a low kitchen girl.

'Happiness,' she almost shrieked, her white face twisted in anger, 'how dare you talk to me of happiness! Our God does not talk of happiness; our blessed Virgin brought our saviour into the world to suffer, yet he was born a man, not conceived in the way you so distastefully mention, he was born of a pure woman without the sins of the flesh, the sins you so disgustingly tasted when you left your marital bed . . . No, Christ did not have the luxury of this thing happiness,' she spat the word, her mouth twisting in contempt.

Fernando regarded his mother with a steady unflinching gaze. He had never heard her speak with such vehemence before. In a way it represented a glimpse of the woman she might have been had she not been so indoctrinated with such a dark vision of the world. Had all that passion been channelled into living and loving, what kind of a woman might she have been? And as he continued to look at her in the awkward silence which followed, a picture of Mary flashed into his mind, a memory of the time they had spent together at her father's house, of the easy playful delight he had taken in her company, how she had awakened in him a dormant childhood, a proper foundation for a man of wisdom and compassion. He realised that somehow his mother had stolen his childhood; she had denied this to him as she now wanted to deny him the love of a woman. Without rancour, he suddenly saw the juxtaposition of the two women in his life and felt they had both betrayed him in their different ways. But with a searing vision he knew he must return to England and he also knew for some reason that he might never see his mother again. Her shrivelled heart was not a thing which would give her a long and happy life. Rather she would be cut off with cold and sudden frigidity from a life never really lived.

It was with compassion that he took a step towards her. She remained tall, erect, unforgiving and ungiving, but he put his arms about her bony shoulders smelling faintly of camphor. He pressed her resistant body towards him and murmured in her ear, grotesquely weighted with the magnificent drop emerald earrings his father had given to her to mark his birth. She pushed him away and with the gesture rebuffed her last chance of any kind of resolution.

'Mother, I am sorry you have had such a lonely life,' he said with unexpected kindness. 'You have sought some kind of perfection; it is a tragedy that my concept of that is so different from your own.'

She knew instinctively that this was goodbye. Her son had come of age, he was his own man, and she no longer had any influence upon his conduct.

'I will not find perfection in this life but I will in the next,' she said quietly. She noticed her son's large shoulders, the tendrils of thick black hair that curled on to the snowy white ruff around his neck, the faint smell of his masculinity and the sandalwood in which he stored his clothes. She looked long and hard at this son who would soon leave her to her rosary. It was the first time she actually saw him as a man, and she saw her own womanhood now passed into oblivion, there would be no more chances for the life she could have had. Fernando returned the look unflinchingly and it seemed to him that she lost height, her head hung disconsolately. He suddenly saw her as vulnerable and a tragic figure who had denied her own femininity. He was overwhelmed with compassion for her.

'Mother,' he said in a more solicitous voice, 'you must understand, there are things I must do as a man, one of them is to understand the frailty of human nature. Sometimes it is the very sin in a man or woman which makes him most lovable. Surely Christ taught us that. Even you, Mother, have sinned, mostly against yourself. I cannot commit the sin of depriving a woman of love and true affection. You yourself are a victim of that. Would you have your own son perpetuate that?'

'No, my son,' she replied tentatively, softening a little. 'I would not, you are right and strong. I wish your father could have seen you now, that at least he would have commended me for.' Consuelo stretched out a bony hand, Fernando knelt. He kissed the hand, his lips lingering a second on her skin. Before she could pull away, he felt a tear drop. He did not look up. There was no more and yet so much to be said and so they parted.

*   *   *

Fernando lost no time with painful farewells, his senses raced with a fanatical urgency to get on with his life. Although he did not admit it, the bitterness he felt towards Mary and his lost love came and went in great waves, alternating in a fantasy that it had all been a terrible mistake and that there must be a perfectly logical explanation. But then with a sinking feeling he would know that horrible though the truth might be he must face up to it. But despite all this he had a desire to see Mary for himself and confront the reality and maybe resolve the anger he felt. He arranged his departure with his usual efficiency, and after a sleepless night in which he had many confusing dreams, some of which still lingered to trouble him with snatches of Mary and his dead wife, he set off on the journey which would eventually take him back to London.

As he approached Lisbon his spirits lifted a little and once again he was reminded just why it was generally considered to be one of the most beautiful cities in the world. He looked at it standing on seven hills like Rome, set in a winding pattern of rivers cascading through wild gorges banked by tall trees festooned with vines, and he breathed in the exotic fragrance of the swords of pomegranate, fig and almond trees that spread as far as the eye could see, interspersed with a foam of orange blossom, mimosa and camellias. In the distance, rising above it all, he saw the ornate spires and roofs of the stately palaces and churches lit by the last magnificent rays on an evening sun.

He thought how he had planned to bring Mary here one day as his wife, and then he wondered if God were punishing him for ever having formed such a dream in his mind while Magdalena still lived. And again he confronted the thought of Mary with a child, someone else's child, the child who should have been his; and yet again Mary's betrayal struck his heart like a dagger. Like a knife in the wound, he heard the first poignant song of the nightingales, for which Lisbon was so famous, trilling their first serenade and he remembered Mary's sweet voice as she had sung in her father's home and as she had amused and soothed the Queen on long winter evenings. He tried to control his emotions but the sadness of it overwhelmed him and, head in hands, he whispered her name and felt his chest constricted with grief.

CHAPTER TWENTY-SEVEN

The London to which Fernando returned shocked him deeply. After the months away he had forgotten how dirty it was. The burning of sea coal left a thick greasy slime on buildings and on dull days, when the sky hung heavily – and this was such a day – the very air had a dank, malodorous, sulphurous smell. Shanty towns still populated the river banks, where the homeless victims of the great fire eked out a miserable existence, and effluent clogged the many small tributaries of the river and the foul water, thick as mud, moved hardly at all.

To his horror the vile pollution had now begun to affect the main river. The many boats, the life force of the once great city, now circumnavigated floating islands of filthy waste. The stench was overwhelming, and the river's dark secrets often revealed a rotting corpse, and as Fernando's coach crossed the rackety bridge at Lambeth to make its way to the Palace of Whitehall the dreadful sight of the bloated figure of a woman floated under the bridge, arms outstretched. He saw it emerge the other side, its face horrible in a rictus grimace, the features hardly distinguishable as human. The postillion called down as the unmistakable stench of decay began to infiltrate the carriage, 'Close your windows, Your Grace, there is more where that came from.'

Fernando put his scented handkerchief to his mouth and nose and thankfully pulled up the glass window of the Queen's coach, grateful for the latest innovation in travel. When he had left London carriages were still open to the elements and the stench of the crowd would be overpowering, so this as least was an improvement.

The coach made its way through the narrow streets, inhabited by a proliferation of starving people. Their progress was impeded by a seething mass of beggars and he was particularly horrified by the children and mothers with babes in arms. He felt totally engulfed by the horror of the city to which he had returned and had it not been for the thought of the Queen who awaited him and to whom his devotion was without question, and had he not been imbued with a sense of duty, he would have willingly returned to his beloved Lisbon at once.

*   *   *

The atmosphere in the palace, with its careless affluence, was in stark contrast to the scenes of hardship on the streets. The Queen received him without delay and as two footmen opened the double doors to her apartments he was greeted by a reassuring scene.

Catherine sat amidst her ladies in an exotic puff of silk skirts. At the centre was some needlework, each of her ladies working on a corner. Two maids stood outside the circle with a selection of many coloured silks draped over their arms. They quietly circulated, extracting the chosen colour and handing it to each lady. There was a low murmur of conversation and a lutist sat on a high stool in the window. The room was suffused with the delicate smell of orange blossom from a group of trees set in large Chinese pots.

The Queen rose eagerly when Fernando was announced, and came warmly towards him. Genuinely pleased to see her again, he smiled broadly and then bent low in the most reverential of bows. Her ladies rose from their work in perfect unison and bent in a communal curtsy, with the rich sound of silk as their voluminous skirts swept the floor. He quickly cast his eye over the group, his heart racing, despite his resolution to ignore Mary with feigned cold indifference should she be amongst them. He saw quickly that she was not there and a strange weight descended on his heart. The challenge of seeing her had been a recurring theme in his mind as much as he had tried to dismiss it.

'It is good to have you back with us, Fernando, my dear

friend,' said Catherine effusively. 'As you will have seen, things are much changed here. The loss of Lord Clarendon is something we feel very deeply and I have need of wise council.'

An anxious look flashed across the Queen's face and she looked meaningfully at Fernando as he thought about Lord Clarendon's shameful treatment.

'Yes, Your Majesty,' he replied solemnly. 'He was a good man, but it would appear he had become expendable, but never fear, Madam,' he hurried on quickly, 'I shall serve you loyally and Portugal's power and influence is much enhanced by Lord Sandwich's cleverly negotiated peace with Spain. There are some things which are not so easily moved,' he reassured her as she led the way to her work table on which lay piles of documents which he suspected had been waiting for his appraisal.

'As you will see,' she said disconsolately, pointing to the papers, 'I have much to do, and there are factions at court that worry me. As you know, my faith . . . our faith,' she went on in a low voice as her ladies resumed a comforting conversation and the lutist continued to play, 'it is the thing from which I cannot waver and I know His Majesty is ever alert to the dangers that lurk in every corner for those who are loyal to His Holiness in Rome. So many good men prohibited from public office by these ridiculous acts of the English Parliament.'

'I feel deeply for your husband, Madam,' said Fernando. 'Lord Clarendon's visionary conception of a balance between The Crown and Parliament has become a poisoned chalice. It is lucky,' he laughed sardonically, 'that no such notion has undermined the concept of the absolute power of the crown in our own country.'

There was a sudden commotion outside the door as the room heard the excited canine squeals that usually announced the arrival of the King. The door opened and a squirming mass of silky spaniels tumbled into the room. It occurred to Fernando, as the King came in exuding the enormous and undeniable charismatic presence, that such a man was uniquely unusual, a man equally at ease with the lowest or the highest of God's creatures, and a man, he thought ruefully, who would inspire unconditional love from a woman.

He observed the Queen's delighted blushes as her husband greeted her, the way she looked adoringly at him, seemingly forgiving of his blatant unfaithfulness but confident in the bond of friendship they had between them. He felt a twist in his stomach as he thought of the way Mary had betrayed him, and he more faithful than the King could ever be. Surely she had realised that he felt nothing but respect for her. Eventually he would have married her and the child she had borne so shamefully would have been his.

'My dear Fernando, how good it is to see you,' the King exclaimed, affecting the room with his casual enthusiasm. He was formally dressed in a dark green doublet and long frock coat, his well-shaped white-stockinged legs ending in elaborate high-heeled shoes with large velvet bows. His thick shiny black periwig framed his dark rather saturnine features with the trace of a slightly ironic smile which always played on his ample lips. There was no denying the sheer animal magnetism of the man and the air of supreme confidence. But it was the man's tolerance which Fernando envied most. He was almost unshockable. 'It is an honour to return and serve Her Majesty,' replied Fernando formally, aware of the trap so often taken by those who returned the King's casualness with like, recalling the many occasions when he had seen the way the royal countenance could so easily turn to icy reproval.

'So . . . ' intoned the King with a long look, 'there are, I hope, other matters which are requiring His Grace's attention, matters he would do well to consider, matters which have caused us concern,' Charles went on, whilst catching the Queen's eye and making a discrete nod.

At first Fernando was genuinely baffled and then it came to him that the King must be referring to Mary. He realised that, much as he would prefer to keep this affair secret, he would do well to explain himself to the King in private. A general conversation commenced and shortly the King took his leave to attend the theatre. The purpose of his visit had been to ask the Queen to accompany him. After a little hesitation she agreed and Fernando was dismissed. Left to his own devices, and after some thought, he decided to attend the play himself, having missed the sophistication of the King's Theatre for so many months.

CHAPTER TWENTY-EIGHT

'I have a note for you, Madam,' said Julia, Mrs Behn's maid. Mary was too excited, getting dressed in her new finery for an evening at the King's Theatre, to think about a note and carelessly pushed it aside amongst the many bottles and brushes on her dressing table. 'No, Madam,' Julia insisted, 'you must read it now.'

Mary reluctantly took the note and read it, admiring a fine and beautifully written script.

'It is from Mrs Behn herself and she is coming here to see me and at once,' she cried in a fluster, looking up at Julia's reflection in the mirror. 'Why did you not tell me, girl?' she asked reprovingly. 'You must know she is a heroine to me. I didn't even know she was in England.'

'I didn't know myself, Madam,' said Julia hastily. 'As you well know, she has been in a disgusting debtor's prison in Antwerp and all for a few poxy debts that were not for her own benefit but for the King's work. It has all happened so suddenly. A benefactor has paid them all off and my beloved mistress is back in England where she belongs.'

Within minutes there was a loud knock at the door of Mary's apartment. Julia rushed to open it and a footman whispered the name of the visitor. 'It's her, Madam,' cried Julia breathlessly. 'Shall I show her in, Madam?'

'Of course,' said Mary, jumping up from her stool, her heart beating fast in anticipation. She could never have imagined such a meeting out of the blue. Mrs Behn had become as a beacon to her, beckoning her to a life of exciting independence. A glamorous figure whose exploits were way beyond the aspirations of most English women. Her mind raced as she considered the possible reasons for such an honour.

And there she was! Aphra Behn. A woman soon to become one of the most celebrated women of her age. There were many moments in Mary's life which would be indelibly etched, but the visual impact of Aphra was one which she would always treasure.

She was dressed like no other woman Mary had ever seen. A dramatic configuration of silks in subtly blended tones of purple, vermillion, peacock blue and emerald green were cleverly swathed from her bodice to her flowing skirt. Emerging from the graceful concoction were a pair of the finest shoulders and a face of striking beauty. Large intelligent dark eyes, a perfect nose and full smiling lips; her luxurious dark hair was casually dressed and caught each side of her head with jewelled combs from which sprung twirling feathers on which many little precious stones danced and twinkled in the light. Mary involuntarily held her breath as she dipped a curtsy.

'Mary Boynton,' said Aphra in a mellifluous tone. 'Please forgive the intrusion, but I am on my way to the theatre, as I know are you, and I wanted to have a chance to speak to you before we met in such a public place.'

'Please do not apologise,' said Mary in a voice rich with emotion. 'I have admired you for so long. There are many things we have in common although not alas your gift with writing.'

'Would you mind if we sat down, my dear, we need not hurry, it is very chaotic at the theatre today. Mr Dryden's new play has had to be reworked and I know it will be very late in starting.'

'My manners have failed me,' said Mary apologetically. 'Julia, fetch us some wine and we will draw our chairs to the fire,' added Mary hastily.

'Now, Mary, if I may call you that,' Aphra began. 'There is so much I would say to you, because I have heard so much about you in Julia's letters, and naturally I know what is going on in your life at the moment . . . ' Aphra paused for moment, observing that Mary was looking down awkwardly. 'I do not mean your private life, Mary, although I do know a little of it,' she went on delicately. 'No . . . that is to say, perhaps I feel protective towards other women when I think of the way I myself have been abused for doing a man's work a deal better than most men could do it.'

'Naturally there are moments when I am fearful about the task I have been given,' said Mary tentatively. 'But the King makes me feel, I hope not erroneously, that I will be well protected. And my own father has risked much in the service of the King. It is if you like in my blood.'

'Let me be frank,' said Aphra. 'I have felt it was my duty to talk to you because if you are in any way thinking that you should perhaps take me as an example I should point out the many differences in both our circumstances and our options.'

Aphra had been carefully informed about Mary Boynton because it was her job to know things about people and she had become somewhat intrigued by this apparently simple English girl who had become one of the inner sanctum of the King's informers. There was also the question of Julia her maid, who would want to return to her service now that her life had been restored. This would be significant loss to Mary and Aphra was a woman of honour and wanted to effect this in a kindly way. But mostly she had taken a view about this young and delightful woman and the main purpose of her visit was to share it with Mary herself.

Mary on the other hand was not of a mind to take any dissuasion. She had become so fired up about her new role, intoxicated by the excitement of it all. She was also enamoured by her new and seemingly close friendship with the King. To acclimatise herself to the idea that Fernando had forsaken her, and she would have to fend for herself, had been a process which had caused her much anguish.

Aphra was now in her late twenties, some ten years older than Mary. She looked at the girl carefully and felt an unexpected rush of concern. She recognised that Mary was in her prime; her beauty surprisingly unaffected by what Aphra knew must have been a series of challenging events. She knew that the girl had borne a child who was now being reared in the country. But there was nothing so unusual in that. Unwanted pregnancies were commonplace and many children were reared in large families where their true parentage was never discussed.

Aphra had never borne a child, despite her now and then marriages. It was a sadness for her, and she had come to accept that motherhood and the happiness of a settled domestic life were never going to be an option for her; her satisfaction would be achieved through her writing and everything that her life had thrown at her was a path to this end.

But Mary was different; Rupert Willoughby was madly in love with her; he would be an eminently suitable match for any girl since his services to the King were soon to be amply rewarded and, besides which, he was no bigot. Given his involvement in the undercover work he had undertaken, he would most certainly know about Mary's indiscretion and it had not, as yet, dampened his ardour. Aphra knew all about the Portuguese diplomat who was almost certainly the father and looking at Mary she doubted that the girl would have been happy with the man. She was so very English, the epitome of a well-bought-up young woman who could rightly expect her life to proceed with a delightful structured happiness, surrounded by family and fortune. This is what Aphra would have liked herself, but for her the road had been so very different. Suddenly she looked at this young woman and wanted to save her.

'Don't do this,' she blurted. 'I had no choice Mary,' she went on while Mary looked at her in astonishment. 'My mother was a humble wet nurse to a noble family, we had nothing, I was brought up with the family, but when it came to the point I had acquired a taste for comfortable living but I had no way to expect it. I have had to live by my wits. The world does not make allowances just because a girl is clever and pretty. Oh no! That is not enough. I have had to do things I would not wish for you, Mary Boynton, and you, my dear, have no need to stoop so low, for that is what it is. Marry your Rupert, have a brood of beautiful children to be brothers and sisters to the child you have, make beautiful gardens. Keep your beauty and your youth . . . how I envy you that.'

Mary held her breath. She was shocked by the outburst, her initial reaction being one of indignation. How dare this woman, for all her fame and brilliance, speak to her so frankly?

'I really do not think you are in a position to have an opinion about my life,' she retorted petulantly, regretting the words almost before they were spoken.

Aphra was not offended by Mary's rebuff, she knew in her heart that the girl had listened carefully to her warnings and she had a feeling that this was not the last time she would speak to Mary about her plans. She took her leave, gracefully kissing Mary on both cheeks.

'I will see you at the theatre,' she said with a bright smile and left in a swirl of exotic skirts. Mary gazed after her with mixed emotions, her thoughts sharply interrupted when Julia handed her her fan and her shawl.

*   *   *

The heat from the many hundreds of candles and an equal number of over-heated bodies hit Mary in the face like the opening of a furnace door. Fantastic as it might seem for one who had been resident in the louche hedonistic court of White-hall with its thespian leanings, Mary had never yet attended the theatre. And she only came now because Rupert had explained to her, 'Mary, you no longer have the option to play the role of a shy young maid, you have to be part of life as it is lived at court, if you are to be of any use to the King.' She reminded herself of his words as she pressed to his strong purposeful back that jostled its way through the throng to get to the upper story of the King's Theatre.

'Stick close to me, Mary,' he called over his shoulder, 'this is one place in the world where rank plays no part.

They forged on and the press of bodies became thicker and orange sellers screeched their wares 'Buy my oranges, Sir,' cried one, thrusting her large over-exposed bosoms into his face with a look that suggested more than the sale of oranges.

'Out of my way, baggage, another time when I am not accompanied by a lady,' replied Rupert with a twinkle.

'My, Sir, that was more than a little familiar,' cried Mary primly.

'A mere jest,' replied Rupert. 'Only a fool would meddle with those jades, not a one of them is free from the pox.'

'Is that so, then I fear for the King, as I understand his latest flirtation is with the pretty Nell whom we shall see on the stage today, and she started life as an orange seller,' said Mary boldly.

They pushed their way up a narrow staircase and made their way to the King's box at the centre of a curved gallery. The seats were of rich velvet plush and the box was heavily decorated with the King's arms and garlands of ornate gilt flowers and cherubs, some entwined in positions leaving little to the imagination. The stage was set for the production of *The Virgin Martyr*, the proscenium arch painted as an allegorical land of the gods, the lush dark red velvet curtains waiting to rise at a sign from the King.

As they took their seats, the crowd below peered round and amidst much pointing Mary realised she was the centre of attention.

'There you are, Mary,' said Rupert proprietarily, basking in the pleasure of escorting such a notable beauty, 'your first taste of the kind of attention you deserve. I meant to say to you that I have never seen you look so handsome. The gown is beautiful, and I am proud to escort you.'

'You are most kind, but I can't think why they are all staring at us, and I am not so sure that I care for it,' said Mary demurely. But she had to admit that she was thoroughly enjoying herself, particularly because the Queen's dressmaker had made her a gown which surpassed any she could see in the other boxes. All eyes were also directed at her, with much flashing of fans and whispering. She began to feel quite heated with the excitement of it all and opened the beautifully painted fan Fernando had given to her on her name day the previous year. Aphra's cautionary words were totally banished from her mind.

As she was fanning her face, Rupert noticed little beads of perspiration on her neck and before he could stop himself, he lifted his hand and gently moved the thick ringlets of hair that Mrs Behn's maid had created in the French style, coaxing them behind her head. Mary turned in surprise and caught his eye. Seeing the explicit and tender expression on his face she felt a thrill of excitement and smiled back at him.

Among the chattering observers was Fernando. At first he had not recognised the beautiful and sophisticated woman in the box, and only when he saw the fan in the flickering exotic light from the candles did he see it was Mary. He caught his breath and watched as the dashing young man at her side lifted her hair in what was without doubt an intimate gesture. Mary turned and as she smiled at the man he knew at once this was the father of the child she had borne and there they were brazenly making a spectacle of themselves for the entire world to see. He felt something akin to hate at that moment, and then he dismissed the emotion and tried to substitute it with indifference, for he knew only too well that such feelings could only erode his own honour. But try as he might any enjoyment he might have had from the play disappeared in an instant.

In striking contrast, Mary was having the time of her life. She was beginning to enjoy this glamorous role that life had so strangely thrust upon her; she was almost giddy with excitement. She looked about her and asked Rupert about the women below in the pit, as she could see one of them pointing at her.

'Why are they wearing masks?' she asked.

'They are ladies of pleasure,' Rupert answered perfunctorily.

'So tell me about this play,' said Mary, changing the subject, not wishing to explore the matter of the women and thinking to herself that there was not much to put between them and the exotic figure of Lady Castlemaine who had just made a dramatic entrance into one of the boxes.

'Upon my word, *The Virgin Martyr* is hardly the sort of play with which Her Ladyship might be thought to empathise,' laughed Rupert, following Mary's gaze.

Before Mary had a chance to reply a wave of anticipation took over and the King arrived with a flourish of perfumed silks and the Queen's jewels flashed in the light from the candles. The audience stood and bowed and curtsied as he and the Queen took their seats.

'Just look,' Rupert whispered as the curtain went up, 'the Lady Castlemiane's jewels far outshine the Queen's and note the King does not acknowledge her while he fondly holds the Queen's little hand.'

As they were whispering, the King looked about him and caught Mary's eye. He slowly bowed his head to her in a gracious acknowledgement. Yet again all heads seemed to turn to stare at her and she felt a heady mixture of unbelievable delight and happiness. She knew that this very public greeting from the King was a significant gesture. Whether she liked it or not she was now one of the inner circle; there was no going back. Instinctively she gave a demure and gracious nod. Of the many people who saw this exchange the two most affected were Fernando and Lady Castlemaine, both drawing quite the wrong conclusions.

While Mary's head whirled the play had begun in earnest, and soon she found herself engrossed in the story.

'The heroine is played by Becke, but you wait, we have treat in store. The King's new mistress, Nell Gwyne, plays the part of the angel and all eyes will be for her because that is why half the people are here,' whispered Rupert.

Mary found herself increasingly annoyed by the noisy chatter from the audience which meant the players had to shout to make themselves heard above the din and then, as if by magic, there was silence as the figure of the angel came down from heaven in a spectacular descent which Mary later found out was achieved with an elaborate system of ropes and pulleys. But it was not just the exquisite elegance with which the beautiful Nell performed her astonishing semblance of flying but the accompaniment of music, a mixture of delicate recorders played with a dextrous skill which made them sound ethereal, a sound so heavenly that Mary felt as if she might faint with emotion. It reminded her of Anthony, of their fresh untainted love with all the starry promise of unblemished youth, so different from the life she had now. For a moment she wished for the quiet of an ordinary life and she thought of Phillip and for a minute thought she might be sick with the unbearable heartache of separation. As the music continued to wash over her, the silence in the hitherto inattentive throng continued and even the rabble in the pit stood transfixed. For the rest of the play the music rang in Mary's ears, she could not take her eyes of little Nell, the King's new mistress.

'She is so tiny but she moves like acrobat,' she whispered to Rupert, 'and just look at the way the King stares at her.'

'She may be tiny but she has the heart of a lion. You will see how the people love her, she shines like a beacon in this place,' said Rupert.

Mary looked at him sharply. 'If I didn't know better I would say you were enamoured of little Nell yourself,' said Mary with a laugh.

'She may be a whore, but for all that she is a good woman, and I would be as discreet and loyal to her as I would to any high ranking lady. But . . . probably,' he mused, 'rather more so.' Just then there was a commotion as a drunken man in the pit where the rabble stood hurled a rotten egg in the direction of Lady Castlemaine. It splattered on a pillar just by her face and a rousing cheer came from below. Mary shot a look at the King who appeared to be enjoying the event hugely.

'Do you see what I mean?' whispered Rupert. 'There is no greater barometer than the people and see how they hate that woman. It is the hypocrisy which will be her downfall.' In that moment Mary paled as she remembered Aphra's words and saw the hard edge of life in the King's circle.

*   *   *

'Madam, His Majesty requires you to attend him in his quarters as soon as possible, I believe the matter is urgent,' said Julia, who had not yet resumed her employment with Aphra. It was late and Mary had prepared herself for bed, but she knew that this was a royal command and she was well aware that the King kept a completely different timetable from that of the Queen, often rising early, before light, to walk in the parks with his dogs, sometimes sleeping during the day and seldom retiring before the early hours. He tended to be at his most active later in the day and meetings would be arranged at a moments notice, long after people had gone to bed. And thanks to his obsession with the many clocks he had collected he was a punctilious time keeper. To be late was to incur incalculable wrath.

'What took you so long?' the King asked as Mary was announced. He stood in his chemise without his periwig, his large features accentuated by his close cropped hair.

'I came as quickly as I could the moment I had Your Majesty's summons but I had prepared for bed,' replied Mary falteringly.

'Come, come, I am merely jesting with you, my dear,' coaxed the King with a laugh. 'Now take a seat here by the table; I sent for you because I have some papers from Antwerp and I have nobody to decode them for me,' the King went on hurriedly. 'I think they are important and must understand them before tomorrow, forgive me my dear . . . for disturbing you at such an hour.'

Mary could feel the King's breath on her neck as she set to work translating the code. The documents used the system devised by Aphra Behn and Mary's knowledge of Greek enabled her to work with a speed which had already impressed the King. There was news of a plot by disaffected Parliamentarians to implicate the King in a Catholic conspiracy and names of several innocent men about whom a web of lies was being woven.

'But these men are noble and loyal. How could any of them be plotting such things?' asked Mary in disbelief. She knew of some of them, particularly Lord Stafford, an old friend of her father's who lived quietly on his estates with his books.

'Exactly so,' agreed the King. 'But the best way of undermining the Monarchy is to spread distrust among friends. You will see that most of these men mentioned are loyal Catholics.'

The room was warm and the relaxed proximity of the King disturbed Mary. Despite this, she was determined to concentrate, and before long all the documents had been deciphered. No notes were taken, and Mary soon realised that the King had a formidable memory and she was soon to find out that this applied to all things.

'Mary, now that we have finished that odious task, tell me something . . . ' His tone was enquiring, he paused thoughtfully and looked at her directly. For a moment she thought he was going to kiss her, her mind raced considering how she might respond. The faces of the three men who had come into her life, two who had left her and the third, the dependable Rupert, who had begun to press his suit, flitted through her consciousness, and then she looked at the King in his chemise, a marked stubble on his dark skin, his handsome, compelling face heavily etched with a map of good living, and she decided in an instant that she would refuse him, knowing full well that her position would at once be compromised, since she had neither the rank of Lady Frances Stuart nor, for that matter, Lady Castlemaine. She knew that the extraordinary friendship she had enjoyed with the King would be dented by such a rebuff. But, as if reading her thoughts, the King surprised her by continuing on quite another matter.

'Your child, Mary. I hear news from your father, he has just delivered another quantity of hemp to the navy and we have been corresponding, we are quite open and he has mentioned your child who fares well, I am told.'

Mary's heart gave a lurch at the thought of her baby, realising that in order to survive the situation she had had to harden her heart in a way that was completely at odds with her true nature; sometimes she could hardly believe her own callousness. She had put off taking time to visit her family at Sailing Hall, knowing that to be parted a second time would be impossible. She had even stopped reading Charlotte's letters with their descriptions of Phillip's progress.

'Yes, Your Majesty. I can hardly bear to think of my son growing up without me. It is so cruel. But I know it is for his own good. He is much loved by my father and stepmother and they have a child of their own not more than a year older,' said Mary.

The King sighed audibly, thinking of his large clutch of children, all borne by his different mistresses and all of whom he loved dearly and kept close to him. He did not like this business of Mary being separated from her child, and, truth to tell, Rupert Willoughby had a pretty good idea of just what Mary's dark secret actually was and the King had not been slow to suggest to the man that regularising the girl's life would meet with the Royal approval and all that implied.

'Well, Mary, I have been thinking about you and especially recently,' the King persisted. 'Your friend Rupert has spoken to me about you, assuming I suppose that I have knowledge about your past. I gather you have told him nothing, although the court, of course, has some theories about you, since to give them nothing is to invite a hornet's nest of gossip. Not a good strategy my dear, misinformation is the best path.'

'Your Majesty is very kind to bother with my affairs, but why should I tell Rupert the details of my past?' Mary asked.

'For the simple reason that he wants to marry you,' said the King with an avuncular smile.

Mary's reaction was twofold, firstly relief that her relationship with the King was not going to be jeopardised by the issue of an unwelcome rebuff and secondly a definite sense of pleasure that Rupert should have seen fit to discuss his proposal with the King. It reinforced the impression that the King had a paternal interest in her and consequently she had enjoyed an implicit protection which was known and respected by the court.

'What do you think I should do?' asked Mary bluntly.

'You should tell him everything. There is no great shame attached, Mary. After all who among the court can safely say who their father is?' he laughed. 'The existence of a gold band does not make the sin any less, if sin it really is,' he quipped.

'Rupert is a good man. How do you think he would feel about another man's child?' asked Mary.

'Firstly Mary, there is something you should know,' said the King. 'His Grace the Duke is back in London. In fact he has been here for some time and I have seen the determined way he has avoided you. In truth I have been amazed at how he has managed it since you are usually in attendance upon the Queen.'

Mary felt herself go cold. The realisation that Fernando had been so close to her, and not sought her out, smacked of cowardice, even if he believed the stories he must have heard, about her child, his child, he had so little love for her that he had believed them all. No instinct told him of her constancy. And now he was free, it seemed to Mary that his entire courtship of her must have been based on a lie; he had made love to her in her father's house within the safety of his marriage and now that that excuse had gone, he did not even have the honesty to come to her and find out the truth for himself.

'I care not that he has avoided me, Your Majesty knows the truth. If a man is to believe false rumours after all that passed between us then he is worth nothing to me,' said Mary with a complete finality.

'That is a decision you will have to make for yourself but often a happy life will grow from a compromise! I know this more than any man living,' said the King.

'You have reminded me, Sir, my child needs me. I will beg leave of Her Majesty to visit my father, and I will talk to him about Rupert. My father is a wise man and his guidance will be the deciding factor,' said Mary, wanting go to her own quarters to collect her thoughts. 'And I thank you, Sir, for all your kindness. I will be your loyal servant.' Mary had stood up. Straightening her skirts as if to leave, she waited for the King's dismissal. He looked at her for a moment, thinking how the girl had grown in stature; she betrayed nothing of the emotions she must be feeling. She would make a fine Duchess, he ruminated.

'A thought, Mary,' he said slowly. 'There are more ways than one to become a Duchess. You may go, Mary, and I shall speak to the Queen. Convey the royal greeting to your father. He deserves a daughter like you.'

Mary stood outside the door of the King's apartment for a moment. She had a picture of Rupert's face, and felt warm sensation of pleasure. It was not like the giddy whirl of desire she had experienced with Fernando. But it was a safe, confident feeling, as if all would be well with the world if he were in it. She straightened her shoulders and walked purposefully towards the Queen's rooms to ask permission to leave for the country as soon as possible. It would give her time to think.

CHAPTER TWENTY NINE

Norfolk, June 1668

'Did you ever see such a splendid boy,' cried Sir Miles proudly. Phillip was celebrating his first birthday. It was high summer and the air was heavy with the lush bloom of early summer. The family was gathered on the grass in front of the house. Jayne had been delighted to discover that Charlotte, her temporary mistress, for that is what she considered her to be, had been reared in the simple country ways that encouraged fresh air and sun for children, unlike the nobility, who hid from it for all manner of ridiculous reasons.

Sir Miles had commissioned a score of men to cut the long grass with shears before the sun was up, a bold innovation, since few houses approved of grass as a place to sit or play. Most gardens consisted of long formal avenues of gravel and shaded terraces, but little Emily now played with her one-year-old nephew in the lush green. The previous week he had astonished them all by taking his first steps, and Jayne had immediately asked Charlotte's permission to shorten the skirts of the dresses that all noble infants wore regardless of sex, the only observable concession to maleness being a little gold earring in the right ear.

'Just look at those sturdy legs,' enthused Jayne proudly.

'Yes, and one day he'll be striding through those hemp marshes like a true Boynton,' Sir Miles added, catching Charlotte's eye.

She in turn caught a nervous glance from Jayne, who looked down awkwardly. Later, when Sir Miles had left the family to go to his study to read some important documents just delivered by coach from London, the two women retired under the shade of a weeping beech tree and watched the children tumbling in the grass. Each was working on a patchwork quilt – tiny hexagonal pieces were now to be embroidered in gold thread with the family crest and initials.

'I worry about him and the child,' said Charlotte, stabbing at the cloth with her needle and pricking her finger. 'He must know that one day Phillip will be taken from us,' she went on, sucking the salty blood from the wound.

'Well, maybe so,' said Jayne cautiously. 'But as time goes on I am beginning to doubt that His Grace will claim the boy now, and in my way of thinking it's for the best.'

'What do you mean, Jayne? Surely you think it would be right for the Duke to marry Mary and give Phillip a father?' said Charlotte incredulously.

'There are more ways to skin a cat,' said Jayne darkly. 'Miss Mary, or Mrs Mary as I must now call her, has found favour at court or she would have come to see us before now, and chances are she has a fleet of fine gentlemen asking for her hand.'

'But what about the child? Do you think all those grand ladies and gentlemen will turn a blind eye to a child born out of wedlock?' asked Charlotte , blushing slightly as she recalled her passionate liaison with Sir Miles whilst his wife was still living.

'It's like this, My Lady,' said Jayne through gritted teeth. 'People are the same, it's just the clothes that are different, and from what I saw, Miss Mary is a paragon compared to those other trollops with their high and mighty ways. If His Grace was a true gentleman he would have seen the goodness in her, but he deserted her and I cannot forgive him for that and I would not want our little Phillip to have such a father.'

Before they could continue, they heard footsteps on the gravel path approaching the grass. They both looked up at the same time. Sir Miles was not alone. He was accompanied by a familiar figure. At first Charlotte did not recognise him and then she stood and curtsied.

'Why Mr Willoughby,' she smiled. For some reason she knew at once why he had come.

'Rupert has come to see me, Charlotte, but he wanted to greet you first,' said Sir Miles.

Charlotte greeted the newcomer, although her mood had become slightly hesitant, a reaction which was reinforced when he bent down to speak to the children. Little Emily gave him a wobbly curtsy, something she had proudly mastered in the last few weeks. And then his eye fell on Phillip, who peeped shyly from behind Jayne's skirts.

'So how old is the little fellow now?' Rupert asked gently.

'He is one year old today, Sir,' replied Emily perkily, on his behalf.

'Upon my word he is a sturdy fellow,' said Rupert.

Charlotte studied Rupert's interest in the child, registering the kindly way he knelt down to speak to the children. She was a good judge of character, and Miles had taken to using her to appraise people about whom he was concerned. As he often remarked, 'She can see into a soul as if it were a window.'

What Charlotte saw, as Rupert walked towards her, was a good, dependable, honest man; a man of courage. After all, he had served his King well on many dangerous missions. But at the same time his clean, almost simple country clothes suggested a desire to be an ordinary country gentleman. In an instant she knew just what he might represent for Mary for that was indeed, without doubt, the reason for his visit.

'Will you be staying with us for long?' she asked him.

'That rather depends,' he replied carefully.

'Oh, I see. I will not ask you upon what, for I dare say there is a matter you have to discuss with Sir Miles,' she answered quickly.

*   *   *

'I would like your permission to ask Mary to be my wife,' said Rupert.

He was alone with Sir Miles in his study. The room brought

back many memories of that fearful night when his friend Jan had been murdered. He remembered the raw horror of it, but through it all the seraphic face of Mary shone with a beauty which even compelled him before he had realised it was a girl and not a young boy who accompanied Sir Miles on the rescue. He had fallen in love with her in a split second and then when they had come to her father's house he had fallen in love with all that as well.

When his own family had fled from Cromwell to join the small poverty-stricken community of Royalists living abroad, the family estates had been confiscated, but later returned to them by Charles at the Restoration, a matter which naturally, in the light of Rupert's request, was of considerable interest to Sir Miles.

'Firstly,' said Sir Miles steadily, trying to keep the speed of his thoughts from betraying too much excitement at what he instantly perceived to be the answer to all the family problems, 'does Mary know that you are here?'

'No, Sir, she does not,' said Rupert truthfully. He could hear the children playing in the garden and his thoughts kept darting to the prospect that there was just a chance that those comforting sounds intermingled with the lazy birdsong from the hot summer afternoon might be a template for the future.

'Well, I am not sure about that,' said Sir Miles. 'Mary has led a very independent life, and it is not for me to familiarise you with her personal affairs . . . certain obligations which would most definitely have a bearing on an answer to your question.'

'If by that you mean your grandson,' said Rupert frankly, 'you need have no fears on that count. His Majesty has told me the whole story. You see, when people are engaged in the kind of work we do for the King there can be no secrets, lives depend on trust . . .' he was about to elucidate but Sir Miles held up a hand to interrupt him.

'If we are speaking of trust you obviously know who is the father of Mary's child,' said Sir Miles with what he considered necessary frankness.

'I do, Sir,' said Rupert, without a hint of embarrassment.

'It is a disappointing tale. You see I trusted the man in the same way that Mary did but it appears I was wrong,' Sir Miles said bitterly.

'I do not know His Grace personally, but I do know that, for whatever reason, he has proved himself to be unworthy of your daughter,' said Rupert crisply.

'And you, do you think you are worthy of my daughter? Remember before you answer she will not come alone,' asked Sir Miles.

'I cannot offer her much in the way of worldly goods,' Rupert explained, 'for I am a younger son, but the King is generous to those who serve him loyally and I am not without prospects. In fact he has generously indicated that I will be given a substantial title very soon,' Rupert assured him.

'I am sure that is true and you deserve it, you are a brave man,' said Sir Miles approvingly.

'But it must be said,' said Rupert quickly, 'that were your daughter to accept me, I would not wish her to continue her work at court. But I have a feeling that she does not quite fit in the murky pool that swirls about the King. Things are not easy at the moment and it is not fitting for a woman to be risking so much, and especially a young mother.'

Sir Miles was pleased at the reference to a young mother. Sometimes he almost forgot that Phillip was not his own son, and the reminder of Mary's responsibilities was timely.

They continued to talk well into evening, and by the time the bell rang for family prayers in the great hall, Sir Miles had formed a more than favourable impression of Rupert; he felt confident that although he lacked the obvious worldly advantages of His Grace the Duke, he was a man of integrity and would care for and love his daughter and her child. There would even be a possibility of life at Sailing continuing in the happy vein established, but with the embellishment of a son-in-law and the return of his daughter.

CHAPTER THIRTY

'Your Majesty,' said Fernando, bowing low and deliberately avoiding the King's direct gaze since he had an intuition that the summons was by way of reproof. Of course he knew he should have requested an audience with the King immediately after his return to London, but his thoughts had been in turmoil. He had, so far, managed to avoid contact with Mary; but he had seen her at a distance and references to her, of which there had been a number, had been flattering and respectful. So much so that he had soon realised that the comparatively unknown girl with whom he had fallen in love had experienced a metamorphosis into a woman of power and stature, an insider in the King's privileged circle.

To his surprise, her personal life was not alluded to, with the exception of what appeared to be a relationship with the young man Rupert Willoughby, a trusted and valued servant of the King who, it was rumoured, was soon to receive a substantial reward for his services.

'Let us not stand on formalities, a glass of wine, my dear Duke,' offered the King.

'I expect you are still thinking about the loss of your wife the Duchess, but a man has to think of the future,' the King went on, stopping abruptly, as if the next thought might not be agreeable to the Duke.

'Thank you, Your Majesty, it was, as you know, a long illness, but now she is at peace,' said Fernando hastily, aware that the King was leading him inexorably down a path he did not wish to explore.

The King nodded and handed Fernando a glass of wine,

taking time to consider the lines that now etched the man's face, and thinking he had aged since he left London. The King was sure that the deterioration in his appearance was not solely attributable to the death of a wife from whom he had more or less been separated. There was something the King wished to find out before they moved on to the pressing political matters on the agenda.

'Forgive me, but there is something I must ask you,' said the King. 'Mary Boynton, why is it that you have ignored her during the time you have been away, and even more mysteriously avoided all contact with her since your return?' The King's words hung suspended in the air. Whilst Fernando flinched and then laboriously formulated a response, the many clocks commenced a jangle of sound as the hour struck seven.

'I cannot tell you, Your Majesty, it would be indelicate,' stammered Fernando.

'Come along, man, such delicacy is misplaced,' said the King impatiently. 'The girl is the mother of your child, a child you have ignored. We look for more from a man of your station,' retorted the King with undisguised irritation.

Fernando stared at him, his face in a rictus of shock. His mind raced. The last thing he had imagined was a confrontation with the King about his private life, and how on earth did the King have such an intimate knowledge of his situation and secondly how could he have been fed such a story? 'Your Majesty,' he answered shakily, 'Mary Boynton's child is not mine; she concealed the event from me, ashamed of her guilt. I may as well tell you,' he stammered on, observing the King's expression change to one of marked displeasure. 'I heard nothing from her after I returned to be with my wife on her deathbed; only when Lord Stoneham came on a diplomatic mission did I find out the truth, the reason for her silence and then there were letters to the father. They were explicit, of a nature which she had kept hidden from me,' Fernando stopped. The King's face had hardened, his mouth tightening angrily.

'Pray continue, for I can see there is more and I will keep my council until you have finished,' said the King ominously.

'She had been unwell, visits to a certain establishment which – ' Fernando cleared his throat and looked away, embarrassed, for he was only too well aware that the King was rumoured to have infected his mistresses with the pox. 'A place,' he continued warily, 'which deals with complaints which would not have been possible had she been true, as I had supposed.'

'Until now I had taken you for a blaggard, but now I see you are a fool,' said the King icily. 'You have been fed a pack of lies and forgeries. I am afraid Lady Castlemaine may have been behind all this, but for you to be deceived by them is beyond me.'

'But I saw the letters. They were in her hand, why didn't she respond to my letters?' Fernando answered, his mind racing as he suddenly became aware of how he had been deceived. He realised at once what a fool he had been. He remembered the convenient arrival of Lord Stoneham and it slowly dawned on him the role his mother had obviously played. He had fallen for it all. He suddenly remembered Lady Castlemaine's face as he had rebuffed her. That, combined with his mother's wicked determination to control his life, had deprived him of his happiness and his child of a rightful father.

'I have no time to discuss this further,' said the King with an air of dismissal, seeing Fernando's ashen face. 'But as a diplomat you must be familiar with forgeries and deceptions. I can only suggest that her letters to you were intercepted by a third party, someone who did not want you to know that you had a healthy son from a woman who was pure and true and whom you have treated shamefully. Children are a gift whether they be born out of wedlock or not. But I do not tell you this for your sake but for the mother of your child, a child whose future is mapped without his father for I fear it is too late for you to make amends,' said the King finally.

*   *   *

'Forgive me, Father, for I have sinned,' said Fernando. He had left the King's apartments as soon as he was able.

Father Rodriguez listened behind the ornate confessional grid. 'Do you want to tell me of your sin?' came the solemn voice.

'I fell in love with a woman while my wife still lived. She is both beautiful and good and I have misjudged her. There is a child, my child, and he is to be given a name by another man. I have lost them both . . . this is my punishment, it was her beauty . . .'

'To love beauty is to love God, my son,' came the voice, 'all things are from God and are God.'

'But there is more. I have listened to the voice of evil. I have allowed my soul to become corrupted by lies and intrigue. I have thought only of myself. I have forgotten the laws of chivalry, I am ashamed at my own weakness.'

'Make a good act of contrition and ask for enlightenment,' said the father. 'I absolve you in the name of the Father and of the Holy Ghost, go in peace.'

Fernando crossed himself and walked down the aisle of the Queen's chapel, to the open door. A cold draft hit him and he shivered as if someone were walking over his grave. He felt anything but peaceful, he felt angry with himself for his own lack of judgement and consistency. A sense of desperation and urgency overwhelmed him. Without thinking, he rushed to the Queen's rooms. 'Tell Her Majesty it is the Duke Fernando,' he cried to the footman at the door. The Queen heard his voice, detecting the urgency of his cry; she came running forward as he entered the room.

'Why, Your Grace, what can the matter be?' she asked in genuine alarm. She could see perspiration running down his face. She had never seen the Duke in such a state. He was normally the pinnacle of calm and decorum and even now, in his obvious distress, he managed a deep bow.

'Mary; where is she?' he croaked breathlessly.

'You mean my maid of honour Mrs Boynton?' she asked coldly. Despite the lax morals at court, Catherine had been very distressed by Mary's plight and certainly disappointed by Fernando's behaviour.

'Yes. Mary; where is she? I have to see her at once,' he replied, noticing the prefix of Mrs, and realising that the Queen must know the whole story. 'She has left Whitehall to visit her family. It was time she did so, there were things which craved her attention, things which might well have deserved a little from Your Grace,' she said quietly. 'Your Grace may have the use of my coach at once, if he so desires,' she announced with hardly a raised eyebrow.

'Pray for me, Your Majesty,' he said gruffly, 'I have been foolish.'

'Your foolishness was in listening to my enemies, Your Grace, and, as ever in life, it is usually the innocent who suffer from such random wickedness. But you are a good man and Satan enjoys his work with men like you, go now and be true to your heart and your God, for the two should be indivisible.'

CHAPTER THIRTY-ONE

Mary was two days ahead of Fernando. She arrived in Norfolk in the evening and as the coach approached the lodge gates, the keepers ran out to see who the arrival might be. Through the approaching dusk they distinguished the royal arms on the side of the door and the driver and footman wearing the Queen's uniform. With cries of excitement they opened the gate as Mary leant out to greet them. They immediately rang the large bell kept to announce the arrival of visitors in order to prepare them at the big house.

Thomas heard it as he was stacking wood beside the fire in the big hall. Even in high summer the evenings were often cool with the sea mist from the marshes. Mary smelt the wood smoke mixed with the musky heavy dew on the garden. It was the poignant aroma of the place she loved. 'Home, I am home,' she heard herself say as a strange kind of unaccustomed happiness overwhelmed her. She had forgotten what real happiness actually was; she exhaled a long breath, as if exorcising herself of all the trauma of the last two years.

Her life since she first left home after Anthony's death seemed to flash past her as if in a dream. She did not recognise the woman who had led that life. It was not the real her. The real Mary was the girl who now jumped down from the coach door even before the footman had had a chance to lower the steps. She let her magnificent velvet cloak fall to the ground as her father, having heard the commotion, came running through the door. He had on his old working clothes and his undershirt was carelessly undone showing his craggy neck and overgrown sideburns. She jumped into his outstretched arms and he lifted her off her feet as she kissed his stubbly cheek, with the comforting smell of tobacco and country air and the joy she showed as he held her in his arms brought a lump in Thomas's throat.

'My dearest daughter,' Sir Miles said gruffly. 'God could not have brought a greater gift, my happiness is complete.'

Mary held on fast for a moment, unable to speak. She knew without question this, of all her homecomings, was profoundly significant. Decisions had to be made, but life was going to run her for once. Her guardian angel, in whom she had always believed, had woken from a long sleep and was there holding her hand. She took her father's arm and went into the house.

'Quick, Thomas, call the servants,' Sir Miles cried. The response was immediate. Bess came running from the kitchens, wiping her hands on her apron, the scullery boy followed, with Ned and Betty lolloping behind. They all came skidding to a halt on the polished flag floor.

The Queen's driver and footman were bringing in Mary's large boxes. 'You men must be in need of sustenance,' said Sir Miles, 'Thomas, send for the grooms to take the horses to the stables for food and water and a well-earned rest. You men will spend the night here. Let it never be said that Sailing Hall sends a man away without hospitality.'

The driver looked on at the happy scene, and felt its warm infectious glow, and while he was asking himself how the Lady Mary could ever have left such a home, Charlotte came running down the stairs and enfolded Mary in her arms. The man saw at once that this must be the mistress of the house, since she began issuing a variety of orders to the ever increasing throng of servants.

'Where are the children?' Mary asked excitedly, half expecting Jayne to come down the stairs accompanied by Emily and Phillip.

'They are in the nursery. They do not know of your arrival. Let's go up at once,' said Charlotte. She was wearing her simple sprigged house dress, and Mary longed to jettison her own ornate gown with its cumbersome sleeves and impractical plunging neck which always left her feeling chilled. She hadn't seen her baby for so long and doubted that he would even recognise her, but she had an instinctive desire that the meeting should establish in his mind a picture of her as she really wanted to be.

'Charlotte,' she said quickly, as they mounted the stairs, 'I must go to my room before I see Phillip and change into one of my old country dresses.'

'I shall come with you to help,' Charlotte agreed.

Within minutes, the old Mary emerged from her room and together she and Charlotte hurried down the long passages to the nursery. Mary's heart beat so fast with excitement she felt it might burst from her chest. Soon they were at the door and, with a flourish, Charlotte threw it open.

Mary was astonished by the cosy scene in front of her. Jayne sat on the floor by the fire with a man whose back view she did not recognise. They were playing a lively game of soldiers, whilst little Emily rocked a doll's cradle. Phillip had changed beyond recognition and his hair had had been allowed to grow as was the custom with noble children. The thick dark curls hid his face and he was so engrossed in the game that he did not look up, but on hearing them Jayne turned and let out a shriek of delight, scattering some of the soldiers on to the wooden floor and causing Phillip to burst into tears. The man spoke softly to him, replacing the figures and restoring calm.

'Good Papa,' said the little boy before turning his solemn face to his mother.

Mary's stomach lurched as she saw him but the words the little boy had uttered threw her into confusion; she thought for one mad moment that Fernando had come, and to her surprise she did not feel the elation she might have expected. The man turned around and jumped to his feet and she saw that it was Rupert. Mary felt completely calm. He seemed to be so very much at ease and, before Jayne could come to her, he had crossed the space between them and taken her hand, pulling it towards his lips. Her body came close to his, her eyes met his and no words were exchanged. Jayne quickly scooped up little Phillip and placed him on the floor by Mary's feet. He looked up at her solemnly and, without prompting, Rupert lifted him and put him in his mother's arms.

The words would not come. Mary felt such a wave of supreme joy when she held her son and gradually became aware of Rupert's arm about them both in a protective arc.

'Mrs Mary, I can hardly believe it. This is such a happy day, what with Mr Rupert here and us all together . . . and the weather being so perfect and . . . oh, I don't know . . . it just feels right.' Overcome with emotion, Jayne couldn't say any more.

Charlotte had been watching quietly from the doorway. Just as she was saying a prayer that things would always be like this, Sir Miles joined her, 'I know what you are wishing,' he whispered.

*   *   *

Later, when the family had gathered for prayers and the evening meal was over, the couple retired to a quiet corner of the parlour where a merry fire blazed, the candles were lit and the servants could be heard clearing up. Both children were sleeping soundly, Phillip exhausted by the attentions of his mother.

'Charlotte and I are going to retire early,' said Sir Miles tactfully, whilst casting Rupert an encouraging look.

'Good-night then, Father,' said Mary. 'It is so lovely to be home, and thank you, Charlotte, for looking after Phillip. He is such a happy child . . . I . . . ' stammered Mary, she had already realised that the child had become part of Sailing Hall, that it was where he belonged.

As Mary sat on the embroidered settle she had always loved, her shawl dropped to the floor. Before she could reach down for it Rupert picked it up and placed it about her shoulders. He did not let go and used it to draw her towards him as he sat down. The cosy warmth of the room and the knowledge that for the moment she could just be, that nobody was around the corner to report on her actions, that here in her home there was no need for accountability had lulled Mary into submission. She felt Rupert's lips on hers.

Throughout their long friendship he had never taken advantage of her loneliness or her vulnerability. In fact it was his very presence, in its practical role, which had, although unbeknownst to her, made her life in the echelons of the court possible. She acknowledged it now but her perception of him had changed. He had arrived at her home and put down his own particular roots and all seemed well with the world. But he was also a young, vigorous man, a man who had proved himself as both loyal and trustworthy, not to mention brave. His interest in her child was genuine and she knew that he was about to offer her a choice which would have to be made. There would be no second chance since he was a man who was not to be toyed with. If she chose him it would make all the people she loved happy; it would lead to a path of certainty and no unknowns. And it was this kiss which told her of the man who would be both a lover and a husband.

'Mary, my dearest, I have loved you ever since I first saw you,' said Rupert after a while.

She hesitated, not sure if the reaction she had was genuine or just a manifestation of all the months she had had playing the coy, unattainable monument to icy perfection she had acquired since the birth of her child, the cruel separation, and the betrayal she had suffered.

'You are silent,' said Rupert anxiously. 'Have I offended you?' he asked.

'No, you have not. I wish you to go on. I liked it very much indeed,' she said in a pressing voice she hardly recognised as her own.

'I will, my dearest Mary . . . ' Rupert replied quickly. 'But only if you are my wife. I cannot offer you riches and power, just a solid, dependable life, for I have played out my role in that world. This time here with your family has confirmed in me my desire to live a good and happy life with a fine woman whom I love. I would like to be a father to your child, a friend to your father, a protector to Charlotte. I would like to help your father love and nurture this wonderful place until Phillip is old enough to do it as your father so wishes. But most of all, Mary,' he went on hurriedly while the words still came so fluently, 'I would like to be your husband, a father to Phillip's brothers and sisters. I would like to restore you to the family. You should never have left for the vain glory of life at court; you are too good for it. For me you have always stood out like a jewel, a bright mercurial light. I have lain awake so many nights with my heart aching with love for you, knowing that it would only be in this place that you could see it for its true worth.'

The answer was on Mary's lips when they heard the sound of horses on the gravelled drive, the clatter of hooves in the cobbled stable yard and the urgent pealing of the bell at the door.

Sir Miles was the first to respond, since Thomas was dealing with the kitchen fires, always insisting on dampening them down himself at night as he had seen so many fires caused by slack kitchen boys. Recently Sir Miles had been suffering from gout and the interruption to his preparations for bed had irritated him. His progress down the great staircase was slow, and as he approached the bottom Mary and Rupert emerged from the parlour.

'Who can this be at this hour?' said Mary as the bell continued to peal loudly.

'Allow me to go, Sir Miles,' said Rupert. 'I am fully clothed and I have my sword at the ready. This is not a time to welcome strangers to your home.'

Sir Miles noticed that Rupert had indeed managed to find his sword and was impressed, since he had no recollection of the weapon in the early stages of the evening and assumed that Rupert had quite correctly placed it in a position where it was easily recoverable.

'Thank you, my boy,' agreed Sir Miles.

Before Rupert could begin to pull back the three enormous

bolts on the door, Thomas appeared, puffing disapproval. 'Stand back, Sir, if you will,' he said firmly to Rupert. 'Let me undo the door and you stand at the ready.'

'Well thought,' said Rupert. 'But firstly I would like the women out of the way. May I suggest, Mary that you withdraw to the safety of the parlour?'

'Of course,' replied Mary, with what Sir Miles observed as uncharacteristic meekness.

Thomas undid the bolts, and slowly opened the great door. There was a gush of night and a figure was revealed. Sir Miles gasped and advanced towards the visitor menacingly.

'So, His Grace has decided to pay us a visit,' he boomed, drawing himself up to his considerable height. 'Never let it be said that my manners have failed me when a traveller has come to my home, but by all I hold sacred I will tell you that you, Sir, are not welcome here.' His voice shook with emotion, and his posture had become even more threatening.

'Sir, I understand your anger,' said Fernando in a low contrite tone. 'I merely ask for the opportunity of seeing your daughter, if only to explain my behaviour. It would be better so, if only that she might understand and that I can make amends.'

'Make amends, Sir, make amends,' bellowed Sir Miles, 'is that what you call it? Well, Sir, I will not give you that luxury, leave my house and never return or I will have you run off the estate like a common criminal.'

Thomas advanced towards the open door, waiting for orders from his master. Rupert had remained silent, his mind racing in turmoil. Just as his life had seemed on the brink of ecstatic happiness, the dark figure of the Duke Fernando had come like a devil from hell to ruin it all, for he knew exactly why the Duke had come. He looked at the man now; he was dressed in black, his gleaming dark eyes picking up the light from the lantern Thomas held aloft. He looked magnificent in his distress and urgency and Rupert would like to have run him through with his sword. He knew that this man would try to steal his Mary from him and her son from the family who had taken the child to their hearts.

And then came the calm clear voice of Mary, 'Let him enter, Father. I would like to hear what the Duke has to say.'

She stood, tall and imperious, in the centre of the great hall and Fernando's heart lurched. He had forgotten the power of her beauty. He noticed that she was wearing a simple country gown and that her hair was loose in a way he had never seen it before. Her figure was more rounded and he saw the outline of her breasts behind the thin cotton of the dress. She extended a hand to him and he saw that she wore no rings. Rupert went at once to her side and put a protective arm about her shoulders. Fernando saw that she did not pull away.

'What would you have me do?' Fernando asked.

'What would she have you do?' Sir Miles exploded. 'It's not a fit question for a lady to answer. This is man's work. You are a blaggard and have ill used my daughter, destroyed her honour, broken you word to me as a gentleman. We are insulted. Leave or I will demand satisfaction.' Sir Miles moved quickly and Fernando was off his guard. Sir Miles lunged and grabbed Fernando's sword. Mary let out a scream as Sir Miles lifted the weapon in Fernando's direction.

Charlotte had been coming slowly down the staircase when she saw what was happening and, aware of the strength of her husband's feelings, she ran down the rest of the stairs towards her husband and seized his arm.

'Husband, stop this,' she pleaded. 'Let His Grace say what he has to say. It is Mary's right to hear it, whatever we may think. Let Mary decide – after all, it is her life, not ours.'

'Thank you, Charlotte,' said Mary. 'Thomas, take a lantern to the parlour and bring His Grace some refreshment. He will not be staying long.'

Charlotte took her husband's hand and whispered quietly. 'Let them alone, husband. Mary will make the right decision. Just look across the room, it is Rupert who is needing our support, the situation is now out of his control, he thinks he may lose the woman he has fought so hard to protect. We must trust in God that your daughter decides what is right for us all.'

'You are right as usual. Was ever a man so lucky as I am to have such a wife?' he asked. 'Rupert, come with us, we will go to the kitchens, where the fire is still warm,' he said, crossing the room as Rupert silently watched Thomas lead Mary and Fernando into the parlour.

'I come to beg your forgiveness,' said Fernando desperately. 'I have been deceived by all about me whom, it seems, wished to destroy me, even my own mother.'

'I wonder if you need to explain everything for my sake or for your own sake, or perhaps for the sake of my child,' said Mary impassively.

'It is because I have been a fool, and I wish to repair the damage I have done, Mary,' said Fernando in a voice thick with emotion. He saw Mary's intransigent face and whereas he had not at first understood the presence of Rupert Willoughby or the extreme ferocity of Sir Miles's reception, he was gradually piecing together just how far he was from winning back Mary's heart. In a dramatic measure he threw himself to the ground on bended knee.

'I think it is too late for that,' said Mary steadily. In fact she could barely contain her confusion. Fernando still had the power to move her, and she was impatient with her own weakness, for allowing him momentarily to disrupt her resolve. She had floated into a world where she would never be comfortable. The tight, cold culture from which Fernando came was one to which she could never adjust. She had even begun to question the Catholic faith to which he was wedded. She had an idea of the miserable unloving childhood which had bred a man who could be so easily persuaded to ignore the inner voices of his soul which should have protected him from the forces which had destroyed his love for her and should she want such a thing for her own son? The irony was that she had decided to accept Rupert as her husband at the precise moment she had heard the sound of Fernando's arrival.

But now, suddenly, there was no question in her mind. She was to remember, later, how it was the exact words that Fernando was fatefully to offer in the next minute which irrevocably made up her mind, added to the fact that he had not seen fit to ask about his son.

'People would soon forget about the past, you would be accepted,' he went on. 'I can offer you a new life, please be my Duchess.'

'Be accepted'? Accepted as what, Mary asked herself. She pondered as to why she should have to apologise for the past, which, with its challenges, had been Fernando's own creation. Rupert exalted in her for all her life, both past and present, he was a man whose code of life did not depend on outward appearances. And then she thought, with a great shuddering sigh, how whatever happens, happens for the best. Now she saw, now more than ever, that this was true. How God had meant her to bring a child back to Sailing Hall, a boy to be a son and grandson. How alien Fernando's world would have been to her, how lonely she would have been, once the first sexual frisson had faded and Fernando had reverted to his haughty aristocratic roots.

'I cannot accept you now, Fernando,' she said gently. 'It is not because of another man, it is because I value myself. I have discovered my own strength because of what has happened. The man I share my life with will be a part of my life. I see now that with you that would not have been possible. I would have had to be all of your life and then one day I might have been left alone and deprived in a foreign country, away from the roots I love, which are as much a part of me as the blood in my body or my heart that beats in my breast. So that,' she said finally, 'is my answer.'

Fernando rose quickly, with as much dignity as he could muster. 'I did not ask about your son,' he said slowly, 'because I did not want you to think it was for him that I came. It was for you both, Mary. But I see that I am too late, so I will leave you and him where I know you will be happy. It is better that I do not see him. I do not deserve him. I have not behaved well but now I shall leave you with honour, and I will not worry about my son, even if he is to be my only one. He will be like his mother, a noble person. You will always be my rose in winter.'

Fernando bowed and left the room. Mary, still standing erect, turned the other way so that he could not see her fighting back tears; not tears of regret but tears for a kind of joy in resolution. Not another minute passed before Rupert came through the door. He came to her with trepidation; she turned towards his hesitant figure.

'I was about to give you my answer before we were interrupted,' she said simply. 'It is yes.'